Water Flow Down

R. P. Poe

The past is never dead. It's not even past. -William
Faulkner

Every man's memory is his private literature.
-Aldous Huxley

If you have to keep reminding yourself
of a thing, perhaps it isn't so.
-Christopher Morley

For Diane

One

Surrounded by people, I was alone. The river, a thread of mercury lacing the valley below us, showed no life as it disappeared around a sharp bend, swallowed by the broad land. Distant hills vibrated under a gray sky. I stood beside Angie's grave and felt myself vanishing into the background like raindrops on sand. Words spoken near me fell to earth, melting the ground beneath my feet. I searched for something to hang onto but found nothing and felt I might soon disappear altogether. I had lost too many of the people I loved. A light rain began to fall just as a raven called from far down the hill, sending me into the very air.

A week later, having passed through a veil of lost time I found myself at home again, feeling as if awoken from a bad dream. As I was prone to, I retreated into my books, texts on the hydrogeology of western Texas that had once belonged to my older brother, Roddy. An unusual choice perhaps but right then I found the solid facts of science reassuring. The truth of the scientific method was one of the few things left in this world I could believe in. The unseen but solid intricacies of plate tectonics and permeable strata were something I could hold onto. I set the book in my lap, thinking of Roddy.

I'd seen a lot of ignorance and stupidity in my time but nothing that compared with the bull-headed men in my family. What can make a man up and leave all that he knows, every person who ever loved him or might have loved him given half a chance, and never so much as a letter or phone call to say where he is or if he's even still alive? Roddy's son Quit was a child of only twelve or thirteen when his father left for work one day and never returned. No reason why or I found someone else or even a half-hearted good-bye. Nothing left except a watch hanging on the door knob of the boy's room as if in trade for his leaving. I never forgave Roddy for that.

Less than a year before, Quit's mother who I loved like a sister had died all of a sudden. She was fine and then caught a cold. None of us thought much of it but before you could blink she had pneumonia and the no-good doctors just stood by helpless. It's a terrible thing to watch someone you love pulling for air like a fish and there's not a thing you can do. We cried a bucket of tears with all that but when Roddy disappeared Quit seemed to fade into himself like a shadow when a cloud passes across the sun. Losing both parents in short order was just too much for him and he never again was the same.

His sister Angie and I did our best to care for him but Quit was a piece of work if I've ever seen one. There wasn't a mean bone in his body yet you could see the anger simmering right behind his eyes. He had plenty to be angry about, I'll give him that and the anger seemed to sweep him along like a wave in the ocean. It's fair to say Quit did his share of flailing about like a drowning man and then with time he seemed to settle in.

I believe he would have come through it alright but Angie was six years older and had her own life to live. She met up with a handsome young man two or three years after her mother passed and her father left. It wasn't much longer, a year maybe, when she decided to get married. I could see the boy was in a state. Quit hid it well but his eyes changed and he seemed to fade into himself again. He managed to make it through the wedding but late that night he disappeared. When he lost Angie to marriage it was like his mother had died all over again and I truly believe he grieved for them both equally.

In spite of the timing of his leaving Angie did everything she could to find her brother. I lost count of the number of addresses she sent letters to. Most of them were returned but not all so she kept up hope Quit would know he always had a place with her, especially after she left her no-good womanizer of a husband. She was a good deal more patient than I ever was and I had all but written Quit off as part of this family by the time Angie died. She collapsed at church during the early service. They said it was a stroke. When she died I felt like there must be some kind of curse we were under. Her passing was a shock, coming all of a sudden like it did, and even more so as she was all the real family I had left except for the boy. But I never expected to hear from him again. I was wrong, of course.

Two

The musty air of an unused home mixed with the fragrance of Angie's favorite soap as I pushed open the door and stepped inside her house, the wooden floor complaining beneath my feet. A dim light streamed through the blinds. Once my eyes adjusted, I made my way down the hallway and into the large kitchen at the rear of the house. A scarred oak table stood against one wall, looking as it always had except for a thin film of dust covering the top. The glass-fronted cabinets filled with blue and white tableware seemed just as Angie had left them. I gazed at the dishes, thinking how her hands had placed them there only weeks before. I had to look away. I ran my palm across the green and yellow tile counter below and suddenly felt tired. Dropping my hat on the table, I sat in one of the worn chairs, the wood cool and solid beneath my fingers. Just then the front door opened and closed.

"Is someone here?" A man's voice called.

"In the kitchen." I called back.

There was a pause and shuffling of footsteps as if the person started back toward the door and then turned again. A moment later Angie's brother Quit appeared in the doorway. I tried to hide my surprise and anger came out in its place.

"So, you decided to come back after all this time." It was a statement, no question implied.

He sat across from me and I stared at him, reminding myself that he was my nephew and Angie had long wanted to see him sitting right there but my anger seemed to sweep me along. I tapped the table with a finger.

"Well, I hope you plan to make yourself useful and do some good around here. Lord knows we could use it. Nothing but one bad time after the other, that's what we've had. Not that I expect you'd have any interest in such things. People that leave for fifteen years or more and don't so much as write a letter aren't likely to care about much outside of their own selves."

He just sat there without a word. Somewhere in the back of my mind I could hear Angie's voice telling him how glad she was to see him, and I vowed to act civil if I could. After so much disappointment from the Goforth men, I knew it would be a challenge.

"I started a diet three weeks and four days ago and I'm not fit to live with." I reached into my coat pocket, pulling out a package of chewing gum and offering it. "I remember you used to love chewing gum."

He shook his head. He was holding a photograph that he kept glancing at.

"You have something important there or just forget how to talk?" I snapped.

"Mazie." It seemed all he could do to say my name.

"I'm glad to see you remember my name because we have a lot to discuss." I interrupted. "Did you come straight here or have you been down to see her already?"

He stared at me. "See who?"

I felt my face turn red in an instant. "You Goforth men couldn't be bothered with us when your sister was alive and you still have no respect, always showing up late or not at all. You're no different than your father."

"What are you talking about?"

"We buried Angie not three weeks ago."

"Now, hold on a minute, Mazie." he held up a hand. "I didn't know about Angie until yesterday. I received a letter from a reverend somebody or other and got here as soon as I could. I travel so I'm hard to reach."

"Hard to reach is right. Do you know how she tried? She wanted to see you more than anything. Why she still cared to I couldn't say but she was a better soul than I'll ever be and too good for the rest of this family."

"Well, I'm here now." he grumbled.

"Then you need to make a visit to the cemetery."

"Alright, I will."

I eyed him for a moment, wondering why he had showed up after being away so long.

"If you think you're going to cash in on some big inheritance, you're in for a surprise. Angie was way more generous than a person ought to be, always helping out somebody. This old house is mortgaged to the gills, and the business isn't much better off."

"That's not why I'm here."

"Then why? Does it have something to do with that picture?" I nodded toward the photo in his hand.

"No, not at all."

"What's in the photo?"

"It's a picture of Josephina Del Toro." he held out the picture. "Do you remember her?"

"Sephie? Let me take a look." I put on my reading glasses and studied the photograph. "I remember. You two were sweethearts for a time. What does this say at the bottom?"

"I believe it spells 'murdered'."

"That's a strange thing to write on a picture of a girl. Where did you get it?"

"Someone left it stuck in the screen door out front."

"That's strange, I didn't notice it. Who would leave it there and why now? They must have known you were coming back."

"Maybe. But why leave the picture?"

"She was sent to Mexico to live with relatives just before your sister got married, if I remember. Is that right?"

He nodded. "That was over fifteen years ago."

"I'm not as young as I once was, but I still have a good memory - too good, really. There are plenty of things I'd like to forget." I rubbed my forehead, trying to remember. "Did you keep in touch with her?"

"No, not really. I didn't know where she was."

"And you didn't do much to find out."

I studied him and thought back to that time. Josephina had been sent away about the time Angie was to get married. I tried to put myself in his place as a teenager that had lost his parents. He probably felt the world was mounted against him and resented it. I guessed that he wanted to get as far as possible from everything he knew.

"It was a long time ago. I had to leave." he looked me in the eye for a moment then turned away. "Okay, I didn't do much to find her."

"It runs in the family, you and your father keeping everyone at a distance."

"What does he have to do with anything?" he sat back, annoyed.

There was a knock at the back stoop. I got up and came around the table as the door creaked opened and Nacho, our nursery manager leaned into the room. I could see he had been working in the nursery. His khaki shirt, stained with sweat, hung loosely over his belt and well-worn jeans. Embroidered with a half-peeled stalk of corn, his cap read "Martin Seeds". A thin layer of dirt covered his boots as he stood by the door, uncertain whether or not to enter the room.

"Nacho, come on in and sit." I nodded toward Quit, trying to sound civil. "This is Quit, my nephew and one of my only blood relatives left in this mean old world."

"Narciso Contreras." he held out his hand. "Good to meet you, Quit."

Nacho sat across from Quit. Winston, our other worker followed and climbed onto a chair next to him without a word. With his army surplus pants and thin orange-hued face, Winston seemed elf-like next to Nacho. He scratched his patchy red beard and squinted at Quit.

Quit glanced at him and turned to Nacho. "Same to you. Buenos tardes."

"Quit, you don't have to speak Espanol to our Nacho here. He's more American that I am."

7

Nacho frowned and pulled his cap low on his forehead. "My grandparents came to the States from Mexico but my parents wouldn't let us speak Spanish at home so I didn't learn much until I was in the Army. It may sound strange to go all the way to 'Nam to learn your family's language but two guys in my unit spoke it mostly. You'd be surprised how fast you can pick up something when your life depends on it."

"Nacho can take us to the cemetery in the truck. I need him to pick up some things over that way." I tapped my index finger on the table and again eyed Quit. "Well, I guess it's your truck now, seeing as how Angie left everything to you. You can drive it yourself if you want. It's just that we need the truck to pick up a few things for the business. Of course the nursery belongs to you too so you could tell us to leave it until later. Fact is, you could tell us to leave altogether."

"No, no, that'll be fine." he waved the air with his hand.

"Alright, then."

"Alright then." he repeated.

I noticed Quit again glance at Winston. "Oh, and this is Winston. He's our rose man. Nobody raises roses like Winston."

He stood and saluted. "Winston Churchill Smith!"

"That's some name." Quit looked from him to me.

"His parents were in London during the blitz." I fanned myself with my hat.

"London blitz!" Winston's voice seemed to have only one volume, loud.

"His parents wanted all the luck they could get and figured naming him after Churchill would do the trick. They made it through the war, so it must have worked. Unfortunately, that's where Winston's luck ended."

"No luck!" he sat again.

"Winston likes anything to do with the army." I put my hand on his shoulder. "When he was four Winston had encephalitis and then had an allergic reaction to the

8

medication for it. He very nearly died. It left him tinged just a bit orange and with lots of energy.

"We like that energy don't we Winston?" Nacho added. "Winston works very hard."

Winston stood, faced Quit and saluted again. "I work hard, sir!"

Quit looked at me and then turned back to Winston, giving him a weak salute. I could see Quit wanted no part of the responsibility that goes with a business. He was flighty as a caged bird. He had avoided getting involved with family for all these years and I could see that the thought of doing so now made his skin crawl. I have to admit it gave me some pleasure to see him suffer. He turned so pale I thought he might pass out so I decided we'd better get him into some fresh air.

"I'm ready to go now if that's alright with you." I put on my hat.

"Yeah, okay." he said absently, turning toward the hallway.

"The truck's back here." I motioned toward the back door. "You need something to eat first? You're looking a little pale in the face."

He shook his head. "I'm alright."

I opened the ice box and pulled out a dozen red carnations, thrusting them in his face. He reared back as if he'd been slapped.

"Carnations?" He took hold of the bouquet.

"We always take flowers." I turned for the door.

Three

I climbed into the rusted pick-up next to Quit and Nacho drove us through the wide streets of the town in silence. I was glad to be away from the house and on the move. I've never been one to sit idly. Besides, I needed to think and I always seemed to do my best thinking in the old truck.

I wondered what Quit must make of me still living in my home town, my life half over and nothing much to show for it. I thought I must look to him like some old eccentric but I decided I'd go ahead and let him think whatever he liked. I wanted to see what he would do now that he was back. More than anything I wanted him to do right by Angie. I had been let down enough and had no toleration for quitters.

The truck slowed, pulling me from my thoughts as I turned to the courthouse with its stone clock tower and sprawling live oaks, their limbs reaching to the ground. It had been weeks since I'd passed the shady square. I wondered what the town must look like to Quit after being away for so long. The businesses had changed no doubt, except for the hardware store and Harry's furniture. Windows were boarded up in a few places where long-time family businesses had vanished into memory.

Past the buildings the rusted girders of the bridge broke the horizon, the river hidden from view beneath steep cliffs. On the far bank, sycamore trees glowed bone-like in the afternoon light. Mats of driftwood wrapped the up-river side of trees, bits of detritus hanging in branches well up the cliff.

Above the river, blue hills fell into themselves and stacked against the sky, hazy in the afternoon heat. I rolled down the window, leaning into the wind and again thinking of Sephie's photo. Quit had no explanation for its

10

appearance and I figured it as a sick joke. Still, I couldn't help but wonder about the two of them.

I tried to picture her the last time I'd seen her but my thoughts only crowded together into a single blurred image. I wondered if Nacho recalled anything. His family had known the Del Toro family before they returned to Mexico. I was about to ask when Quit turned to Nacho.

"Alright if I call you Nacho?"

"The only one that calls me Narciso is my mother. It was her father's name so she wasn't too happy when everyone started calling me Nacho." he chuckled. "In 'Nam nobody in my unit had a real name. There was a guy named Turtle and another one they called Chispa. It means spark, like in a fire. They were a pack of wild men."

"Do you keep up with any of them?"

"No. I was hit and ended up in a hospital in Germany." he lifted his cap and motioned towards the left side of his head, pulling aside his hair to show a curved two-inch scar.

"What happened?"

"Shrapnel ricocheted off my helmet. Otherwise I'd have been a dead man. It still left me in a coma for three weeks. They told me my brain swelled so they had to open up my head to let out the pressure. That's what the scar is for. They brought me in with barely a scratch but I had to learn to talk all over again. The funny thing is the Spanish the guys in my unit taught me came back on its own."

"You wouldn't know it now."

"I still have trouble remembering things unless I write them down." he held up a left palm covered with writing. "You ever in the service, Quit?"

"No, the draft missed me."

"Hell, I joined up. Can you believe that? I was young and didn't know any better." he laughed. "It wasn't my first mistake or my last."

"I made my share of mistakes when I was young too. In fact, I've been thinking a lot about that time. There was a photo of someone I knew a long time ago waiting for me when I got to the house." he looked to the horizon. "You ever know a Josephina Del Toro? She went by Sephie."

"I knew that family. I was friends with a cousin." he looked over at Quit. "I heard stories about the Del Toros, like they had to leave town all of a sudden because they were in some kind of trouble. I lost touch with the cousins when I went to 'Nam so I don't know much since then except I did hear that later the family came into a bunch of money. Folks said it was drug money but I don't believe half of what I hear out of my Mexican relatives."

The truck slowed and turned in front of the stone and wrought iron gates of Wilke Cemetery. I was glad to see that the grass was freshly mown, even if it was brown in spots from the summer heat. I liked to think of Angie in a nice-looking place.

"I heard that Sephie had a baby down in Mexico, a daughter." Nacho let the thought stand and nodded towards the gate. "I'll let you off here while I go pick up some materials at the hardware store, if that sounds okay."

Quit opened the door and we got out.

"We'll see you back here when you're done." I slammed the door.

We walked the short distance to the gravesite and stood, saying nothing. The sky, white with heat, rose wall-like above the distant juniper-covered hills. Quit kneeled and ran his hand over the low granite marker, tracing the words etched across its surface. The letters spelling out his sister's name stood in sharp contrast to the polished stone and were deep in shadow. He placed the flowers on the fresh earth, wiping the sweat from the back of his neck and then looking down the hill toward the river, a thin edge of silver beyond the tree line.

Angie loved this place. I again wondered why, unlike Quit and most everyone else they knew, she had returned home after her divorce to make a life for herself here. A dim memory of her holding Quit's hand in front of their mother's gravestone took shape in my mind. The three of us knelt there together. Behind us Roddy stood watching, leaning against the car and chain-smoking cigarettes. He turned as Angie cried silently, the click of her tears on stone the only sound.

Roddy could never tolerate a display of emotion and it made him a poor father. With no wife to soften him he had become angry and overbearing, finding fault with his children and ignoring their needs. Angie somehow managed to protect Quit from the worst of Roddy's anger. After he left, Angie and I cared for Quit as his mother had, making his breakfast and helping him with schoolwork. But it felt to me as if that time had passed in a moment and then was gone.

Quit and I walked through the cemetery grounds and down the hill to a grove of cottonwood trees, their broad leaves flickering in the dappled shade. Standing beside him at Angie's grave had affected me in a way I was unable to explain, even to myself. I had an overwhelming urge to walk away without looking back. I suppose I was afraid to again hope for something approaching a family. After Angie died I had nothing left to hold me. I had lost contact with people little by little and after she was gone it suddenly became clear I was alone. For a time I tried to convince myself I had matured beyond something as trivial as socializing. But I had to face the truth that there was something about me, something people wanted to avoid. We communicate whether or not we speak a single word and my message was to leave me alone. I wanted to run from that sad fact but I had nowhere to go, no way to escape from myself. I looked at Quit and wondered what he was trying to escape.

He turned as an older model sedan pulled to the curb and Angie's priest, Father Gus stepped out. Short and round, his clerical collar bright and slightly off-center in the afternoon sun, he walked directly to Angie's grave. As we were a distance away from the gravesite we went unnoticed. I again thought of Quit and Angie and their fractured childhood, and I watched the priest approach with a mixture of anger and gratitude.

We looked on as Father Gus pulled at his sweat-stained shirt, puffing out his reddened cheeks. I was in no mood to talk but his round face framed by a thin beard had a disarming quality. He wiped his forehead with a wadded up handkerchief and knelt beside the headstone. Quit started toward him and then stopped, stepping back into the shadows. We could hear the priest's muffled voice but were unable to make out what he said although it was clearly filled with emotion. He stood, reaching out and touching the marker with three fingers. It seemed almost a caress. Quit stepped out of the shadows, walking toward him as the priest turned, his eyebrows raised in question.

I knew Father Gus only through his friendship with Angie. Now, I'm no fan of organized religion. I'm too stubborn and independent to tolerate all the rules and false niceties, and I'm suspicious of religious types in general. They always seem to want something, like your money or your soul. Still, Father Gus had been good to Angie and he did find Quit so I decided I'd cut him some slack. Even so, I was annoyed to see him there at that moment. I had hoped some quiet time at the graveside would make Quit realize his obligations to Angie's memory. I still had a suspicion he only returned home to see what he could get for selling the place and the thought chapped my hide. I hesitated for a moment and then followed.

"I take it you knew Angie." Quit called out as he approached.

"I knew her, yes." he tugged at his collar. "I don't make a habit of visiting the graves of my parishioners, but I, ah...well she was, ah...I was lucky enough to know her for far too short a time."

"And you're a priest." Quit interrupted.

"I'm Father Gus." he shook Quit's hand energetically. "Am I right in guessing you're Quentin Goforth, our dear Angie's brother?"

"You'd be right there, Father."

"Please, just call me Gus." He looked back at the stone marker. "Angie was well-loved and had a very big heart that will be missed by many."

"That's what I've been telling him." I stepped beside Quit.

"Hello, Mazie." He smiled at me and turned back to face Quit. "But this must be doubly hard for you, she being your only sister."

Quit shifted his gaze and studied the ribbon of river below us. "We went through a lot together."

I was annoyed that was all he could think of to say. He glanced at me as I eyed him, returning my stare by turning away. I thought I spotted a hint of shame on his face but he chose not to add anything to what he had said. The priest sensed his difficulty and changed the subject.

"Quentin, I understand you travel a lot."

"Call me Quit." he turned to face Gus. "I traveled. It had to do with the work I used to do. I've been wondering how you managed to track down a mailing address for me. That can't have been easy the way I've moved around."

"We church types have our ways, including contacts all over the world." he chuckled. "To be honest, I know a young priest who is very computer savvy and he found it for me. I have no idea how he did it."

"Well, it was good of you."

"I'm sorry it took so long but I'm glad you're here. I know Angie would be pleased to see you back home."

"I left a long time ago and to be honest I don't know why I'm back. I may only be here a short while."

Needless to say that last comment irritated me. I wondered again why he had returned. If he didn't know, it was unlikely I'd be able to figure it out. On the other hand, while I could see the priest's comments made him uncomfortable something about the man made Quit want to talk. I realized right then if I could make him understand why his sister had returned home he might find a reason to stay. Gus seemed to sense it too. I could tell in the way he spoke to Quit.

"Well, I'd be sorry to see you leave." Gus again mopped the sweat from his face. "Angie loved this place and the life she had built. She talked of it many times and hoped you would come to love it as she did."

We turned as Nacho edged the pick up through the cemetery gate.

"Well, our ride is here and I'm guessing he needs to get back to the house." Quit shook his hand. "It was good to talk to you, Gus."

"Would you be willing to meet me for a drink later? I like a drink in the evening. It's good for the system, you know." Gus patted his belly. "I know a bar that has decent Scotch and ice cold beer. What do you say we meet at five?"

Quit hesitated, looking down the hill again. One thing I can't tolerate is an indecisive man. I wondered if he was thinking about his sister and her relationship to the priest. I also wondered if he had an urge to walk away from it all like I did or if his thoughts were as confused and unsettled as mine or both. One thing I knew for sure was that we could all use a drink, the sooner the better.

"You're not a teetotaler, are you?" I barked.

"Alright, I'll meet you." he turned to the priest. "Where is this bar?"

"Just ask Mazie for directions. She knows the place."

"Hell, I'll take him myself." I called as I opened the truck door. "Move over, Nacho, I'm driving."

Talk of the past got me to thinking again of my own. On top of all that had happened, Len Simmons my lost love from college had shown up out of the blue. I thought I'd long ago given up on men but then there he was still looking delicious and before I knew it I was all twisted up about him like I'd been transported back in time. One minute I convinced myself he was not worth the trouble and the next I was looking up his address. I had no idea what I might do next but either way I was terrified. Still, I couldn't help thinking about when we first met.

Four

The air was unusually warm for October the afternoon Len called asking me over to his house. We were in the same biology class and had gotten to know one another working on lab assignments. After a while we started studying together, trading lecture notes and drinking coffee late into the night. It made the class more interesting and to my surprise I found I liked Len.

I had first met him one summer several years before when he was dating a good friend of mine, Hannah Ambrosian. Back then Len never seemed particularly talkative or friendly. In fact it seemed like he went out of his way to avoid me. Just the same, I saw him often enough at parties or whatnot. When summer ended I left for a job in another town, so that was that.

 I eventually grew tired of my job and the small town where I lived so I decided to return to school. I was hoping to find something else I could do for a living. I moved back to Austin to register for a few classes and that's when I ran into Len. I was nervous about returning to school so it was a nice surprise to see someone familiar. Not only did we know each other from that summer, at least a little, but we were older than a lot of the other students and we had that in common as well. As it turned out, we made a good team.

I got to Len's house about six that evening expecting to finish up a final project due the following Monday but when he answered the door he had the stereo on, a beer in his hand and the table set, complete with candles. He handed me a longneck and led me to the kitchen. I was surprised, to put it mildly. We were just study partners. On the other hand, I often found myself staring at the side of his face while he tried to reason out the double helix or why calico cats are almost always female. Len wasn't much good with genetics but that was part of his appeal.

He planned the dinner to thank me for helping him make it through the class.

Hannah had broken up with Len a month before so I didn't see a problem with the two of us studying together. It was no different than what I would do with any other classmate. We were both interested in the class and we enjoyed talking about it so it made sense that way too. But when I saw the dinner he made I had a strange feeling, just for a moment. I couldn't put my finger on it or maybe I didn't want to. I think deep down I hoped that we might be more than friends. Still, it wasn't like I was doing something wrong. I *had* helped him, more than a little. You see, even though Len was good-looking the logic of recombinant DNA somehow escaped him.

He sat me at the kitchen table and we peeled avocados, sliced limes and chopped onions for a guacamole salad. Then he filled a baking dish with spinach and mushroom enchiladas and I put it in the oven. It felt so exotic. The peacock blue kitchen cabinets and black and white octagonal tile countertops gave the night a festive feel, not that it needed any help. I had downed that first beer in record time and it went straight to my head. I wouldn't admit to myself that I was attracted to Len because the thought was thrilling yet terrifying. I'd never dated a friend's ex before. Even though she had broken up with him, I worried what Hannah might think. I got so nervous that when the radio started playing Jerry Jeff Walker's *Sangria Wine*, I couldn't help but sing along. Then I had to make up for it by downing another beer.

The dinner was surprisingly good and everything seemed ordinary enough. I thought maybe I had been imagining Len was interested in me other than as a study partner. That is, until we sat on the couch. I should have known that would change things and it did. We sat there for the longest time talking about nothing in particular. I'm sure I made no sense. What with all the thoughts swirling around my head I'm surprised I could talk at all. Later, after I had a chance to think about it I realized Len was pretty sly the way he steered the conversation around to the genetics of eye color. I thought he was seriously interested in the subject. He turned and looked at me for a moment.

"So, what color are your eyes?" He leaned toward me.

"Well, they're mostly green but sometimes in a certain light they can look almost blue." I blinked at him. "That's because they have a blue center."

"Well, which is it, blue or green?" He leaned a little closer.

"Len, you should know by now that when it comes to genetics brown eyes are dominant and blue eyes are recessive." I started to get on my high horse. "My mother has blue eyes and my father has brown, so the recessive genes came through in my case. They're not sure but they think green is sort of a shade of blue."

"I don't think I've ever seen anyone that has both green *and* blue eyes."

He stared at me, making me a little uncomfortable although I couldn't say why and then he leaned closer. I thought he really wanted to see my eyes. The next thing I knew we were kissing like teenagers. I seemed to just float away into some other world. Soon we were laid out on the couch and Len's hands were everywhere. At least that's how it seemed. In a flash it hit me what we were up to and I jumped off that couch like it was on fire. The sad truth is I was the one on fire. I was so flustered I couldn't put two words together straight so I grabbed my purse and ran out the door before Len had a chance to talk me out of it.

I wandered the neighborhood trying to figure out what to do. It wasn't that I didn't like Len. I did, more than I wanted to admit. But I couldn't get Hannah out of my thoughts. She was my friend after all. I kept telling myself that she broke up with Len rather than the other way around. Still, I wanted to talk to her. I think I had convinced myself she would tell me not to worry and to go ahead and date Len if I wanted to. I turned around and headed straight for the house she shared with three other girls. I couldn't get there fast enough.

In the dim light of early evening, yellow leaves drifted from the tall pecans lining the street, littering the broken sidewalk like giant confetti. After such a warm day the look of autumn was disconcerting. As I hurried beneath the street lights the damp night seemed heavy, as if paused in anticipation of fall. I approached Hannah's house and a little voice inside my head told me to turn and walk away. I should have listened. Instead, I ignored it as always and walked up the concrete steps to the small house, painted an uneven brown with a dull yellow trim. I'd spent so much time in that house I almost felt like I lived there.

Walking through the open door without knocking, I wandered down the narrow hallway and past the front bedrooms until I came to Hannah's room. The other girls were out. I found Hannah standing in front of her dresser mirror, hurriedly brushing her hair. She pulled it into a pony tail and wrapped it in an elastic band. As soon as I realized that she was wearing her waitressing outfit I felt relieved to have caught her at home. She finally noticed me.

"Got a minute?" I mumbled.

"I didn't hear you come in." She searched for a shoe. "Sorry, I have to get ready for work."

A pair of men's briefs sat on the chair next to the dresser. Hannah grabbed them, giving me a quick glance as she stuffed them into a drawer.

"Whose are those?"

"They belong to a friend. A guy I met."

"A friend?"

"It's just sex, Mazie, nothing more."

"Anyone I know?"

"No. So, what were you saying?"

"I just need to talk to you. It won't take long."

"I'm okay on time. What's up?"

21

I realized I had no idea where to start so I just jumped in. "Len and I are in the same biology class and we've been working on projects and labs together."

A strange thought then struck me: Prior to that moment I had never talked with Hannah about studying with Len. As much as I saw her it should have come up at least once. I realized both of us had avoided the subject, consciously or not. That made me more than nervous and I paced the floor like a one-eyed cat.

"I heard." She stopped tying her shoe.

"I've seen… He's been… We've spent a lot of time together studying."

"Why are you telling me this, Mazie?" She stood with only one shoe on. "What's going on?"

"We've gotten to be good friends." I continued pacing around the room even though I didn't want to. "Maybe more than good friends."

"I don't want to talk about this."

"But, I think he wants us to date." I made myself say it.

"I have to go to work." She began forcing her foot into the other shoe.

"But we need to talk."

"No." She walked to her dresser.

"I didn't plan this, it just happened." I tried to get her to look at me. "Talk to me, Hannah."

"There's nothing to talk about."

"I don't know what that means."

"It means I don't want to talk about it." She put on her name tag.

"But what am I supposed to do?"

"That's not my problem." She glanced at me.

"Talk to me."

"No, I'm not talking about it."

"I'll meet you after work and we can talk then."

"No, not then, not ever." She grabbed her purse. "I have to go now."

She rushed past me and out the back door. I watched through the kitchen window as she climbed into her car and drove away. I trudged back through the house, gently closing the door behind me as if trying not to wake someone. I wandered the neighborhood, regretting I had left Len's house in such a rush. He would doubtless think me some kind of nut and want nothing to do with me. Worse, I realized the thought scared me. I knew then I was taken with him.

I ambled along narrow sidewalks crowded by massive live oaks and parked cars, lost in my thoughts. Now and then a full moon peeked over the silhouettes of rooftops. I walked to keep moving, to avoid sitting still. I needed to feel like I was doing something. The next thing I knew I was standing in front of Len's house.

The home had been divided up into apartments and his door was up a short paved walkway set back and to the side of the front entrance. Overgrown bushes lined the walk, giving the doorway a closed-in feel. Yellow light from a nearby window cut the lawn into dark rectangles. I hoped the light meant Len was at home as I knocked on the door and stepped back into the dim glow of the porch. I could hear steps on the wooden floor just inside and then the door opened and I found myself facing a woman I had never before seen. I wanted to turn and run. I wanted to slap myself for being stupid enough to think that Len was interested in me. He already had someone and was just playing the field. That made me the field, which didn't help my attitude any. The disappointment on my face must have been obvious.

"Oh my... can I... is there... are you looking for Len?" The woman stammered.

All I could do was nod. I stood unmoving as my mind ground to a halt, taking with it my ability to make any decisions. She opened the door and took my arm, leading me to the couch.

23

"I'm Shirley. Can I get you some water or something? You look a little pale."

I was feeling light-headed so I nodded again, but mostly to give myself some time. I needed to think, if I could manage it. I wondered how I could have misled myself so completely about Len. On top of everything else, I had probably forever lost Hannah as a friend. I felt angry at myself, angry at Len and angry at the world. It amazed me the way life could go from hopeful to disastrous in such short order. The thought took the air right out of me and I sank into the couch, feeling like I was going to cry. I didn't want that.

Shirley came back carrying a glass of water and a bowl of eggs and I went from confused to clueless. I stared at the eggs as I sipped the water and wondered if I was hallucinating. Shirley noticed my stare or maybe that I was still about to cry and sat down next to me.

"Can I ask your name?" She held the bowl like an offering.

"I'm Mazie. Len is in my biology class. I had a question about genetics I was hoping he could answer." I lied. "I didn't think he'd have a guest."

"Oh, Mazie, I'm not a guest." She held up the bowl. "I'm over here boiling eggs for supper. I live next door and have a two year old that loves boiled eggs, but our stove went out. Len is over there now helping my husband fix it. There hasn't been an explosion so I hope that means they found the problem. I'm going back now. I'll tell Len you're here. I know he'll be glad to see you. All he does is talk about you."

My face must have gone even paler because she reached out and touched my arm. That was more than I could take. I started crying like a six year old as Shirley did her best to comfort me but I'm sure she thought I was touched. I was beginning to think so myself. She set down the eggs, led me to the bathroom and left me there to clean up as best I could. I guess she told Len to wait a bit because I was more or less back to my old self when he walked through the door. By that point, I had no idea what to expect.

He sat down on the couch without saying a word and kissed me. Then he took my hand and led me to his bedroom and before I knew what was what I was floating again in that other world. It was wondrous. I'd had boyfriends before but this was different. I felt like I had become part of Len and him part of me. His breath was my breath, my skin was his. We drifted on a warm sea.

Then I was having the strangest dream. I sat working on a little lattice-covered house, the kind they use for cuckoo clocks. I was hammering away at a nail, tapping and tapping, but the nail bent like rubber, first one way and then the other. I kept tapping away at it, feeling more and more frustrated. Finally, I gave it a good whack and the little house shattered in my hands like glass. I awoke with a start.

For a moment, I had no idea where I was. Moonlight streamed in through the windows and up the far wall. The ceiling fan hummed overhead in an off key. I could see well enough to know it wasn't my room and then I remembered where I was. I reached over the covers to touch Len, finding him just where I hoped he'd be. That was reassuring. Strangely, I could still hear the tapping and it seemed to be coming from the window behind me. I pulled up on one elbow, leaning toward the sill and squinting through the dusty pane when suddenly I found myself face to face with Hannah. I gasped so loud that Len sat up, blinking the sleep from his eyes. He turned toward the window just as Hannah screamed loud enough to break glass. Len hopped out of the bed like he'd seen a snake. I did the same and grabbed whatever clothes I could find, dressing in record time.

"What should we do?" Len whispered.

"I don't know." I growled. "I can't believe this is happening."

We could hear Hannah stomping through the back yard, yelling something unintelligible. The clock on Len's dresser read three-forty. One of the empty beer bottles Len kept in a barrel near the back gate crashed against the side of the house. That sobered me up. I looked out the window and realized what I had to do, whether I wanted to or not.

"I'm going out to talk to her." I slipped on my sandals.

"No, I should go." Len paced the room without a stitch of clothing.

"Put some clothes on and wait here. This is between Hannah and me."

I was surprised at how sure of myself I sounded. I was as far from confident as a person can be. In fact, rather than confident I felt I must have some sort of emotional whiplash from all that had happened in one day; that and my own personal black cloud. I stepped out the back door and down the steps, turning up my collar against the chill. Heavy dew glistened across an overgrown lawn scattered with moonlight. I scanned the yard for Hannah just as a beer bottle exploded on the garage door next to me.

She came walking around the corner, her coat hunched up around her shoulders, saw me and stopped, staring through the cold mist without a word. Then she began to pace, facing the ground and mumbling a litany of crimes against me. I didn't know what to do. Finally, I walked over to her.

"Hannah." I began.

"Don't start trying to explain yourself, Mazie." She held up a finger.

"But, Hannah."

She stopped and stared at me, shaking her head. "How could you, Mazie? How could you?"

"I don't know. It just happened." I held out my hand.

"These things don't just happen."

"We were just study partners, honestly, and we got to be friends. We didn't plan to get involved. It just happened."

26

"You really expect me to believe that? You've had your eye on Len from the start. It doesn't just happen." She picked up another bottle and hurled it at the garage.

"No, Hannah, there was never any plan. I never wanted to do something to hurt you. But I did and I'm sorry for that."

"Don't you dare talk about my feelings. You have no right, Mazie!" Her voice cracked. "How could you, Mazie? I thought you were my friend."

"I am your friend, Hannah."

"No, friends don't cheat on each other." She kicked the ground.

"But, Hannah, how can it be cheating? You broke up with Len."

"That didn't mean anything. Len and I had been together forever. I just wanted to date a little before we got married."

"Before you did what?" I stepped back, unbelieving. "What about the men's underwear in your room?"

"Don't try to change the subject. Len and I were going to get married."

"You could have told me."

"I did, remember? It was when you came back to school."

"But, Hannah, that was months ago. I thought it was over between you and him."

"I can't stand this!" She yelled. "You have an answer for everything, Mazie. But you're just trying to make yourself feel better. What you did was wrong!"

"I'm sorry, Hannah. I wish you had told me." I shivered in the chill air.

"Don't say you're sorry! Nothing can change what you did. I hate you!"

She stomped off, slamming the gate as she left. I stood there, feeling more alone than I ever had. Pale moonlight, sliced by the trees, fell in shards at my feet. I shivered again, not knowing what to do, and then Len's arms

27

wrapped around my shoulders. A thought crossed my mind that this was a bad beginning but I pushed it aside like an empty bowl and turned to face him. I had made my decision.

Five

Memory is a map, a map tracing the past, a map to the future, the blue highways of a life. Memory traces the crooked line from then to now, the course of an experience, where we were once, where we are now. We find meaning in time passed in all we've seen, in who we were and have become as best we can recall. Even if we try to break from that past, our next step depends on what we remember, affecting what we do like the spin on a curve ball, whether we want it to or not, whether we realize it or not.

The decisions I had made wasted no time in catching up with me. Len and I did our share of bar-hopping in those days. I was living in a rooming house north of the university owned by an elderly woman whose family had emigrated from Germany before the turn of the century. In spite of living all her life in Texas, Mrs. Ebeling still spoke with a noticeable accent. She rented to both men and women but she had strict rules about visitors. The sprawling two-story house, divided down the middle, had two large upstairs bedrooms. No men were allowed in the women's side, and no self-respecting woman would show her face in the men's side, according to Mrs. Ebeling's view of the world. The truth was she had little to worry about because the two men renting from her were gay and, although they rented separate rooms, a couple. I could hear them through the thin walls cavorting about on their side of the house. Every now and then, I'd hear one of them, Marcos, yelling "Oh, Fernando!" in a wavering falsetto. While friendly and polite to a fault, they had a wild side that occasionally made me wonder what was happening over there.

Mrs. Ebeling kept her silver hair in a bun and wore a blue calico apron over her thin flowered dresses regardless of the season. If the house held a chill, as it often did, she donned a grey sweater with brass buttons up the front that smelled of cedar and camphor. Although she tended the flower beds along the front porch, I never once saw her venture beyond the yard on her own. Every Sunday her son, Herman came by in his white Olds to take her to church and dinner before buying her a week's worth of groceries. Otherwise, she seemed always to be at home.

Frail and birdlike, Mrs. Ebeling reminded me of my late grandmother. She was kindly to me as the only other woman in the house – the other room was rented to a woman who lived with her boyfriend but wanted her parents to believe otherwise – and though somewhat forgetful, Mrs. Ebeling seemed to sense when I was feeling particularly blue. At those times she would ask me to the kitchen where she would brew a pot of tea and sit across the table talking of her life growing up on a small ranch west of the city where wolves prowled the fence line looking for wayward lambs and Austin was merely a dim glow in the night sky. She allowed me to talk if I wished but never asked about my personal life. Listening to her stories about her family calmed me like nothing else and I soon grew fond of her.

After the first of the year, I began to notice her forgetfulness seemed to be worsening. She would leave clothes on the line for days at a time or tell me the same news two or three times in an hour. At first I thought it was just due to her age, but I began to worry when I found the stove on or a faucet left running for no apparent reason. Then one morning I came back from class to find the house full of a choking smoke. The smell was awful. I ran from room to room calling for her and finally found her sitting at the kitchen table completely unaware that a pot of cabbage was burning on the stove. Not long after, her son moved her to a nursing home. She died less than a month later.

About three weeks after, Len decided to take me bar-hopping. He liked to drink beer on Saturday afternoons and had heard about a saloon in a small town an hour west of the city. He had a particular interest in out of the way places, especially bars that had a history to them. The weather was warm and spring-like that morning even though it was less than a week before Valentine's Day. February can be like that in central Texas. I was sitting on Mrs. Ebeling's broad porch when Len drove up in a pickup he had borrowed from his mechanic friend, Elton Stiles. Len's beat up VW bug was about as reliable as the weather and Elton argued him out of taking it and into using his truck instead. In terms of practical matters, Elton considered Len's hold on reality suspect and was more than a little protective of me in a way I never fully understood. I was wondering about that as I hopped in the passenger seat and we headed west.

Len and I had seen each other nearly every day in the months since Hannah surprised us in the middle of the night. That nightmare still haunted me. Of course, she told everyone she knew the whole sad story and I soon found myself without a friend in the world. I had crossed a line and there was no forgiveness on the other side. Most considered it a horrible betrayal, with me as the betrayer, and would have little to do with me. Hannah never mentioned that I had tried to talk with her beforehand and she refused me, or that Len and I had become friends over a course of months with no intention of falling in love, or that she had broken up with him weeks earlier and was seeing other men. All of that was lost and I was left as the scheming, underhanded betrayer. I soon realized any attempt to explain myself only sealed my guilt and there was no future in it.

The ordeal pushed me closer to Len, maybe too close, as I soon lost all perspective. He seemed to be all I had left in the world. My brother Roddy, cool and distant as always called only when something bad had happened or he wanted to complain. I was leaning on Len more each day. Somewhere in the back of my mind I felt the level ground

I'd always had with men falling away. I knew it was risky yet I let it happen. I had lost all confidence.

I tried not to think of all that as we drove through the low rolling ranches edging the west side of town and up the escarpment into hills dotted with limestone and granite. Elton's blue pickup rattled over patched blacktop roads that followed dry creeks and shallow, winding rivers. Fields of blonde grass moved behind rusted oil-pipe fences. I leaned back in my seat, watching endless lines of barbed wire and gnarled cedar posts clicking off the miles. Small town high schools, their parking lots crowded with pickups and yellow buses carrying basketball teams passed in and out of our sight. Stunted rows of dormant peach orchards stretched toward the distant tree line.

We followed the curve of the highway past an old jail and through a town square anchored by a solid courthouse of brick and limestone topped by a copper dome. A giant cement pecan stood above the lawn on blocks. Across from the courthouse, dusty windows of a hardware store held stacks of feed and tin cattle troughs. Next door a barber shop scrolled its candy cane sign.

Len turned at the intersection and pulled up to a red brick building that held an outdoor barbeque pit as big as a kitchen. We climbed out, inhaling the wonderful smell. Smoke poured from the pit, circling the metal lid in slow eddies. As we neared, the cook pulled a weighted cord, lifting the top and revealing chicken, brisket, sausage and even a steak or two sizzling on the wire grill. Len looked at me and pointed to the brisket, and I nodded. After helping ourselves to pinto beans and ice tea, we sat at one of the long tables next to an older couple. Len set the butcher paper holding the brisket on the table and cut a thick slice for us both. At first bite I was in heaven.

After we finished off the brisket Len left the table without a word, returning a moment later with two cans of beer. We toasted the road and the nearby older couple, who had their own cans. They had escaped the snows of

Montana and were on their way to the Rio Grande Valley where a daughter taught school. They had been married for forty-three years and had the similar appearance of some older couples. I noticed they were holding hands beneath the table and wondered what it must feel like to live with someone so long and still want to hold their hand.

My thoughts were interrupted as a noisy group passed our table on their way toward the door. I looked up and suddenly I found myself face-to-face with Hannah and her family. She stopped and glared at me in disbelief, a mixture of horror and disgust on her face before stifling a scream as she rushed out. Her parents stood for a moment looking from me to Len, then turned and followed her out. I stared across the table at Len's stunned face and wondered if my bad luck would ever end.

We drove in silence for miles. I had no words for how I felt and instead let my mind empty into the clear sky above the reddish, cedar-covered hills that stretched beyond the narrow road. The world outside my window seemed pristine and pure in the clear air, devoid of people or sign of civilization. I wished that I could enter that world and start over, escaping the mess I had made of my life. Part of me knew those thoughts were nothing more than fantasy but I needed to dream.

The truck shuddered and slowed, pulling me from my thoughts. Len turned onto a narrow, brush-lined road and we soon came to several buildings arranged along a tight curve. He parked next to a low wooden hut that had once been a post office. The weathered exterior had rarely if ever seen paint and the metal roof, streaked with rust reflected a weak winter sun. Picnic tables and cast-off folding chairs sat under sprawling Live oaks. I climbed through a narrow door and into a dimly-lighted room, the wooden floor sagging beneath my feet. I paused, letting my eyes adjust.

Len stepped past me and to the bar, ordering two longnecks from a rough looking woman in braids and flowered headband. She wore turquoise earrings and a rolled up red bandana around her neck. Her rugged, deeply-lined face made it clear she would put up with little in the way of unruliness from customers. Len paid her and turned, handing me a beer. I studied the colorful posters advertising upcoming concerts plastered helter-skelter across the unpainted walls. To our left a pot-belly stove radiated heat in spite of the warm weather. Two older men in felt Stetsons played dominoes on a wooden barrel in one corner while a woman dressed entirely in black leather made out with her ponytailed boyfriend in the other.

I wandered out the door, followed by Len, and on to a nearby empty table. Discarded bottle caps crunched beneath my feet somehow lifting my low spirits a bit. On the tree next to us a flier touted the upcoming mud dauber festival celebrating the approach of warmer weather. I tried to imagine the lime green of emerging leaves, the warm breezy afternoons, the feeling of hope carried in the smell of spring but the dry lifelessness of winter instead filled my mind. Then I felt the touch of Len's hand on mine.

"We can't let what happened control our lives. The past is over. We have to move on."

"It's not so easy when everyone you know hates you."

"I don't hate you."

"Don't you see? You're just a guy who used to date Hannah? I'm the friend who let her down."

"Hannah made her choices but she'd rather blame you than herself."

"I feel blamed."

"So, what are you going to do now? Are you going to feel bad about what happened forever or leave it behind and live your life? It's up to you, Mazie."

He made it sound so easy. I had no idea what I was going to do but I didn't want to be one of those pitiful people I'd seen that let one mistake ruin their life. I had to decide one way or the other. No one could make that decision but me and, although I still had little idea how to go about it, I knew Len was right. I had to find a way forward.

I looked at him for awhile and then held up my beer. "Alright, a toast to moving on."

"To moving on."

He stood and drained his beer. "Another round to the future, then."

"To the future." I tried to sound convincing.

As Len vanished into the bar several people walked up and sat at the other end of the table, two women and a man. Both women wore grimy jeans and black t-shirts saying something no longer legible. The man's stringy hair poked out from beneath his dirty ball cap. Spending my days around grungy college students, I was used to casual dress but these three were in another league altogether. In no time, the man turned to me.

"You got any spare cigs, darlin'?" He held up a plastic cigarette lighter.

"No, sorry, I don't smoke." I glanced at the bar, hoping to spot Len.

"So, are you here all by yourself? 'Cause if you are, you can just join up with us. We're here by ourselves, aren't we?"

The women nodded and smiled, unafraid to show the gaps in their yellow teeth. They moved a little closer to me.

"Oh, he's just getting another round." I nodded toward the bar. "But thanks."

"He don't smoke, I guess." The man again held up his lighter.

"No, sorry."

"That's okay, we'll keep you company. Have you all been here before?" The man moved a little closer.

"No, we never have."

I glanced at the bar again, wondering what in the world could be taking Len so long.

"Well, you'll have to come back next weekend for sure."

Just then I noticed Len standing next to me. He set the bottles on the table and sat across from me, next to one of the women. He nodded to the man.

"What's next weekend?" Len glanced at me.

"It's the funnest thing they do around here all year. It's called the Hug Fest."

The women nodded in unison, the one closest to Len looked like she might climb onto his lap any second. The man leaned back, stuffed the lighter in his jeans pocket and pulled out a can of snuff, tapping it against the table and then stuffing a large wad inside his bottom lip. He turned, spit into the dirt and wiped his mouth with the back of his hand before continuing.

"They do it for Valentine's Day. They give out sheets of stick-on hearts in all different colors, and then you go around drinking beer and sticking the hearts on whoever you hug. Just the babes - I don't hug no guys." He frowned and shook his head.

"I do." The woman next to Len leaned towards him.

I could see where we were headed and downed half my beer at once. The man looked around the table smiling then slapped his knee with the palm of his hand.

"I got a idea. We could start early." He turned to me.

The woman next to Len grinned. "Yeah, darlin', we could start right now."

I drained my beer in an instant while trying to think up with an excuse to leave. The man looked at me and smiled, black grains of snuff dotting his teeth. He turned and spit. I looked at Len, who seemed unnaturally calm considering the situation. He winked and stood.

"You folks won't want to be hugging us, I don't believe."

"Why, sure we do honey." The woman looked up at him.

"We might expose you to what we have. It's very contagious but only if we have close contact with someone."

36

"You all don't look sick." The man looked from Len to me.

Len held out his arm, pulling up his sleeve and showing them a large reddish mark on the inside of his arm. The woman next to him moved away.

"What is it?" The man grimaced.

"It's a tropical skin disease I got while working in a biology lab. It can spread over your entire body if the medication doesn't work."

"Does it hurt?" The woman asked.

Len nodded. "It's extremely painful, especially if it spreads to your sensitive areas, if you know what I mean."

"Sensitive areas?" She repeated, wincing.

"That's right. The medication doesn't always work." Len rolled down his sleeve.

She stood and stepped away from the table, closely followed by the other woman. The man watched them for a moment and then rose, stuffing the can of snuff in his back pocket. He turned and spit before turning back to us.

"We'll leave you to it, then. You all have yourself a nice day."

"Sensitive areas?" I looked across the table at Len, trying not to smile.

"Well, a birthmark can spread, can't it?"

"You and your birthmark better get me out of here before I burst out laughing and get us both in trouble."

Six

I tried to focus on the here and now as I climbed out of
the truck and watched Nacho wind down the rutted gravel
drive that ran from the house to the nursery. Quit stood
nearby surveying the property. Grass growing high
between the wheel paths and beyond drifted before a light
wind, the land spreading out below us in a gradual slope.
Granite boulders peaking through the earth in places
glowed pink in the low sun. Behind us, Angie's house
stood nearest the street while to our right the small frame
bungalow Quit's grandfather built in 1939 from a Sears
and Roebuck kit sat perched on a thick limestone
outcropping. He had named it the "Little House". In the
waning light of early evening, we could see a figure
moving from window to window.

Beyond the small bungalow, a low stone building faced
away from the street, connected to the two houses by a
winding gravel walkway. Further down the hill, the
dilapidated barn Quit would remember from his childhood
stood restored and surrounded by potted palms and cacti.
Near the entrance, Nacho began unloading bags of peat
moss.

"Someone's here about a job." A voice came out of
nowhere.

I jumped even though I recognized the voice. "Do you
like sneaking up on people like that, Naomi?"

I turned to her. Naomi's square face, framed by short,
bristling hair and silver stud earrings always seemed to me
both friendly and vaguely threatening. She rarely smiled.
She wore a red t-shirt with partially rolled up sleeves,
faded jeans and heavy work boots. Self-contained and gruff
as a rule, she was hard to read but a talented landscape
designer.

"This here is Bean McEwen." She handed over several sheets of paper.

"Bean McEwen." I repeated the name, trying not to smile.

"Says he needs a job, Mazie. I expect you can use the help."

A young man stood at her elbow. His compact frame appeared ready to take flight. He glanced up at Quit but otherwise kept his eyes to the ground.

"What kind of job?" I studied the boy.

"In the nursery, of course." Naomi barked. "That's what you people do around here. So, what do you want to do?"

"We'll take it from here, Naomi." I nodded toward Quit. "This is Angie's brother, Quit. I'm telling him about the business. Naomi is a landscape designer. She rents an office from you."

Unsmiling, she nodded at Quit. "That's what I do and I have a big project for the golf course so I'd better get back to it."

Naomi turned and walked toward the office before Quit could say a word. I handed him the papers and let him look them over for a moment. The boy seemed nervous as a cat, looking here and there and anywhere but at me. When I thought Quit had taken enough time, I spoke.

"So, what do you want to do?"

"Hold on a minute." Quit thumbed through the papers again.

"Are you going to talk to him or just stand here reading all night?"

He looked at me for a moment. "Well, Mazie, this is all new to me, should we hire him or not?"

"We need the help but you're the boss now so you get to decide."

"Well, I don't know how we can hire someone named Bean when we already have Nacho working here." He looked up and smiled. "The town will think we're a bit strange and that would be bad for business, now wouldn't it?"

The boy raised his face and squinted, looking Quit in the eye. "I go by Cam. It stands for Campbell, my middle name."

He had a defiant air about him and a clear edge to his voice. I wondered if he'd be trouble but decided to ignore the thought. Something made me want to protect him in spite of his prickly demeanor.

"I'm glad to hear it. I guess you're hired then. When can you start?" Quit handed me the papers.

"Right now. The fact is I got nowhere to go and nowhere to stay. I was hoping I could start work now and you'd let me sleep in that barn down there." He nodded down the hill.

"Nowhere to go?" Quit frowned.

"My step-father kicked me out of the house. I can get a place once I save a little." He stepped back, anger flashing across his face. "Unless you're going to tell me I don't have a job now. That would figure."

"Hold on now." I held up a hand. "Give us a moment here."

I moved a distance away and motioned Quit to join me. We stood together looking at the boy.

"What are you thinking?" Quit leaned towards me.

"We do have an extra room down there with a cot in it. It doesn't get used for anything but storage now. I think it would be alright for him to stay there if you can agree to it."

"He's seems awful edgy to me. Do you think it's a good idea?"

"This is your business we're talking about, not mine." I whispered. "But that boy is asking for our help. I can see that he's had a bad time of it and it's hard for him to ask for much of anything, much less a place to sleep. Angie would've helped him. Now I know you're not her and you are in charge but I think we ought to give him a try. So, there you have it. What do you say?"

Quit straightened up and faced Cam. "Come on over. We've decided."

Cam hesitated. "You're not going to tell me to go back home are you? I won't do it."

"You sure do jump to conclusions." Quit looked at me and nodded. "But we're going to hire you anyway."

I wondered what we were getting ourselves into but decided I'd have to think it through later. I felt sure Angie would have helped the boy and I was determined to do the same, if I could.

"Go on down and help Nacho unload the truck." I pointed at the truck. "Tell him I said to open up the storage room so you can clean it out. That's where you'll stay. We'll be down later to help you get settled."

The boy hesitated, looking at Quit expectantly. I might have taken it personally but I could see the boy was used to taking orders from men. He stood waiting for an answer.

"It's okay." Quit waved him toward the barn. "Do what she says, Cam."

I faced Quit. "Angie would like that boy."

"I don't know. He could be trouble."

"You did your share of causing trouble so I guess you can handle him. It'll be good for you."

We watched the boy walk through the tall grass toward the barn and I wondered what Quit would decide to do with all of this, the house, the barn, the office. I loved the place and the business, mostly because Angie put so much of herself into it. I missed her more than I could say and felt close to her here. I was about to bring up the subject again when I noticed him looking toward the house.

"So, who else works here? I saw someone in the Little House. You're living there, aren't you?"

"That's still the house my father gave me and I still live there." I waved my hand down the slope. "Everything else belonged to Angie and now it belongs to you. She and I did alright in spite of the wayward men of this family."

"Travelling was part of the work I did, Mazie."

I studied him as he surveyed the scene. Although his dark hair and sharp cheekbones lent his features a cool reserve, his deep-set eyes belied a hidden intensity, as if an unspoken truth struggled for control.

"You know, it surprises me how much you look like your father when he was your age. You're thinner. He had let himself get a paunch, but otherwise it's eerie how much you look like him."

He frowned. "Why do you keep bringing him up? I haven't wasted time thinking about him and I don't want to start now. Besides, he's long dead, no doubt."

"It's just something I noticed, Quit. No need to get touchy."

He again looked toward my house. "You still haven't told me who else we have working here. If I'm the owner now, like you keep reminding me, then I should know what's what."

I needed to talk to Quit, and what we needed to talk about was important, but I was waiting for the right moment. I knew it would be risky to rush into news that was likely to affect him in ways I could scarcely imagine. I wanted him around long enough to understand how important this place was to Angie and I knew that would take time. I figured if he understood, then maybe he'd stay. Still, I realized I'd have to face the music and tell him sooner or later. The question was when. I hoped that I'd know when the right moment arrived.

"Well, you can see that Nacho's a good man, except for a memory problem that kept him from finding work until he came here. And you met Winston." I tried to get my mind off the secret I was keeping and focus on his question. "He works with Nacho in the nursery. He has to take off occasionally for appointments at the state hospital across town. It's a mental thing."

"I could see that."

"Winston is a good worker when he's with us. He's just a little addled."

"I'm beginning to feel a little addled."

"Nacho is solid, except when his memory acts up. We rely on him. Winston can swear like a sailor. That's one reason he couldn't hold a job before Angie hired him. We have to remind him to do certain things and not say certain things, especially when other people are around, but you'll get used to him."

"Quite a crew we have here." He forced a smile.

"You could say that."

"Do you work for the business, Mazie?"

"In a way. I've taken care of the books for years."

"You're an accountant?"

"Not exactly, I just keep the books. I taught Science at the high school for years but they ran into financial problems and I was laid off. So, I decided to help out around here. I'm using Angie's office, across the hall from Naomi."

The back door of the house opened and closed, and Grita stepped into the dim porch light. She looked around for a moment, waved and began walking towards us. Grita had been working for us a month and though friendly she seemed evasive, as if she had something to hide.

"And here comes the rest of the crew." I waved back.

"So, we have four working in the nursery?"

"No, she helps me out."

"Oh, you mean around the house, that sort of thing?"

"You could say that."

"I'm surprised you'd let anyone do your housework for you. You seem too independent for anything like that."

"You mean ornery, don't you?" I pretended to frown. "Don't answer that. Anyhow, I didn't say she did my housework, you did."

"Well, whose housework are you talking about then?"

Once Grita drew closer, the beauty of her dark hair and tea-colored skin was obvious even in the fading light. For an instant her gray eyes searched Quit's face, as if she recognized him. I wondered how long I could wait before telling him why she was there.

"Mazie, we're finished and I'm ready to start dinner if you want me to." She kept her eyes to the ground.

"Grita, I want you to meet my nephew, Quit." I nodded in his direction.

"Good to meet you." Quit bent forward, trying to get a better look at her.

"Hello." She glanced up at him. "I heard you were coming."

"Don't believe everything Mazie tells you." He tried to hide it, but he sounded uneasy.

"Go ahead and start getting dinner ready, honey. Quit will join us."

Quit held up a hand. "I promised to meet Father Gus for a drink."

"I forgot about that. Grita, can you save it for us? We'll be having a late dinner tonight."

"Well, okay. It's a pot roast so I'll leave it in the oven."

She faced Quit as if to say something but instead turned towards the house, a look of disappointment in her eyes. A little voice inside my head was trying to tell me something and I paused, trying to listen when Quit spoke, interrupting my thoughts.

"Have you known her for long? She reminds me of someone. It's strange, as if she's familiar but not quite."

"She has been a big help to me." I stalled.

"Who was she saying she's finished with? Do we have someone else working here? I thought you said she was the last of it."

I ran a hand across my cheek, trying to think of what to say and how to say it. I had no problem telling Quit about her work. What worried me was what I'd have to tell him after that. The last thing I wanted was him running off before we had a chance to get started. He looked at me like he expected bad news so I just gave up and blurted it out.

"I hate to surprise you with this Quit but I hired Grita to help me with your father. He's living here, recovering from a bout of cancer." I took a deep breath. "I know he left you and your sister high and dry, but he came back and Angie took him in. That was the way she was. Even though Roddy is my brother, I had no use for him after the way he treated you and Angie, and I told her so. But she wouldn't turn him away so I won't either because of her. I owe her that much."

"All these years I thought he was dead and now here he is fifty yards away?"

His face went pale and I reached out to steady him but he pushed my hand away. I could see it was a shock to learn his father was alive after nearly twenty years. He faced me without speaking, his eyes glazed.

I lightly touched his arm. "He's changed, Quit. Why don't you come see him?"

"No." He ran his hand through his hair. "No, no, no. I need some time."

He shook off my hand and began to pace a tight circle. I could see he wanted to leave.

"Does he know I'm here?"

"I haven't told him."

"Well, don't." He looked from me to the house and took a deep breath. "I'd appreciate it if you didn't just now, Mazie."

The back door to the house opened again and Grita stepped out, looking our way.

"Mazie, he's asking for you. He says he wants to see you right now. You know how he gets."

Quit shook his head. "He hasn't changed much. Tell me how to get to the bar Father Gus mentioned. He said you'd know which one."

"It's Dizzy's Ice House, on Cherokee just off Main. I'll take you, just give me one minute. You're not the only one who needs to get away from here."

I left Quit with his own thoughts and made my way toward the house while the fading light of dusk reflected in the windows and then vanished. As often happened, the close of the day held a dull sadness that stretched across me like a shadow. I tried to focus on what had just occurred but found no order to my thoughts and was left to wonder why Grita looked familiar to Quit and why she seemed to know him. Nothing made sense. And Len's image kept drifting through my mind at random. I needed to talk but not being the religious type I disliked the idea of talking to a priest. On the other hand, I needed a way to reason through the situation. I also needed a drink.

Seven

As I drove the dark road into town, my thoughts of Len shifted to puzzlement over Sephie Del Toro. Why leave her picture at the house with the ominous "murder" scratched across the bottom? Was someone trying to threaten Quit or warn him? Did the photo have a meaning or was it a cruel joke? I have to say the whole situation baffled me.

Something else bothered me too but I was unable put my finger on it, try as I might. I had no idea what Gus had on his mind other than Scotch and I wondered what questions Quit might have for him. In his role as priest, I figured the Father would have heard what went on around town so I decided I'd ask him about Sephie. Then I thought, why not ask Quit?

"I can't get that picture of Sephie off my mind. What do you make of it?"

He didn't answer at first. I glanced at him as his face, reflected in the dashboard lights, seemed to stare into the distance. The courthouse loomed into sight, its light bouncing off the low clouds overhead. Dizzy's Bar was just beyond.

"There's someone following you." Quit finally spoke.

I thought he was kidding. "Don't mess with a woman over forty, Quit. You might get hurt."

"I know what I'm talking about." He glanced at the side mirror. "You don't work in a war zone for long without developing a sixth sense for being tailed. You won't last long without it."

I turned trying to get a better look but Quit grabbed my arm and jerked me the other way.

"Don't let on you've spotted them."

"There can't be anyone following us. Why would they?" I forced a laugh. "I think you must have jet lag."

"Mazie, what kind of car does Grita have?"

"She has a beat up, gold Ford sedan." I kept glancing at the rear view mirror.

"The car following us is a sedan, but I can't tell the color."

"Why on earth would you think it's Grita?"

"No reason, I just had an odd feeling when I met her."

A block past the courthouse I turned left onto a short gravel road that ended abruptly in a steep drop-off, known locally as Drunkard's Drop. Below us the trickle of a small creek flowed toward the river two blocks beyond. To our right, stood a two story granite building with a finely carved stone archway that was once the town's only hotel. Dizzy's Ice House, aglow with neon beer signs, occupied one side while the other held Des Clymer's law office. In its day, the Shandua Hotel was popular with wealthy politicians and their female companions up from the capital to carouse, hunt and fish, in that order.

"I can't help but notice that no one is following us now." I quipped.

"You don't follow someone into a dead end." He barked back.

Quit waited at the rear of the car while I reached in to grab my purse and phone. Light from the bar fell across us in dim rectangles of blue and red. I could see a couple through the window making their way toward the exit. A moment later someone laughed and the door to the building slammed shut, echoing in the stone entryway like a gunshot. The next instant I was on the ground with Quit huddled next to me, his back against the car door and his eyes white with alarm.

"Good lord, Quit, why'd you do that?" I said between gasps. "If you're planning to tackle me, at least give me warning."

"Didn't you hear the gunfire?"

"That was no gunfire. It was only the door to Dizzy's place."

"How do you know?" He rubbed his face.

"I saw that couple over there walking out."

I got up as Quit craned his neck around the bumper to face the building, where a man and woman stood staring at us as if we were criminals. I waved, not knowing what else to do.

"We're just checking the tire here." I lied. "The car was making a strange sound."

They turned and walked away and I looked down at Quit. I could see he was shaking something awful. After a moment, he managed to stand.

"What just happened?" I brushed the dust off my coat and glared at him.

"Nothing." He avoided my eyes. "I thought I heard a gunshot and I took evasive action. There's nothing wrong with that."

"Not everybody reacts that way to loud noises."

"It's the only sensible way to act if bullets are flying." Anger flashed across his face. "Damn it, Mazie, we're outside a bar in case you haven't noticed. Bars and guns tend to go together."

"You sound paranoid, Quit. It was only a door that slammed shut."

"I'm not paranoid. We were being followed, remember?"

"Why would someone follow us?"

"I don't guess you owe anyone money, do you?" He grinned through his teeth, his eyes still full of anger. "Maybe you owe someone that gets upset if they don't get paid."

"You mean someone other than the bank?"

"Well, do you?" He said as we started for the door.

I was irritated at the question and his attitude and said nothing as I followed him toward the building. He stopped on the stairs and faced me, waiting for a reply. I can be more than a little stubborn when someone gets under my skin so I stared back at him. After a moment, I began thinking about his work overseas and what it might have done to him so I finally gave in.

"No, I don't owe anyone money." I mumbled.

"Thank you." He turned and walked into Dizzy's.

Gus sat at a window overlooking the creek, the windows behind him reflecting the dim red and blue lights of the bar. Next to him sat Des Clymer talking in his typical exuberant fashion, using his hands as much as his voice. I had known Des since grade school. We were involved once when we were a good bit younger but for some reason I could never explain whatever was there had faded over time. Although I found myself more than a little attracted to him on occasion, when I heard he was involved with Hannie Hereford, a widow over in Cherry Spring, I figured that was that. Quit sat on one side of the table and I took the chair opposite, still annoyed with him.

The bar had changed little since I had last seen it. Crowded with tables of varying sizes and paneled in a dark wood that matched a massive bar covering the far wall, the room seemed smaller than I remembered. The bar's carved wooden columns framed a tarnished mirror running the length of the counter. At one of the barstools an older man in chaps and spurs slumped before an empty shot glass and a longneck, his dusty Stetson on the chair next to him.

Des turned as I pulled out a chair. "Mazie Goforth, what brings you to Dizzy's? It's not like you to be out on the town."

Des had a disarming smile, impossible to dislike. Once handsome in an off-kilter sort of way, he was still good-looking in spite of his angled nose and thinning hair. Everything about him seemed to smile at once. He cocked his head to one side, taking my hand in his, studying me with his lively blue eyes. I thought it a wonder Des had never married, charming as he could be. I felt more than a little awkward sitting there, knowing what he said was true. I had kept myself locked up like a nun for the last year, maybe longer. Lately, I'd had a hard time keeping track of

50

time, what with Roddy back home and Angie gone. My life had become filled with other people's concerns, leaving time for little else. As I stared at Des, looking so relaxed and happy, I wondered if there was something wrong with me. I hardly ever seemed to smile.

"You're like expensive Scotch, Mazie. You only improve with age. Gus was just now holding forth on the merits of Scotch so I know what I'm talking about."

"You mean old Scotch, don't you Des?" I pulled my hand free.

"No, I mean the well-aged kind."

"I feel well-aged most mornings." I nodded towards Quit. "Des, this is my nephew Quit."

They shook hands as a waitress wearing too much makeup walked up to take our drink orders. As she moved closer, I could see the makeup was meant to cover a black eye and I wondered if a husband or boyfriend gave it to her as a reminder of who's in charge. So much for the power of love, I thought. I ordered a glass of wine. Quit stared at her for what seemed a long time, as if he was trying to remember something, before he finally ordered a beer. I thought again of Sephie and the disturbing combination of her photo and being followed, and I turned to face Father Gus.

"I have a question for you Gus." I had never called him anything except Father before but decided to follow Des' lead. "What do you know about a Josephina Del Toro?"

"Do you mean Sephie Del Toro?" Des held up an index finger.

"Well Des, I didn't think to ask you but if you know something I'd like to hear it."

"I handled some paperwork for her about a year ago." He pointed to the far wall. "It had to do with a ranch that she inherited way out west, near Presidio."

"If it was that far from here, why were you involved?" Quit leaned toward him.

"Although the land is in western Texas, she was living here. There was some animosity within the family about the land and she wasn't sure who she could trust. She wanted someone close by, someone she knew, involved in the transaction."

"She was living here?" I wondered how that fit in with the photo.

"That's right, the last I heard."

"Do you know anything else?"

"Mazie, you sound like a lawman." He chuckled. "That was the last contact I had with her."

"One more question. Did she have any family here?"

"A daughter, I believe but I never met her." He held up his hands. "That's all I know, sheriff."

The waitress returned with our drinks and Quit studied her again. Once she became aware of his interest she hurriedly set our drinks down and left. After what had happened in the parking lot, I worried he might get up to follow her but it was Des that stood.

"I'm sorry to leave such good company." He pointed to the door. "There's a realtor's meeting at the Ranch House Café and I have to introduce the speaker. Some yahoo from the Land Commission is going to talk about the State selling off land out west in the Christmas Mountains. Why the State would want to sell such a beautiful piece of Texas, I have no idea. I'm just the guy that gets to introduce the speakers. I don't know why, maybe they like my voice."

"It's because you always have a new joke to tell, Des."

"I do have a good one, Gus. I wish I could try it out on you but I'd better go." He hurried toward the door.

"Why are you two so interested in Ms. Del Toro?" Gus finished his drink and waved for another.

"Someone left this picture of her at the house, stuck in the door frame." Quit pulled the photo out of his shirt pocket and handed it to Gus.

Gus studied the image. "What do you make of it?"

"I have no idea. Sephie and I spent a lot of time together the summer before Angie got married. Then her parents sent her to live with an aunt in Mexico and I never saw her again."

"You were in love with her?"

"Well, we were both young but I thought so at the time."

He handed the picture back to Quit and stared at the table for what seemed like a long time, chewing his mustache and saying nothing. I looked at Quit and shrugged, not sure what to do. Finally, I couldn't stand it anymore so I spoke up.

"What is it, Gus?"

"I'm trying to decide what I can tell you." He pulled at his ear.

"You know something about her?"

He nodded. "I do."

"All this mystery worries me, Gus. What's it about."

The waitress returned again and set down drinks for all of us but this time Quit scarcely glanced at her. I tried to imagine what Gus could mean but could think of nothing. He pulled out a yellowed handkerchief and rubbed the sweat from his forehead, then downed half his Scotch in one gulp. He set down the glass, slapping the table with his palm.

"Alright Mazie, what do you know of the girl I sent a few weeks ago to help with your brother?"

"What do I know about Grita Sifuentes? Even though it's been over a month, she doesn't often talk about herself so I don't know much. She seems smart and she works hard. Now and then I get the feeling she's hiding something."

"She's a good worker?"

"She's been a great help to me."

"So, you plan to keep her on?"

"What should I know about her, Gus?"

"I don't want to say anything that might jeopardize her job."

"I plan to keep her around as long as she'll stay."

"Alright, here goes. This may be hard to believe but she's Sephie Del Toro's daughter."

I turned and looked at Quit, trying to understand what we'd just heard. Was it only coincidence that Sephie's daughter had come to work for us? It had to be. There was no way she could have known we needed to hire someone. On the other hand, she must have left the photo in the door frame.

I faced Quit. "She left the photo for you. It had to be her."

Quit turned to Gus. "But she has a different last name."

"After Grita was born, her mother married a man who was not her father. Although the marriage didn't last she kept the man's name for her daughter."

"What else can you tell us about her?"

"There was talk but it's little more than speculation."

"You mean gossip." I interrupted. "But let's hear it anyway."

"Grita was born in a town outside Mexico City. She never knew her father and her mother refused to talk about him, although she hinted that he was from Texas. Eventually, Grita and her mother moved back to Texas. Grita's mother died recently in an accident while visiting the property she inherited."

"How old is Grita?" Quit squinted, his eyes unfocused.

"Well, she's smart but she left high school in order to work. I'd guess she's about sixteen."

"But, Gus, she told me she's eighteen." I replied.

"It's possible but I don't think so. She's in a bad place for a girl so young. Would you lie about your age if you needed a job?"

"I see what you mean."

Quit leaned his elbows on the table. "She doesn't have any idea who her father was?"

"Not that I know of. Why do you ask?"

Quit sat staring into space, saying nothing, and all at once I realized what he must be thinking. I nearly jumped out of my chair.

"Lordy, Quit, you think she's yours don't you?"

"I don't know what to think." Quit pulled at his fingers. "Gus, did Sephie ever mention me?"

"I was told that she spoke well of you and said you were once close. I would guess that she said the same to Grita. Nothing ever came up about you being Grita's father."

"Grita must think so, if she left that picture of Sephie for you." I sat back in my chair. "But, why would she think her mother was murdered?"

Gus held up a hand. "Coincidentally, Des and I were just talking about the struggle over water rights in the western part of the State. Water has always been a point of contention out there. According to Des, there's an interest among developers in building resorts, complete with golf courses that require a lot of water. Des said there have been threats made toward land owners reluctant to sell."

"Would they murder someone just for water, Gus? I find it hard to believe."

"Greed is a powerful motive to do harm, Mazie." Gus leaned across the table. "Are you feeling alright, Quit? You're looking a bit pale."

"Is it possible that I'm Grita's father?" Quit stared into the distance.

He sat back in his chair, looking as if he'd been slapped. I thought he must be in shock, having so much thrown at him all at once. In one short day, he'd taken on an ailing business, a sick father and the possibility of a daughter he never knew existed. Gus left the table and returned a moment later with a half-filled glass. He placed it in Quit's hand.

"Take a good swig, Quit. It'll do you good."

I patted Quit's arm. "I don't know that I've ever had a stranger day than this one."

Gus smiled. "God likes to keep us guessing."

Eight

The sheer greed of humankind never ceases to amaze me - or disgust me. Otherwise law-abiding people will take the rug right out from under you if they want it and think they can get away with it. The more I see of life, the more grateful I am for the few trustworthy souls I've been lucky enough to know. The sad truth is people are prone to an avarice and underhandedness that seems taken right out of Dickens even when it comes to, of all things, water. You might think something as plentiful and essential to survival would be looked upon differently but you'd be wrong. We humans have a long history of fighting each other over water. Texas is no exception.

Now, if you happened to be traveling through the western part of the state you could look out your window at a landscape so dry and desolate you'd be tempted to think it must be without moisture altogether. The truth is, parched as it may be, the area contains dozens of underground aquifers with names like Bone Spring, Rustler and Capitan Reef. In some places the aquifers reach the surface creating artesian wells like the Kokernot, Davis and Phantom Lake springs, just to name a few. They once flowed clear but no more.

It's a sad fact that those springs went dry and aquifer overuse was a major part of it. What is known as the rule of capture is the law of the land and that means property owners can pump as much water as they like and their neighbors can't do a thing about it. Comanche Springs, in the small town of Fort Stockton went dry, resulting in a landmark legal case involving groundwater. The springs had been around since at least 1684. Then a local landowner started heavy pumping from a nearby well during the big drought of the 1950's and eventually the spring dried up. The county even went to court to stop the pumping but judges decided the rule of capture applied and that, as they say, was that.

So, when Gus brought up water as a motive in Sephie's death I decided I'd go right to my brother Roddy. Having read a few of his hydrogeology texts, I figured he had to know more than a little about aquifers and I wanted to see what he had to say on the subject. He was trained as a geologist, after all. I wasn't sure he'd be willing or able to talk, considering he'd had a brain tumor but I was never shy about imposing on family if I had a reason. I wanted to know if what Gus had said at Dizzy's could be true.

As we were leaving the bar, Quit had walked up to the waitress and called her by name. I wondered how he could have known since she never mentioned it but the Scotch had brought him out of his shock and made him almost friendly. She looked at him for a moment and then her mouth flew open and I could see she had just then recognized him. She reached up to cover her black eye.

"Mercy, Quit Goforth, how long has it been since I saw you last?"

"Too long to remember." He nodded toward me. "Zoe Finn, this is Mazie."

I shook her hand. Beneath her makeup, I could see she was naturally pretty, with blue eyes that tended toward purple. Her dark auburn hair lay thick about her shoulders. She looked as if she'd rather disappear than be seen in her current state. Finally, she let her hand drop.

"I'm sorry I had to run into you just now." She looked from me to Quit. "I know how bad I must look."

"I'd say other than a shiner you're looking good, Zoe." Quit leaned against the bar. "What happened?"

"You're not going to believe it." She reached up to her face again. "I own a horse, Rosie, a reliable and good-natured mare. We were lining up for the Frontier Days parade last Saturday night when someone came up behind us leading a llama covered in blinking Christmas lights. Rosie nearly jumped out of her skin. I was leaning forward to check the bridle and got an eye full of horse before I knew what had happened. I never saw the llama coming but I'll bet Rosie thought it was some sort of a ghost horse. Whatever she thought, that llama startled the both of us but good."

"That sounds like it hurt, Zoe. But I guess it could've been worse."

"That's easy for you to say, Quit. You're not the one with a black eye. I managed to keep from getting thrown, at least. Rosie is a gentle horse. She and I do equine therapy at the county barn on Thursday afternoons."

"Equine therapy? Is that what you need when your horse gives you a shiner?" Quit smiled.

"You should come to my house, Zoe." I winked at her. "I know a few folks who could use some therapy."

"It's what I love. I just wait tables to pay the bills." She turned to Quit. "Quit, why don't you come see what it's like? I could use the help."

"I don't know anything about horse therapy." He shook his head.

"You know about horses." She turned to me. "Mazie, Quit and I used to ride together at my parent's ranch. He got to be pretty good on a horse."

He rubbed his jaw. "I'd forgotten all about that."

"Come with me next Thursday and see Rosie in action. She's really good with the kids." She grabbed an order pad from the counter. "I've got to get back to work."

On the drive back home it struck me how little I knew of Quit. Had he ever been married? Did he have a girlfriend or maybe even a child back in Europe? What exactly was his work over there? I was determined to find out but I decided to let it go for the moment. I was more interested in what Roddy might tell me about underground water.

Nine

When Angie first asked if I would be willing to share my little house with Roddy, I nearly fainted. I told her I'd think about it. I was still angry with him over leaving the way he did, and I was angry with her for asking me to take him in. If it had been anyone other than Angie, I might have said no but I could never refuse her for long. Once I saw Roddy in person, frail and thin as a post, I felt differently. We soon had him set up in the spare bedroom.

Although it was late by the time we returned from Dizzy's, Roddy was still awake when I knocked on his door. He was a good bit older than me but not what you'd call old. Still, he looked positively ancient when we moved him into the house. All of his hair had fallen out during the treatments, even his eyebrows, and then it came back a wispy, pure white. With his round, tinted glasses on, he looked just like a baby owl. He looked up from his audio book as I walked into the room.

"What book do you have now?" I sat on the bed.

"It's Turgenev's *Fathers and Sons*."

He held up a hand as if blessing me. Since his surgery, Roddy had taken on a habit of doing odd things with his hands when he spoke. He sometimes looked like he was directing a symphony, other times like chopping wood. I suppose a person that loses his sight due to a brain tumor can develop mannerisms as a result of the blindness, the tumor or the surgery. All I knew for sure was that using his hands to speak the way he did was necessary. I once asked him to try and keep his hands still while we were talking and I sat there for a full minute while he contorted his face this way and that without managing a single word. I never asked again.

"Turgenev is worth reading." I sat on the bed.

"I have trouble keeping the Russian names straight. They tire me out."

Another strange habit Roddy had acquired was that he would never ask a question. If he wanted to know something he would sit, waiting, his white eyebrows arching like twin question marks. It had taken some getting used to but I had become fair at figuring out what he wanted to ask. I wondered how long I'd have to continue our guessing game. The doctor had said some of his mannerisms would go away in time so I hoped he'd lose this one.

"You're probably wondering why I came by, late as it is."

"I'm wondering why you came by late as it is." He repeated. It was another new habit.

"Do you remember much about the geology of western Texas?"

"Do you remember? I can't tell you what happened yesterday but geology I remember."

"If someone owned land that had water under it and you needed that water, could you get at it without owning the land or would you need to own that land to get to the water?"

"Would you need that land?" He repeated, cutting the air with his hand. "Some of the groundwater out there is in big aquifers that can be tapped by multiple landowners, but some are very contained. If you didn't own the land over the aquifer, you would have no way to access it."

"You're probably wondering why I'm asking. I'm trying to understand why a person might kill someone to get at their water."

"To get at their water, I don't know about. It's not geology. I do know that water is everything in that part of the world. In some places you have to drill over a thousand feet before you reach an aquifer, if you reach one at all. Even then, the water may be so filled with minerals as to be unusable." He bent down and passed his hand across the

61

floor several times as if feeling for something. "On the other hand, land out there isn't worth much without water. It's just too dry."

"So, if you have land over an aquifer it's worth a lot."

"Worth a lot, but the problem out west is there isn't enough rainfall to sustain an aquifer if it is being pumped at anything close to a significant rate."

"It sounds like a person that needed water might do just about anything to get at it."

"Anything to get at it. West Texas has an ancient geology that works in its own way. No one can change that." He set aside his book and stood. "I'm tired now, Mazie."

Roddy had done away with social niceties since his surgery, not that he ever had much in the way of warmth and hospitality. Still, he seemed to want companionship in spite of his cut and dry manner. I sensed it more than I could actually see it. I moved to the door.

"Can I help you with anything, Roddy?"

He stood in the middle of the room, perfectly still. I could see from his eyes that his mind was working, so I waited. He started slowly shaking his head, as if denying something. Then he held up a hand.

"When I lost my sight it felt as if time had stopped all at once. There was only darkness, like a never-ending moonless night, and what was happening then didn't seem as real as what I could remember. I felt trapped in the past, within my memories of what I'd seen, what I could recall." He let his hand fall.

"That sounds frightful, Roddy."

"I wanted to let you know, Mazie."

I didn't know what to say. "Is there anything else you want to tell me?"

He shook his head and moved to the bed. I stood, trying to think if there was something I should say but I could think of nothing.

"Should I turn out the light?"

"I wouldn't know the difference if you did, Mazie."

"I know Roddy, it's just a habit." I pulled the door to. "Good night then, and thanks for the help."

He made no answer as I walked away. I sat at the kitchen table puzzling over the turns a life can take. Quit and Roddy had come home much changed from who they once were yet somehow still familiar. I wondered if in truth they were at all like they once were or if I saw in them what I wanted to see. Was I just looking for whatever fit my memory of them, trying to make sense of what I saw, to connect the dots? I wanted to do more than that. I wanted to know what I should say to Roddy. I wanted to understand what had happened to Sephie Del Toro in that beautiful, desolate part of the world. I wanted to imagine what it must be like for Grita to be alone so young. My intuition told me that under her calm demeanor she was terrified at all that had happened and all that might happen still. Maybe that was what she was hiding from. I decided to find out.

Ten

Early the next morning, I took a cup of coffee and two biscuits down to the barn, planning to leave them outside Cam's room. I thought he might appreciate some breakfast on his first day of work. Before I had a chance to knock, I spotted him through the wide doorway already at work repotting young sabal palms into large barrels we had stacked behind the barn. Angie had developed a specialized nursery business growing and selling palm trees to landscaping firms in the city, and Naomi's contacts kept enough orders coming in to keep the business afloat.

I set the coffee and biscuits on a work table and started to call to Cam when something caught my eye. I turned to see Grita walking away from Cam's room, the door now open. She hurried up the hill as if she hoped no one would spot her. I suppose I was surprised at first but after I thought about it, I wondered why I would be. They were young and had a life to live just like everyone. I turned back to the doorway and called to Cam.

"Would you like to have a little something to eat?" I nodded toward the table.

He glanced at me, shook his head and kept working on the pots with an intensity that bordered on violence, rope-like veins trailing down his sunburned neck. He looked as if he was expecting someone to jump him at any moment. I stood there wondering what to say next.

"It's just coffee and biscuits. No charge." I thought I'd try to lighten the mood. "My biscuits aren't the kind you'd want to pay for anyway, but I promise they won't kill you. I can't promise you won't break a tooth."

He shook his head again and kept working so I walked through the doors into the yellow sunlight and sat on an overturned barrel. I tried to imagine what might be going through his mind and decided he might need a friend.

"I'll tell you what I'll do. I'm going to leave them on the table so if you get hungry later you'll know where they are." I shielded my eyes from the morning sun. "My brother Rand would never have any breakfast other than coffee. He said he just couldn't stomach food early in the day. You remind me of him a bit. He was all business when it came to work, too."

"I just need this job." He looked up at me. "I can't go back home."

"You won't lose your job if you take a coffee break."

"I don't want to take any chances. I'm not ever going back."

I studied him for a moment. "Don't you miss your home, Cam?"

He stood upright, red in the face. "I don't want anyone feeling sorry for me. I don't need anyone's pity. I can take care of myself."

He glared at me but only for a second, then he began stacking the bags of peat moss Nacho had unloaded the night before. I leaned back, trying to imagine what it must be like to be young and have no home to go to. I decided to give him time to settle in. I was rushing things, as usual.

"Those biscuits are hospitality Cam, not pity. We're glad to have you here." I stood, thinking of Angie. "You have a place with us as long as you want it."

I turned and started toward the barn. Just as I got to the door he spoke, so quietly I could scarcely hear.

"It takes me time to get used to people."

I stopped and turned beneath the doorway. "Some people can be hard to get used to."

"People make me mad more than anything."

"They can make me mad too but more often they disappoint me." I surprised myself saying it.

"People will always let you down sooner or later." He looked away.

"I've been let down more times than I'd like to admit, Cam, and when it happens I don't want to have anything to do with anybody for a while. But there are some people I can count on."

He looked at me again. "Like your brother, the one I remind you of?"

"Well Cam, Rand died many years ago during the war in Viet Nam."

"He was a soldier?"

"No, he was a pilot. His plane was shot down."

Even after so many years I felt the sadness as it passed across my face. I could see in his eyes that Cam saw it as well.

"I'm sorry, Mrs. Goforth."

"Thank you, Cam. Please call me Mazie so I won't feel so ancient."

"Do you have other family?"

"My older brother Roddy and Quit are all that's left."

"I don't have any brothers or sisters."

The look on his face worried me. "Cam, you know there are people you can count on, don't you?"

"I count on myself." He sounded unconvinced.

"What about your parents?"

I knew it was a mistake as soon as I said it. His face seemed to stiffen and he turned, looking down the hill toward the river. There was no anger in his voice, only disappointment.

"I'd better get back to work." He picked up a pruning saw. "Nacho asked me to prune the big palms down the hill."

I was mad at myself for pushing him and afraid of making things worse, so I said nothing as he walked down the rutted drive past the greenhouse. I thought again of Rand and the silent anger he sometimes held after we argued, and I wished he was here to tell me what to do. Men have their own way of communicating, inadequate as it may be. Even still, I understood a little too well what Cam was feeling. There were days when the space between me and other people seemed a distance infinite and

66

impassable, like the desert east of El Paso. I felt alone yet bothered by people. Maybe it had started after my falling out with Hannah. Maybe I was too independent. I had been disappointed more often than I wanted to admit. I had lost too much. Yet hearing Cam talk, I felt like I was listening to myself and I didn't much like what I heard.

Eleven

After my conversation with Gus I had intended to talk with Grita straight away but a mistake came up with a shipment of pots and then there was a problem with the greenhouse and it simply slipped my mind. One afternoon I realized over two weeks had passed. I had spent bits of time with her here and there while she worked with Roddy and had grown to like her, yet I still knew little about her. The thought crossed my mind that I had avoided talking to her because I hoped she would come to me first. I decided it was time for me to make a move.

Nacho was waiting for me as I stepped out of the office, his face lined with worry. We'd had little contact with each other before Angie died, but after she was gone I had gotten to know him well as we worked to keep the business afloat. I knew I could count on him for an honest opinion and I knew he'd get straight to the point. That's just what he did.

"Something's wrong with Quit. He nearly lost it after Winston couldn't find an order, yelling at him and cussing him. Before I knew it, Cam was in there defending Winston and then Quit got into it with Cam. He, Quit, was out of control. He had Cam up against the wall and for a moment I thought someone was going to get seriously hurt. I managed to break it up before it went too far, but not by much."

I motioned him to follow me. "What do you think is bothering him?"

"I don't know. It seems to come out of nowhere. He never talks about himself so he's hard to figure. Believe me, I've tried." He pulled at his mustache. "He reminds me of some of the guys in 'Nam who had seen too much."

"Too much?"

"They'd seen so much death and violence they were walking time bombs. You never could tell when they might explode."

"What do you think we should do?"

"I don't know but I'm worried. Cam has his own short fuse. Between him and Quit it could turn ugly quick."

I knew he was right. Quit was rough with Cam the way Roddy had been with him. A few days earlier Quit had been overly harsh with him and it was all I could do to get Cam to walk away. I saw that wild look in his eye and I shuddered to think what might have happened if I had been somewhere other than there at that very moment.

I stopped at the door to my house, turning to face Nacho. "I'll try to talk to him, Nacho. Thanks for telling me."

I stepped inside the house, trying to put Quit out of my mind and figure how I might strike up a conversation with Grita. She was still working with Roddy so I sat back for a moment, watching her help him through his physical therapy and wondering what Cam might see in her. Sunlight streamed through the living room windows, falling across her satin-like black hair. Her gray eyes and long lashes seemed to fill her face with mystery, and the thought came to me that she had the beauty the young have but rarely realize. As she took hold of Roddy's elbow, her hair fell across her face in a dark wave and she pulled it back, tucking it behind her ear in one motion, never taking her eyes off him. In spite of her skillful way with him she seemed less focused than usual. She walked him to his room and then returned, sitting across the table from me.

"Can I talk to you, Mazie?" She tugged at her middle finger.

"I thought you might have something to tell me."

Her eyes grew wide. "Did I do something wrong?"

"You just seem a little preoccupied."

"I try to do a good job."

"You do fine. It just looks like something is bothering you."

"I feel safe here." Her voice was barely above a whisper. "I don't know what I'd do if you let me go."

"Let you go? Grita, you're good with Roddy and I think he's getting better because of it." I leaned toward her. "What's on your mind?"

She tugged at her finger again and took a deep breath. She looked as if she might cry.

"I don't have anyone I can talk to."

"Is it about Cam?"

"What?"

"I saw you leaving his room one morning last week."

"Oh, God!" She sat back, looking at me in disbelief.

"There's no reason to worry, Grita, you have a right to live your life the way you want to."

"I don't know what happened. I thought we were just friends. Something upset me and I went to talk to him and the next thing I knew we were kissing." She rubbed her forehead. "But it's not about that."

I was shocked at how similar her story was to mine when I was her age. I tried to hide my surprise.

"What is it, then?"

"I think someone is watching me." She glanced out the window.

I thought of what Quit had said the week before about being followed but I was skeptical of his judgment. I figured Grita's concern more than likely had to do with an ex-boyfriend, her imagination or both. Still, I wanted hear what she had to say.

"You mean someone is stalking you?"

She nodded. "Something like that. The phone rings but they won't say anything when I answer. At night, I feel like someone is out there watching."

"Who do you think it is?"

"I have to tell you something else first." She clasped her hands together. "When Father Gus referred me here I had no idea where he was sending me. Then I saw Quit's picture on your bedroom table and recognized it as the same photo my mother had always carried in her purse. She wouldn't tell me his name but said he was someone from her past, someone special. I could never get her to tell me anything more.

"When Father Gus told me Quit might be coming here, I couldn't believe I was going to meet the person I had wondered about for so long. I found a picture of my mother when she was young, put it in an envelope and stuck it in the door so he would find it. I was hoping he would want to help me."

"Help you with what, Grita?"

"That's what I wanted to talk to you about. It's what I'm worried about."

"I don't understand."

"You know that my mother is dead." She stared into the table top. "We moved here a few months before the accident and I left behind everything, everyone I knew."

Her gray eyes seemed to grow dark and I thought of Quit and Angie alone in the world at a young age.

"You're young to lose a parent. It's hard enough when you're my age." I leaned down to see her face. "What's worrying you, Grita?"

She stared at the table in silence.

"Who is watching you?"

"I don't think it was an accident. I think my mother was killed."

"Why would you think that?"

"She inherited land that her relatives in Mexico believe belongs to them. I think they wanted her out of the way. That's why I wrote 'murdered' on the photograph. I thought Quit might want to help if he knew and still cared about her, but I'm afraid to ask him. Can you help me talk to him?"

I wondered if blaming her relatives was just Grita's attempt to make sense of her mother's death. We want a solid reason rather than random chance to explain the bad things that happen to us and our imagination will sometimes supply that explanation.

"What do you think Quit can do?"

"He could help me find the truth about my mother. He could help me find out who's following me."

"Have you seen any of your relatives around here?"

"No."

"Have they contacted you?"

"No."

"But you think they're stalking you?"

"I think so." She looked up. "I don't know, maybe."

"But why wouldn't they just offer to buy the land from you?"

"Maybe they don't want to pay for the land because they think it should have come to them. What if they think I'd never sell it? Maybe they want me out of the way too so they can get their hands on it."

"If you haven't actually seen anyone, how do you know you're being watched?"

"I don't know." She leaned across the table. "I just feel it."

"But you're not sure? Maybe it's something else."

"You don't believe me, do you?" She stood. "You think I'm lying!"

"No, it's just that sometimes our imagination plays tricks on us. Maybe it just seems like you're being followed."

"Why won't you believe me?" She paced the floor. "I came to you for help!"

"I'm trying to help, Grita."

"No, you're not. You don't trust me." Her voice quavered. "Why would I lie?"

Footsteps sounded behind me and I turned to see Quit in the doorway. He looked from me to Grita and then turned as if he might leave.

"Come on in, Quit." I called to his back.

He turned around, his face pale as an apparition and lined with worry. I was glad he was there. I had no idea what else to say to Grita.

"Maybe I should come back later."

"Take a chair and join us." I waved him in.

"No, I just…I thought…I think I'm in the way." He stammered.

"Nonsense, we were just talking about you." I pulled out a chair for him next to Grita.

Grita jumped from her seat and stumbled back while Quit held tight to the door frame. I looked from one to the other, wondering what in the world they were thinking but before I had a chance to say anything else, Grita bolted through the door.

"I have to go now." She mumbled on her way out.

She brushed by Quit while he backed against the wall as if trying to become part of it. I jumped up and gave him an expectant look, hoping he might call to her but he just stood there silent as a stone. She was out of sight before I could utter a single word so I sat down with a sigh, eyeing Quit where he pressed against the wall like a sentry. I waited for him to explain himself but my patience gave out in no time at all. I'd had enough of his indecision.

"What's wrong with *you*, then?"

"I didn't know what to say to her."

"Well, what did you *want* to say to her?"

"I don't know."

"How about 'I'm your father'?"

"Are you crazy?"

"Never mind. Whatever it was would have been an improvement on what I said."

"What did you say?"

"Nothing helpful. Let's go find her."

"What for?"

"Are you afraid of her or what?"

"I don't know."

"Is that all you have to say? Men are all action and no talk. Don't you know a woman needs to be talked to?"

"It didn't look like you were doing such a great job."

"Don't you think I know that?" I slapped the table. "Look, we're wasting time. Let's go find her."

I grabbed him by the arm and headed for the door but by the time we made it to the porch, Grita's car was heading down the drive. I noticed a note on the truck windshield and pulled it from beneath a wiper blade as Quit stood by.

"Here's what she wrote: 'I can't stay here if you think I'm lying. I've gone to find out what happened to my mother. Tell Roddy I'm sorry.'"

"Well, that's that." Quit started walking toward his house.

"I didn't mean to say she was lying. I was just trying to help her think things through." I stared at the note. "No, that's not true. I was skeptical and didn't try to hide it. I don't know why. What on earth is wrong with me?"

"It sounds like she's made up her mind." He called over his shoulder.

"You're not going to do anything?"

"Go ahead. I won't stop you."

"Quit, you can't just let her go like you did Sephie."

He stopped and turned, clearly annoyed. "Look Mazie, I let that comment go once but not again. You have no business bringing up my past. I don't owe you or Grita anything. Besides, I didn't ask her to leave."

"You think I did?"

"You were the last one to talk to her."

"She could be your daughter, Quit. Are you going to stand there while she goes off on her own to God knows where?"

"She's free to do as she pleases. I don't know that she's any relation to me and I'm not responsible for her. Let her go." He waved toward the road. "I don't like teenagers, anyway."

"How can you be so cold? She could be in danger."

"Why would you say that?"

"She thinks she's being followed."

"Where did you get that idea? Did she tell you someone is following her?"

"I'm afraid I didn't believe her. Not that she was lying, but I thought she was making more of it than it was. I thought she was having boyfriend troubles."

"Grita has a boyfriend?"

I nodded. "She and Cam."

"Cam? You mean the Cam that works here?" He walked back toward me.

"That would be the one, not that I've come across any others...ever."

"Boyfriend troubles." He repeated.

"Quit, I'm afraid she's going out to West Texas where her mother inherited that property. Out there she could get into a different kind of trouble. There's not much for a young woman who's on her own to fall back on in that part of the world, not much in the way of people, not much in the way of the law. It's a harsh, empty land. Anything can happen."

"And I'm supposed to go after her? What if I was to find her? I never know what to say. A woman would know what to say, not me."

"You sure scare easy for a man who worked in a war zone."

"War is easy compared to women."

"Quit, she came to me but she wanted to talk to you. She knows you and her mother were close. I wonder if she's guessed you could be her father. In any event, she wants *you* to help her, not me."

"I'm not her father."

"You don't know that. Either way, she needs your help."

"Help with what?"

"I'm not sure. I think she wants to find out what really happened to her mother. Can you blame her for that?"

He paced the gravel walkway, mumbling to himself.

"Look, Mazie, I don't know what I'm doing here or why I came back. I don't know how long I'll stay but probably not long. I don't need to get mixed up in Grita's life, or anyone else's for that matter. I like to travel light, and this is about as far from that as you can get. You go on. I'll look after things around here while you're off searching for Grita. That'll give me time to decide what I'm going to do with all this." He waved his arm toward the barn and houses.

"I can't just leave. Who'll look after Roddy?"

He rubbed his forehead and then looked up. "Ask Cam, he's close by."

I knew there was nothing more I could say to Quit and it irked me to no end. He was turning his back on Angie and everything she had worked for and he seemed to have no more care about it than Roddy did the day he left the both of them. I was mad enough to kick a dog if I'd had one to kick.

Twelve

An overcast sky roiled low in the west, its rough clouds breaking the dim horizon like torn paper. Shafts of light impaled the gray hills below. Triangles of bald cypress traced the unseen river in dark lines as I stepped out the door, stopped and took a deep breath.

As much as I wanted to avoid it, I felt responsible for Grita. If I had done a better job of listening, she might have been able to think through the situation and figure out what to do next. Instead I had grilled her like an overbearing mother, believing I knew best. She confided in me and I had let her down. It was no surprise she left like she did.

As I walked toward the barn, I decided I'd ask Cam if he knew where she might go. I had a rough idea of the location of her property but would need more than that to find her. I knew I could go to Des Clymer but I also knew lawyer confidentiality could be a problem. When I walked into the barn I found Cam's door open and him stretched out on the cot.

"I'm sorry to barge in on you, Cam, but I need your help. Grita has run off. I think she's gone to West Texas to find out what happened to her mother." I could hear the worry in my voice. "I'm going to go find her. Do you have any idea where she might be?"

He sat up on the cot. "You're going after her? Why do you want to do that?"

"I'm worried about her going out there all by herself. It's not safe."

"You'd really go find her?"

"We can't just let her go."

"I should go after her."

"No Cam, I need to be the one to go. It's my fault she left. She tried to talk to me and the only thing I managed to do was upset her. Besides, I need you here to keep an eye on my brother, Roddy."

"Keep an eye on him?"

"He's had brain cancer and it cost him his sight. He manages but he's not yet ready to be on his own."

"He's blind?"

"That's right. Would you stay close by and keep watch? He doesn't need much. Just check on him now and then. I couldn't leave him right now without knowing he was safe."

"I don't know anything about blind people but I'll do whatever will help Grita."

I was feeling time slip away. "What can you tell me about her?"

"West Texas is a long way from here. Her car will never make it."

"So you're telling me she'll end up stuck in the middle of nowhere with a broken down car? How will I ever find her?"

"You should ask Caspar Michnic. He's the old man that owns the garage apartment where she lives. I think he's Czech or something. He also keeps her car running."

"He's a mechanic?"

"No, he just likes Grita. They understand each other."

"He takes care of her car because he likes her?"

He held up a hand, seeing my confusion. "You'll have to meet Caspar to know what I mean."

"You think he'll know where she is?"

"It's only a guess but that's where I'd try first. I'll go talk to him if you want me to."

"Like I said, this is something I need to do. Just tell me how to find him."

A short while later, I peered out the windshield as I angled the truck down a narrow gravel road and across a dry creek before turning onto a short street bordered by massive pecan trees. Yellow leaves drifted confetti-like through the air. October was only days away and the smell of damp leaves reminded me that autumn would soon arrive in spite of the warm weather. I pulled up to a white frame house set on a slight rise, its green shutters framing windows adjacent to the front door. An empty porch swing rocked in the wind.

On the near side of the house, a man in gray overalls stood with his back to me, raking leaves into small piles. Every few moments he leaned to spit. I waited and watched him work but he turned only after I slammed the truck door. He reached up and touched one ear, and then shook his head as he began limping toward me. A tan line of snuff trailed down the front of his blue shirt.

"I done turn my hearing aid off and it gets so peaceful I just forget all about that damn t'ing." He spit and wiped his mouth with the back of his hand. "Can I help you wit somet'ing?"

I held out my hand. "I'm Mazie Goforth. I'm looking for Grita Sifuentes. I understand that you know her."

As he shook my hand I noticed he was missing the fingers on his right hand. He still had most of his thumb. I looked at his other hand, finding it identical. I wondered how in the world he was able to hold something, much less rake his yard or work on cars. He saw me looking and held out both hands, palms up.

"My hands they got caught in a mattress-making machine when I used to work out there at that dang state hospital. They can still do some good if I let them." He lifted his cap and scratched his closely-cropped hair, eyeing me. "Grita, she's a good girl. What do you want wit her?"

I grabbed Sephie's picture from the truck dashboard and held it out to him. "You are Caspar Michnic, aren't you?"

"Who else would I be then?" He looked at the photo.

"Grita has been working for me for the last month or so, ever since her mother died in a car wreck. That's her picture. Grita thinks someone killed her." I took a quick breath and continued. "I'm afraid she's on her way somewhere near the Mexican border to try to find out what really happened and I'm worried about her wandering around that part of the world on her own."

He gazed at the photo, absently rubbing his stiff hair. He stopped and looked at me with his cloudy blue eyes. I could see he was deciding whether he could trust me.

"I have the damn cancer in my back and I can't stand too long no more." He nodded toward the house. "Please come sit wit me."

I followed him up the concrete stairs and onto the porch while he ambled along, wincing now and then in a high-pitched wheeze. As we passed the screen door, the yeasty aroma of baked bread filled the air. A painted wooden crucifix hung on the door frame. We made our way to several metal chairs crowding the far corner of the porch and I sat facing him. I thought it might help if I gave him some time to get to know me, so leaned toward him and spoke.

"Have you lived here long, Caspar?"

He nodded. "My family was Czech mostly, but my mother's people come from Poland. My parents, they bring me over to Texas when I was a youngster. Then when it was my time to leave home, I come here."

"Do you have any children?"

"I have a daughter. She moved to New York City so I don't see her too much."

I sat back in the chair. "I hope I'm not wasting your time, Caspar."

"When you get old like me, you got plenty time to waste."

"Since you have a daughter you can understand how it must be for Grita to suddenly lose her mother."

"I t'ink I can understand." He rubbed his forehead with the stubs of his fingers. "I done buried plenty of my family."

"Sometimes it seems I've lost everyone that was ever important to me." I started, again surprised at what came out of my mouth.

"This damn old world can be a hard place sometimes, especially for the young people like Grita."

"Have you seen her? It worries me to think what might happen to her."

He sat back and looked at me for a moment. "I t'ink I can help you wit finding Grita."

"I have a map in the truck." I stood.

"I don't need no map." Caspar chuckled.

"A map might help." I started down the porch.

"I t'ink I can still find my own kitchen."

I stopped and turned. "Your kitchen?"

"You smell that fresh bread cooking?" He stood. "That there bread is in my kitchen. I don't need no map to find it, only my old nose if it still works."

"Grita is here?" I nearly jumped out of my skin. "Why didn't you say so?"

"I got to be careful with Grita. She's alone in this world, you know."

"Can I talk to her?"

He nodded. "You have some pie too."

I followed Caspar as he limped through the door and into a small living room crowded with cut glass bowls, porcelain vases and lace coverlets. A cuckoo clock ticked loudly on the far wall. He paused and held to the hall doorway. I thought he might be in some kind of pain but then he reached up to touch a photo of a young woman. He let his hand rest on the frame.

"I ask my Dora to help me with Grita."

"Is she your wife?" I leaned for a closer look at the beautiful, pale face.

He nodded. "One year ago she died."

We continued down the narrow hallway and into an overly warm kitchen. Grita ignored us as she leaned into the open oven, pulling out a fat loaf of bread. She placed the loaf on a cooling tray next to a freshly baked apple pie. She continued moving around the kitchen without looking up as I stood there trying to think what to say. I wanted to tell her I was glad she was safe and not stuck alone on some desolate back road. I wanted to tell her I would listen.

"Grita, I done brought someone to talk to you. I don't want you to go off some place you might get yourself hurt."

She looked up at me for a moment and her eyes flashed with anger. I walked to the far side of the table, studying more photos as I went and giving her a moment to think about what Caspar had said. Finally she spoke.

"I need to know what happened to my mother." She faced the floor. "I'm going to find out the truth."

"Okay." I stepped toward her.

"I'm going to find out what happened to her and no one can tell me not to."

"Let me help you, Grita."

She looked up. "Now you want to help me?"

"I want you to be safe, Grita. I want you back with us."

She leaned against the counter and stared at me. "I thought I had lost my job, leaving like I did."

"Like I told you, you're good with Roddy. He needs you."

"I don't care if someone is watching me. I can't just stand by without finding out the truth about my mother."

"Let's see what we can find out before you drive halfway to El Paso."

"Did you think I was going all the way out there? I'd like to but my car would never make it."

"That dang car I have to work on all the time but I don't mind if Grita cooks me some apple pie sometime."

She looked over at Caspar. "Caspar lets me come over and cook when I'm missing my mother. It feels safe here."

"I hope you'll still feel safe with us too." I looked at her for a moment. "Grita, I think you should talk to Des Clymer. He might be able to help."

"Who is Des Clymer?"

"Des took care of the paperwork when your mother inherited the land. He's an old friend and I think he'll help you if he can."

"Will you go with me?"

I tried to imagine what it must be like for Grita, alone and unsure who to trust. I could know a person for years without trusting them. I didn't want to think what that said about me.

"You're sure you want me to?"

She nodded.

I managed a half-smile. "Alright, but only if I can have some of that pie."

Thirteen

I followed a winding blacktop crowded with cedar and sumac, past bone-white stone bluffs and spring-fed creeks running clear and fast. Granite boulders splotched with lichen appeared for an instant and then vanished as I sped past. Subtle first colors of autumn dotted the cliffs ahead. The air, fresh and cool as it streamed through the window and across my face, left an acrid mix of limestone and Live oak on the back of my tongue. I breathed in the dry lightness as if it could relieve me of the weight I felt.

Somehow, Len's return had brought my many failings into stark focus. The more I tried to avoid them, the more obvious they became. The daily sight of Grita and Cam standing close, talking in hushed tones, only heightened the feeling. I'd had relationships in the past but none lasted more than a few months, some only days. Something would inevitably happen and I'd find myself pulling away.

By chance, I heard from a friend in real estate that Len lived about fifteen miles from town, near one of the jade-green lakes that stretch up through the hills like jewels on a necklace. I decided I needed to see him, though my reasons were less than clear. When we had run into each other at the grocery store, I was leaving and he was walking in. I stared in surprised disbelief as a smile so slight I might have missed it passed across his mouth. We talked, but only for a moment. He had someplace he needed to be and I had ice cream melting. I felt as awkward as a teenager with acne yet once I had a chance to think I realized I wanted to find out who he had become. Although I remembered him as creative and fun-loving, I wondered if he had become staid and conservative like so many men I knew. Still, I wanted to hear his voice and listen to the way he used words. I wanted to know which ideas he considered important, what beliefs he held as true. I was afraid of what he might see in me but I also wanted to know.

Before I ran into him at the store, the last time I had seen Len was years before, not long after the white heat of August had given way to the warm days of late September and celebrations marking the Bicentennial were beginning to wind down. Children had returned to school and swimming pools had closed for the year. Football was on the news.

We had been living together and were for all practical purposes married, even to the point of wearing matching rings, but it mattered little on that day. We sat on a park bench overlooking the town lake. Len looked across the windblown water and said that he needed some time on his own, that he had to figure out what he wanted in a relationship, that as first born he was never able to live the free life of his dreams and now was his chance. He needed to "get out his ya-yas", whatever that meant. He said our separation was only temporary but I could see there was no room for me in his future. Leaving me was as easy for him as taking off an old coat and I was the one left standing in the cold.

I tried to put aside my memory of that day as I turned onto a red gravel road that followed the edge of the lake and wound around a tight bend. As the underbrush fell away, the road widened and the lake opened before me in a sweeping arc. Len's house, all gables and windows, stood on a gradual rise to my right, a hundred yards from the lake. I stopped to check the address. Len had no phone number listed, if he even had one, and I wondered again if he would see me as a guest or an imposition, or if he'd see me at all. I drove up the long asphalt driveway, parking beneath a hulking oak.

The stone house loomed over me as I stepped onto a broad deck fronting four sky-filled windows that stretched to the narrow roofline. I paused and turned to see the lake, mercurial in the light haze, reflecting the low hills beyond and nondescript puffs of cloud overhead. I recognized them as cumulus humilis, the smallest of the fair weather class of clouds. Angie had never tired of teasing me about my cloud-spotting obsession and for a moment I wished she was there with me sharing the view.

I turned back to the house and knocked on the front door, stepping away and trying to look relaxed, as if I had nothing on my mind but the weather. As I waited I studied the house. I had a hard time imagining Len living in a place so ostentatious. The massive door, covered with intricately carved Hindu gods, antique cast iron fittings and an enormous brass lock, was likely pilfered for a hefty price from some ancient burial site. Above the door, stained glass windows of saints and angels in what looked like the original stone Gothic arches pointed toward the sky. Gargoyles stared at me from beneath the tile roof. Palms in clay pots as large as bathtubs covered the deck in green fronds. A fountain splashed noisily in the yard below.

I knocked on the door again with more force but the heavy wood seemed to absorb all sound, so I leaned toward the door. I could hear music playing lightly somewhere inside. As there was no doorbell, I knocked once more with little effect and stepped back, feeling relieved but at the same time disappointed with the lack of response. I wondered again why I wanted to see him considering the way he had once treated me. I turned to walk down the stairs toward my small sedan, looking like a disheveled, luckless relation next to the well-dressed luxury of the house.

As I reached for the car door a voice called, seemingly out of nowhere.

"Can I help you with something?"

I turned to see Len walking down the drive from the rear of the house. He looked better than ever. I stood there without a word and soon found myself thinking about what it would be like to be with him again. I'd seen in the news how couples sometimes reunite. Old sweethearts meet up again after many years and strike up a new romance. I thought I must be delusional. As he came nearer, the same slight smile passed across his lips and then a puzzled expression settled on his handsome face. He squinted and pulled at one ear.

"Mazie Goforth, how did you find out where I live? This address isn't listed anywhere that I know of."

"Just luck." I lied.

"Just luck, is it?" He frowned.

"I don't mean to show up unannounced but I couldn't find a phone number. I'll leave if you want me to."

I tried to sound disinterested but how could I? I had sought him out, after all. He had left me, some would say cruelly, and here I was years later chasing after him. It was as if all the time that had passed since that day ceased to exist and I again felt humiliated and angry with myself. I was tempted to speak my mind but wanted to maintain some bit of dignity.

"No, no." He held up a hand. "I'm just surprised to see you here."

"I didn't think anyone was at home so I was about to leave."

"I'm glad I saw you then. I was back of the house packing my car."

"You're leaving? I thought you just got here."

"I have to take a business trip but only for a couple of days." He nodded toward the house. "Come in for a moment."

I followed him through the creaking door and into a soaring, light-filled room that looked more like the inside of a chapel than a home. Against the far wall a rough-hewn altarpiece topped by a sinewy crucifix reached halfway to the ceiling. Stain glass-hued sunlight danced across the dark wood. A gilded mirror filled the wall to my right, its smoky glass reflecting the scene in sepia tones. Crosses of various sizes covered the opposite wall above an overstuffed leather sofa flanked by two hand-made walnut tables. I avoided the couch and found my way to a thick wooden chair that sat next to a coffee table scattered with painted Mexican pots.

"Can I get you a drink?" Len stood at the bar, pouring himself a Scotch.

"No, I can only stay a short while." I decided I wanted to keep him guessing.

"Only a short while? Well then, let's catch up while we can." He sat on the couch. "Don't you want to join me over here where it's comfortable? It'd be just like old times."

"That's funny, Len." I leaned back into the chair. "No, I don't think so."

"So, what do you do for a living around here, Mazie?"

"We have a landscaping company." I embellished. "What about you?"

"I have an importing business. I deal mostly with Mexico and Central America."

"So, that's how you afford a house like this." I waved my arm across the room. "I feel like I'm in church."

"This is about as close to a church as I'll ever get. The house belongs to a client. I live in Chicago." He leaned toward me. "What happened to you, Mazie?"

"What happened to me?"

"You had such big plans for yourself. I thought by now you'd be a rich doctor living in some posh neighborhood, not a little backwater like this."

"How do you know I don't live in a mansion like this?"

"It's still in the middle of nowhere."

"I've never thought of it as nowhere. I was born here."

"I know that. I just never imagined that you'd come back."

"I realized that this is where I wanted to be." I turned and looked out the tall, soaring windows. "This part of the world is beautiful."

"There are many places more beautiful."

"Maybe, but the only family I have left in the world is here. I can't find that anywhere else."

"Don't you get tired of it? Isn't it incredibly backwards out here away from important people and events, from where people with power create the future, from where you can surround yourself with the cutting edge of culture?"

"What are you doing here, then?"

"I'm here to make money but this place is so god-awful I'm not sure it's worth it."

"Well, I like it just fine." I sounded less than convincing.

"This is nowhere, Mazie. You must be bored out of your mind. Why won't you admit it?" He looked at me, a smug smile on his lips.

"I'll tell you what bores me." I felt blood rush to my face. "People who think they know what's beautiful and what isn't, who think they know what's important in life when they don't have a clue, who want to be close to so-called important people because it's the only way they ever feel important. You want to know what bores me, Len? Well, that's it!"

I was angry at his pompous, know-it-all attitude. I could never stand that in a person and it was so unlike what I remembered of him. I found it hard to believe he was the same man I had once known. The thought crossed my mind that perhaps neither of us was anything close to what we were back then but I ignored it. I was disappointed at what Len had become and what I had become, and I was angry I had fallen for some juvenile fantasy that he would match my impossibly perfect image of him. I knew I had to be a disappointment to him as well. I decided to leave.

"Why are you here, Mazie?"

"I thought I just said why." I grabbed my purse.

"I mean here, now, in this house."

"I need to go." I stood, not wanting to continue the conversation.

"Are you sure? There's a huge four-poster upstairs surrounded by Mexican mirrors placed so subtly you only notice once you're in bed."

I turned and the hint of a nervous laugh escaped before I could stifle it. I could feel the blush running up my cheeks. He had propositioned me without even blinking. I would have slapped him but I didn't want to give him the satisfaction.

"Don't flatter yourself, Len." I began walking toward the door.

"You still look good Mazie, sexier than ever."

"I can't say the same for you." I lied.

"You're tempted. Go ahead and admit it."

I turned to face him. "I made that mistake already."

"It was no mistake."

"I'm leaving now."

"I don't mean to offend you." He changed his tone.

"I'm not offended." I lied again.

"I'd like to hear more about you and what you're doing these days, Mazie. You could come over for dinner. I'll fix my special enchiladas, the ones you like."

"I lost my taste for enchiladas a long time ago."

As I turned toward the door, light reflecting off a framed photo caught my eye. I glanced down for a second and kept walking but something in the image made me stop. I stepped back and bent down to get a better look. Hannah's face smiled back at me from a sandy beach, the blue-green water behind her sparkling under a tropical sun. In the background a banner read "Happy 30th". I stared at the photo, transfixed by her features, older but still pretty. Unable to understand why her picture would be here of all places, I stood frozen in place, feeling as though I had become detached from all sense of time. The face in the photo was the same face screaming at me from outside Len's bedroom so many years before. Len's words brought me back to reality in an instant.

"It's the beach at Cabo. Our kids gave us a trip down there for our anniversary."

"Your children?" I turned to him, unbelieving.

"Cabo is a paradise, especially compared to winter in Chicago. Have you ever been?" He smiled like a kid.

"You and Hannah are married?" I felt like I had been slapped.

Len's smile vanished. "Thirty years last January. I just assumed you knew."

"How can it be thirty years? That means you were married right after..." I left the thought unfinished.

"I can't believe no one told you."

"You've been together all that time?" I felt like I was dreaming.

"Hannah and I get along well."

"What about needing to get out your ya-yas?"

"I had to say something. I couldn't tell you I'd been seeing Hannah again, now could I?"

"And you have children?"

"A son and a daughter, both grown."

"You left me for Hannah." I laughed to myself. "That's perfect."

I turned and walked through the door, thoughts coming at me from every direction. Had I really cut myself off from my past so well that no one bothered to tell me Len had married Hannah? Did they feel that sorry for me? Or did no one care enough to make the effort? I was almost feeling sorry for myself when Len's voice called from the doorway. I turned to face him.

"Don't forget my offer." He smiled suggestively.

"Lordy Len, you're married!"

"We could have some fun, Mazie." He held the door open.

"You're married to Hannah, no less! Have you forgotten everything?" I was so mad I could hardly breathe.

"You have to seize the moment, Mazie!"

I stared at him in disbelief before climbing into my car.

As I drove toward home, shadows cut the blacktop into a patchwork of blues and grays. A lone hawk spiraled against a dome of sky lightly streaked with clouds. As the road topped a rise, opening onto a broad expanse of grassland that seemed to move in the autumn breeze like a blonde-hued river, I spotted the waning gibbous moon low in the west, barely visible beneath a light haze. I felt time passing in the change of season and wondered how I had come to a place so different from what I had always imagined. Here I was middle aged and never married, with no children, few friends and the bare bones of a family. I didn't even have a real job. I looked back into my past, trying to see what I had done to earn such a life but I found no answers as another day slipped by like lines on a highway.

Fourteen

The weather that fall was as predictable as the people in my life. One day was cool and damp, filled with the smells of autumn, the next blazing hot. I rolled down the car window and leaned out, allowing the warm breeze to blow through my hair. The general sensation was not unlike wind blowing through straw. I glanced at Grita, her long hair floating about her head like strands of black silk, and wondered what had happened to my once-soft curls. I still had them when I was Quit's age. He should have been in the car with us. Why he was trying to run from his past was beyond me. I knew better than most the ways a life can circle around back on itself like a dog chasing its tail. Len was a perfect example. It had been less than a week since he propositioned me as if I'd jump in bed with him without a second thought. As much as I imagined I'd enjoy hearing those words, the entire scene took me so by surprise that I went into a sort of shock. Later, I regretted not giving him a piece of my mind before I left.

Staring through the windshield I found myself thinking that men were not to be trusted, a worrisome thought considering we were on our way to meet Des. As we drove past the courthouse, several shop windows lining the square caught my eye, their broad panes painted in colorful slogans supporting the high school football team. A printed banner welcoming hunters fluttered in the light breeze even though deer season was still a month away. A pickup selling late-season cantaloupes from Mexico sat beneath a sprawling oak.

I pulled up to Des' office and parked next to a dusty flatbed truck with a mottled, black and white cow dog chained to the bed. The truck belonged to some rancher with a thirst for Dizzy's, no doubt. As we got out of the car, the dog lifted his head and looked at us with mild interest. Grita reached over to stroke his head and he gave off a low growl. She jerked back her hand in a flash.

"That's just what we need Grita, another ornery male." I walked with her to the stairs. "I surely do hope Des will be an improvement on the sex."

She stopped and faced me. "Thank you for helping me, Mazie."

I looked at her for a moment, unsure of what to say. In the weeks since confiding in me she had seemed young and vulnerable, almost fragile. The sad look I could see in her eyes worried me. I was determined to avoid making things worse.

"Now Grita, try to look at this as an experiment. We want to see what Des can tell us but don't set your hopes too high. It may end up being a waste of time."

"It doesn't feel like a waste of time."

"Yes, well, the important thing is that you're doing something. We'll see where it takes us and then decide what comes next."

We climbed the stairs and pushed through a heavy wooden door to the chaos of Des' office. State and county maps of various sizes and colors covered most of one wall. Yellowed rolls of paper, the ends cracked and torn, lay scattered across a low counter. File cabinets crowded one corner in haphazard fashion. A desk lined with thin map drawers sat beneath three louvered windows overlooking the courthouse lawn. Nearly every level surface in the office was covered with paper of some sort: maps, file folders, well-used magazines, old newspapers. Des had no secretary and it was clear his office lacked a woman's touch. I turned to find him standing in a doorway that led down a short hall. He smiled and cocked his head to one side.

"Mazie Goforth is actually in my office. It's a miracle."

"I'm glad to see you cleaned the place up for us, Des."

Des held up a hand and began to gesture about the room in his usual expressive style.

94

"Now Mazie, we must be honest here of all places, a place of the law. Are you suggesting this office gives off a certain impression upon entering?"

I nodded.

"And what would that impression be in one word or less. The truth must be brief and to the point."

"Slobbery."

"Slobbery? You mean I've been drooling?"

"Not lately." I held back a smile.

"Might you mean the place is slobbish or has a slob-like quality of appearance?"

"You get the idea, Des."

"Point taken, Mazie but please note this is the office of a hardworking attorney." He stroked his chin. "Come to think of it, that's why you're here, isn't it?"

I glanced at Grita. "Des, this is Grita. Like I said over the phone, she is trying to find out what happened to her mother out in Brewster County. We thought we could start by learning about the property she inherited."

Des made a quick bow. "Hello, Grita. Please ignore your cleanliness-obsessed companion."

Des motioned us into a second room located at the end of the hallway. Crowded into the room was an oak desk stacked with accordion files and legal reference books. A low table covered with maps of various sizes sat next to it. Des pulled a rectangular, multicolored map from beneath the pile and spread it on top of the others, smoothing it out with his hand.

"I've done my homework and here's what I found. Your mother's land is here, north of the town of Alpine." He circled an area with his finger. "It totals about five hundred acres, not a lot in that part of the State but located over a relatively small unnamed aquifer adjacent to the Marathon Aquifer, a larger water source for the region. Your property is the only access to that unnamed aquifer, and because water is so scarce your land is worth much more than it would be otherwise."

95

"That's good news, then." I bent over the map.

"Well Mazie, yes and no. It's good to have access to a water source, especially on that part of the planet. On the other hand, having the only access to an aquifer may cause people who want that water to do whatever it takes to gain access, legal or otherwise."

"That's why my relatives wanted my mom out of the way." Grita stared at the map. "They want that land and thought I'd give it up for nothing if they could scare me."

"You mean by stalking you?" I turned to her.

She nodded. "They think I won't know anything about the value of the land because I'm young so they can get me to sell it to them for nothing, especially if I'm scared."

"I'd be careful about assuming too much, Grita." Des swept his hand across the map. "There are a lot of people that might have an interest in gaining access to that aquifer."

"People who would kill to get it?"

"I don't know about that. It could be your mother just lost control of her car." He pointed toward the courthouse. "I called in a few favors with my public safety friends and hope I'll soon have something new to tell you about the accident."

"It was no accident." Grita placed a hand on the map. "I need to know what really happened to my mother."

"I want you to think carefully about what you just said." Des leaned toward her. "Sometimes people start digging and find things they never wanted to know."

"I want to know the truth, whatever it is." She stepped back, crossing her arms. "I don't mean to sound ungrateful but why are you doing this for me?"

"Why? Because Mazie asked me to, of course." Des cocked his head and smiled. "How could I ever resist such a good-looking woman?"

"Des, you sound like you've already made a trip across the hall. It's a little early to be visiting Dizzy's, don't you think?" I gave Grita a wink.

96

Des could be as charming as anyone but I'd had enough of men for the time being. I wanted to do what I could for Grita and I was having trouble seeing our next move. She *had* learned something more about the location and value of her property. Still, I was unsure how it might help her understand what had happened to her mother. I looked at her as Des pointed to the map, again explaining the important points, and wondered how she would come to terms with all that had happened in her young life. Does anyone ever understand all that happens to them? I knew I was nowhere close.

The sky had clouded over by the time we were headed back to Grita's apartment. A brisk wind vibrated through the tall pecans and broad Live oaks lining the street. As we drove the narrow road, Grita seemed lost in thought, her head leaning against the passenger window, her eyes half-closed. Des had agreed to contact her as soon as he heard from his highway patrol contacts. I wondered what she thought of the meeting.

"Was talking to Des helpful?" I glanced at her, looking for a reaction.

"I don't know."

"At least you know more now than you did before."

"Maybe, but what do I really know? The land is so far away from here it seems like it's on another planet."

"It is like another planet in some ways. The western part of Texas is beautiful but harsh. It can turn dangerous if you're not careful."

"I feel like I'm a long way from understanding anything."

"Des may find something else that'll help."

She turned to me. "I think he's sweet on you."

"Des is that way with everyone." I sounded less than convincing. "It's just his nature. He likes to flirt."

"It seemed like more than flirting to me." She looked out the windshield. "Can I ask you something, Mazie?"

I nodded.

"How did you and your mother get along?"

I realized, a little shamefully, how long it had been since I had thought about either of my parents. When I was young my mother and I were so different in temperament that we got on each other's nerves constantly. She was a true lady, polite and proper under all circumstances, never giving offense except to her own family and only in private. Living on a farm with two brothers, I grew up too rough for such social niceties and became a source of embarrassment for my mother. I slowed the car, stopped and turned to Grita.

"I loved my mother but we had our differences, plenty of them."

"I know how that is."

"How did you and your mother get on?"

"Okay."

"Well, that's good."

"No, it wasn't good. We fought just before she left for Alpine." She whispered. "The property has a house out in the middle of nowhere and she planned to move there. We argued and I finally told her I'd never go back. I got so angry that I said things I shouldn't have, that she was a selfish witch and that I hated her."

"People say things they don't mean when they're angry, Grita. Lord knows I have often enough."

"I wish I could tell her how wrong I was to say what I did." She put her hand to her mouth. "There are so many things I wish I could say to her."

"Try not to be so hard on yourself, Grita. People argue if they're around each other enough, especially family." I searched for what to say. "Your mother knew you didn't mean it."

"I know I can't take back what I said but I want to try to make it right. I want to find out what happened to her. It feels like her life was left unfinished. Only the truth of what happened can finish it for her." She turned to me. "Will you help me find out?"

98

"I don't know that I'll be much help but I'll do what I can."

She searched my eyes for a moment and then turned back to the window with the sad look of someone lost. I hoped I was helping rather than hurting and that I'd know the difference between the two.

As we pulled up to the house, Caspar waved from the porch swing and started down the steps, smiling and carrying a wooden box. I stepped out of the car as he limped along the drive toward us.

"I hope you like them sweet potatoes because I got some good ones here for you, fresh from my old garden." He held up a slatted apple crate. "You fix this here up wit some ham and turnip greens and have one good dinner."

Grita wandered over to the porch where a large black dog, his muzzle gray with age, lay next to the steps. She knelt and stroked his broad head. The dog raised his watery eyes to her while his tail slapped the ground. Caspar stepped closer, leaned his head toward mine and then nodded toward the porch.

"Old Priddy there, he is almost old as me. My wife found him in the alley out back one day and he adopted her even after she done give him a girl's name. He has been not so good since she passed on. I think soon I will lose him too." He turned his lined face to me. "You take good care of my Grita, will you, Mazie? She done kept me going since she came to this here house."

I thought how it must feel to become old and alone, pieces of your life falling away one by one like autumn leaves. I found it a frightening thought. Grita had been the opposite for Caspar, an adding to instead of taking away. I suspected it held true for the both of them. I looked into Caspar's cloudy eyes and nodded, wondering how my life would be at his age.

Fifteen

As I was leaving Caspar's, I turned to see Grita hurrying across the lawn and waving me to stop. She seemed a young girl as she leaned into the window, head down and panting. I gazed at the dark hair falling across her face and realized with a start that I wanted to lay my hand on her shining head and tell her everything was going to be alright. I wanted her to have the normal life of a teenager. I wanted her to know what had happened to her mother. She took a deep breath and looked up, a pained look on her face.

"Mazie, now tell me the truth. Is Quit mad at me for some reason?"

"I don't think so." I was surprised by her question.

"Ever since that day when I got so upset, he's been avoiding me. He won't even look at me if he can help it. What did I do?"

"You didn't do anything."

"I don't want him to be mad at me if he's…" She stopped herself.

"I don't know what's wrong with Quit. In the last week he's hardly said more than two words that he didn't have to."

"I must be me."

"It's not you, Grita. I think he's bothered by something and he doesn't know what to do with it. Don't you worry. I'll have a talk with him."

"You won't tell him what I said, will you?"

I shook my head. "I'll let you know if I learn anything."

The sun had disappeared behind a towering thunderhead as I pulled up to my house. I had spent the drive back from Caspar's thinking about Quit and what I wanted to say to him. As I sat in the car gathering my thoughts I caught sight of him down the hill, rounding the barn and walking toward the open door. I stepped out of the car, waving him toward me. I glanced over at my house, wondering if he had spoken to his father yet. Roddy had never mentioned it, so I guessed that Quit was avoiding more than just me and Grita.

As I stared at the house, Cam passed in front of a window and then disappeared. After I'd first asked, he had continued going on his own to see Roddy and I could see that he had taken a genuine liking to Roddy. Roddy responded by loaning him several of his old books and even teaching him to play chess. I turned as Quit walked up and leaned against the car.

"You need something, Mazie?" He spoke between breaths, irritation in his voice.

"Do I need something?" I was in no mood for his attitude. "No, but I wonder something."

"Is there a point here?"

"I can't ask a question?"

"I still have work I need to finish." He stood and turned as if about to leave.

"Don't walk away from me, Quit Goforth."

He faced me as if he was about to speak but then checked himself. I could see I was going to have to get right to the point.

"You haven't told Roddy that you're back here, have you?" I could see I guessed right and held up my hand. "Don't answer, just listen. You've been avoiding him and me and, if I were a betting woman, I'd say you've been keeping yourself as far away from Grita as you can."

"What did you tell him?"

"I haven't told him anything but I'm about to go see him and I think you should come along."

"I don't have anything to say to him."

"He'll find out you're here sooner or later."

"He's not my problem."

"Quit, leaving you and Angie like he did was wrong but he's still your father."

101

"He was dead to me a long time ago. I don't owe him anything."

"Well, Angie didn't think so. She took him in and gave him a chance."

"I'm not her."

"No, you sure aren't." I took a breath. "Quit, he's changed. You can't just turn your back on him."

"Watch me."

That made me angry. "What happened to you in Europe or wherever you were? You don't care about anything but yourself!"

He turned his eyes from me as if looking to a spot far in the distance. I waited, wondering what thoughts might be going through his mind and what I should say next. I had sensed that his coming here had as much to do with leaving something behind as with Angie's passing and I could see I was right. A door opened behind me and his eyes refocused in an instant.

"Nothing happened." He turned away, again leaning against the car.

"Mazie, he told me to ask if you can find his copy of *Great Expectations*." Cam called from the doorway. "We've been talking about Dickens and he wants to loan it to me."

I held up my hand. "Just give me a minute, Cam."

"Quit!" He yelled. "Quit, did you see the new shipment of baby palms? They were delivered while you were at lunch. Hey, Quit!"

"He heard you, Cam." I called toward the house and then turned to face Quit. "You know, when a person loses their sight their hearing usually improves."

"Is that right?" He crossed his arms and stared down the hill.

"There aren't a whole lot of folks with the name Quit."

"I never much liked that name."

"So, what are you going to do now? He must know you're around."

"I'm going to do nothing." He stood and began walking back the way he had come.

"You can't avoid your life forever." I called after him. "What am I supposed to say to him?"

"Not my problem." He yelled over his shoulder.

I walked to the house and through the door, silently cursing the stubborn men in my strange and dislocated family. Surveying my small living room crowded with faded chairs and couches, the shelves on two walls crammed with books and knickknacks, I thought over what I wanted to tell Roddy. I was tired of the secrets, innuendo and second-guessing that seemed to inhabit my life. I wanted to face what happened in the world head on and see it clearly, whether good or bad, even in my past. I wondered if I could manage it as I grabbed *Great Expectations* from the shelf and walked into the kitchen where Cam sat hunched over a well-used chessboard, across the table from Roddy.

Roddy leaned back in his chair, his eyes darting here and there as he considered possible strategies. I looked at him, thinking of the progress he had made in the last couple of weeks. While his physical therapy was clearly paying off, Cam's presence seemed to have had the most effect. He and Roddy spent nearly every weekend afternoon talking or playing chess. Recently, Cam had started reading his favorite books aloud to him after supper. He had even taken Roddy for several tours of the property, orienting him to the paths and walkways and teaching him about the peculiarities of palm trees. Roddy seemed to enjoy the time. He had stopped repeating what was said to him and would even ask a question if he was given the chance, although he kept to his strange gestures. He turned to me, leaned on one elbow and cut the air with his hand. I realized with a shock how much he reminded me of Des.

"Did you find my Dickens?" He leaned back again.

"Here it is." I set the book on the table.

"Cam, we can start on that whenever you're ready." He looked up at me. "Cam and I have a deal. I'm loaning him my books and he's helping me learn to get around the property."

"I heard."

Cam shook his head. "You don't need my help anymore, Roddy. You know your way around here just fine."

"Not so, Cam." He held up a hand and blessed us both. "Besides, I still have a lot to learn about the plant business. Botany was one of my favorite classes in college. With your help I'm relearning what I forgot, which is almost everything."

Cam looked up at me. "I'm not much help, Mazie. I never had a botany class."

"You know more than you think, Cam. Just keep reading." Roddy passed his hand across the table like a magician.

"I'm almost finished with that book on monocots." Cam tuned back to the chessboard.

I looked on with amazement. Cam was nothing like the boy that barely looked at me the first time we met. He seemed to trust Roddy without hesitation. Roddy was equally changed. I had never seen him so willing to help someone other than himself. Quit could have used that help years ago, I thought. I remembered my intention to tell Roddy about him.

"Roddy, the doctors must have given you a dose of patience along with your chemotherapy." I sat. "I know you must be wondering about who Cam was talking to a minute ago."

"Why would I wonder? He was talking to you, Mazie." He smiled.

"Don't be smart, Roddy. You know what I mean. You hear everything."

"You must mean Quit." He snapped his fingers. "That's old news, Mazie."

"You knew?"

"I may be blind but I'm not stupid, at least not any more so than before I lost my sight. I know some of what goes on around here. Cam has been good enough to fill in the gaps."

Cam turned to me. "Did I do something wrong?"

I shook my head. "No. He and Quit haven't talked to each other in years. I thought it was Quit that was too stubborn to try but now I see one's as bullheaded as the other. It's a shameful way for a father and son to act, Cam."

Cam's face clouded over in an instant. "Some fathers don't deserve to be talked to."

"Cam, are you going to side with Mazie now?"

"No Roddy, I didn't mean you." He mumbled.

I tried to get Cam to look at me. "I didn't mean to bring up a sore subject."

"I just don't like talking about it or thinking about it." He fingered a chess piece.

"Well Roddy, I suppose it's between you and Quit. You can leave Cam and me out of your feud."

"You tell Quit I'm ready to talk whenever he is."

"Oh, that should help. He'll say the same and you'll both be back where you started." I stood. "We've had enough of this macho nonsense, haven't we, Cam?"

He kept facing the chessboard. "I'd rather not say, Mazie."

"Well, I have more important things to do than referee a pissing contest." I turned toward the door. "Roddy, if you decide you want to act like an adult and actually do something about this, let me know."

I slammed the door on my way out. I decided to head for Dizzy's. Going out was something I hadn't done much of in recent years, especially to a bar and especially on my own, but after all that wasted talk I needed to get away from there.

Sixteen

Darkness had settled on the street but occasional flashes of lightning silhouetted the roadside trees like paper cutouts as I drove toward town, a low fog hanging just below fence posts lining the highway. Thunder split the night. A moment later a lone car raced up behind me, its headlights flashing off the side mirrors, nearly blinding me. I felt a wave of panic as Grita's talk of being followed raced through my mind. Squinting into the mirror but unable to get a clear view, I decided to head straight for the sheriff's office when the courthouse lights loomed into sight and the car swerved left, speeding off into the night.

I walked into Dizzy's still a little shaken and took a seat at the bar before I noticed Des at a nearby table, his back to me. He sat talking to Zoe Finn. She wore dusty jeans and boots, and had her hair back in two tight braids. A sweat-stained Stetson lay on the table next to her. She leaned back listening to Des with the hint of a smile on her lips. Des stood, slapping the table top with his hand and laughing. He turned and looked around the room until his eyes fixed onto me.

"In the same room with Mazie Goforth twice in one day. I don't think I can stand it." He waved his arm. "Come join us, Mazie."

I walked to the table and sat across from Zoe. Her black eye had faded and beneath the warm light of the bar she was even prettier than I remembered. Her thick hair shone a deep red against her pale skin and striking blue eyes. I could see why Quit had trouble taking his eyes off that face. She reached across to shake my hand.

"Quit's not with you tonight?"

"No, I came here to get away from him. When he was a boy, I could see he would eventually drive someone to drink. I just didn't know I'd be the one." I could feel the blood rush to my face.

"Mazie, you look even prettier when you're mad." Des tapped the table with his finger.

"Knock it off, Des." I frowned at him.

He held up both hands. "Not that I want to be the one to make you angry."

"What did Quit do?" Zoe leaned toward me.

"Oh, you don't want to hear about it."

"I'd like to if you'll tell me."

I looked from her to Des, thinking I should keep my mouth shut. I started to shake my head but then my anger got the best of me and I started talking without a thought to what I was saying, rarely a good idea.

"He can't get over that his father left him and his sister when they were youngsters."

"How old was Quit?"

"About twelve or so."

"And he's still mad at his father?"

"Yes and he's mule-stubborn about it. Not long ago he - Quit's father, that is - got sick and nearly left this world for good but Quit still won't talk to him."

"Some things are hard to get over."

Zoe looked me in the eye. I knew almost nothing about her but could see she spoke from experience. The look on her face softened me and for a moment my thoughts returned to Grita and the difficulties a young person can face. An idea struck me out of nowhere.

"Zoe, would you be willing to teach someone I know about your horse therapy?"

"Do you mean Quit?"

"Lord knows he could use it but I was thinking of Grita Sifuentes, the girl I hired to help me with my brother Roddy, who also happens to be Quit's father."

"Oh, I see." She looked disappointed. "Well, we always need help. Des and I were just talking about the program. Did you know that he's on the board of directors?"

I looked at Des, shaking my head. "You're just into everything, aren't you?"

"Somehow I don't think you appreciate my contributions to this community, Mazie. I even bought a wild mustang to save her from the glue factory." He leaned toward me. "I love this town, but mostly because you're here."

I ignored him and decided I'd better change the subject. I turned back to Zoe.

"I noticed your boots. Have you been off riding?"

"Some of the girls were practicing barrel racing and I decided to join in but instead found my time for racing is over. I'm already sore. Tomorrow, I'll have trouble walking from here to the bar and back."

Des slapped the table and stood. "Well Zoe, you need some medicine for those aches and pains."

While he went to the bar, I looked at Zoe and wondered if she'd be willing to help me with my plan. Beneath the dust and her good looks, I thought I could see tenderness and I meant to use it if I could. I leaned toward her.

"When do you do your horse therapy?"

"We have a clinic tomorrow. Why don't you come by and see what it's like?"

"I'll do that. I can tell Quit about it, if you'd like."

"Would you? I think he'd enjoy it."

"Would it be alright for me to bring Grita along?"

"Sure you can. If we have more volunteers, we can team them to do things we can't otherwise."

"Alright. I can't promise anything but I'll do my best to get Quit there."

"Thanks, Mazie." She blushed.

I heard voices and looked up to see Len and a young woman walking through the door. She wore a tight, low cut blouse and black jeans that looked painted onto her long legs. My heart sank. As they approached the bar, Len's hand slid down her back and past her waist as he surveyed the room. He spotted me in an instant. Leaning to the woman's ear, he whispered something that made her laugh, and then they ordered two shots of tequila, downing them in one swallow. The woman stole a quick glance in my direction as Len ushered her back out the door. A moment later, Zoe's voice snapped me out of my trance.

"Mazie, you don't look so good. Do you know those people?"

I could barely speak. "I only thought I did."

Des returned with three glasses and a bottle of Scotch, handing one glass to Zoe and one to me. He poured a liberal amount in each. I rarely touched hard liquor and had no taste for it but I downed the glass in one gulp. Already feeling dissatisfied, all I needed was the sight of Len and his long-legged friend to push me over the edge. Instead of being grateful for what I had, I could only see what seemed to be missing. I might have started feeling sorry for myself again but Des leaned across the table, holding the bottle and grinning like a boy. He poured a liberal amount into my glass.

"Mazie, do you like horses?"

"I don't know a thing about horses, Des." I drained my glass and watched as he refilled it.

"Neither do I but since I own one I'm trying to learn. Why don't you come see my mustang? I have her out at Race Brewster's horse farm."

"It's hard to imagine you with a horse, Des." I said as I downed half my drink.

He jumped up and bolted out the door without a word. I turned to ask Zoe what was wrong with him but she was up at the bar visiting with the bartender. I drained my glass and was about to join her when Des returned carrying a large photograph.

"Here she is at Race's place." He set the photo on the table.

"Did you say his name is Race?" I was beginning to feel a bit woozy. "Nobody has that name."

"They do if their full name is Horace and they live in Texas."

"You have a point there, Des."

When I said his name it came out sounding like "Desh", so I tried again with the same result. I started to giggle until I noticed Des leering at me.

"So, what do you say, Mazie?" He leaned closer.

"About what?"

"Will you come see my new horse? I named her Edain, after the Irish horse goddess. She's small but you can tell she's smart. Race says so too. He's training her."

"I don't know, Desh. That sounds an awful lot like a date."

"Are you going on a date?" Zoe appeared in her chair as if by magic.

"No I'm not, Zoe." I slurred.

"Mazie, it's just a friendly invitation to have some fun. There's nothing complicated about it." Des held up both hands as if physically holding the thought.

"Race's stable is right next to the county fairgrounds where we do the therapy. Why not go by to see the horse afterwards." Zoe looked at us both, her eyebrows raised in expectation.

I thought over the offer and realized it would give me an excuse to keep an eye on Quit and Grita. I was determined to get Quit talking to her. I looked at Des for a moment, thinking about what he'd said. I reminded myself that he could be charming and handsome in a certain offbeat way. He cocked his head, smiling at me.

"Alright, Desh, I'll go." I held up a hand. "But first, tell me what you've heard from your trooper friends."

"Mazie, you read my mind. I was just about to tell you."

"Good newsh or bad?"

"The officers were hesitant to say anything in the negative about other law enforcement types, but after a little persuading I got them to talk. They're skeptical of the report on the accident. The sheriff's office out there has a reputation for botching investigations. Some troopers even think the sheriff is in the pockets of the drug runners and land developers."

"Did they say what Grita should do?"

"That's the bad news. They said there's nothing she can do at this point. I'm not even sure you should tell her."

I slapped the table. "I said I'd help her and I mean to be honest with her about it."

"I'm sorry for her and what happened to her mother. I wish there was more I could do."

"You've done plenty, Desh and I thank you. Grita thanks you too." I stood, a little unsteadily. "I'm going to go home now."

"Can you drive okay, Mazie?" Zoe stood up next to me. "Maybe I should give you a ride. I'm going that way."

"No, you're sweet to ask but I'm just fine." I leaned toward her. "Desh here has been trying to get me drunk so he can take advantage of me."

I reached for my purse and the room began to move around me. All at once I felt like I was dancing a waltz faster and faster. I had trouble focusing on Zoe. Thinking I could walk it off I turned, losing my footing in an instant. Luckily, a chair was close at hand and I sat down hard. I took a deep breath, irritated with myself.

"I'm not used to liquor." I frowned. "You're a bad influence, Desh."

"I was just trying to cheer you up, Mazie. I hate to see you looking so sad. Don't be angry with me."

"Was I looking sad, Desh?" I looked from one to the other. "Am I that obvious, Zoe? I don't want to be sad."

I realized I was about to cry. Making a show was the last thing I needed right then, so I grabbed Zoe by the arm and stood. She stood up with me.

"Zoe's going to take me home now, Desh."

"I'd be glad to be your chauffeur, Mazie." Des stood. "It's the least I can do for pushing the Scotch on you."

"No, us girls need to stick together. I'll see you later."

111

"Is that a promise, Mazie?"

"Sure, Desh, just no more Scotch."

I stumbled out the doorway, clinging to Zoe like a child. The next thing I knew, she was helping me into my house. She sat me down in a kitchen chair and took the one opposite. In the bright light and linoleum, my surroundings soon stopped spinning and I focused on Zoe's pretty face as she looked around the room. I studied her profile, trying to remember what it had been like to be her age. She eventually turned to face me.

"How are you feeling, Mazie?"

"I'm much better but I'm glad I didn't try to drive home. That could've been a disaster. Thanks for giving me a ride."

"You'd do the same for me." She studied me for a moment. "So, you're alright then?"

"Don't I seem alright?"

"It's just that you looked like you were about to say something."

I studied the skin of my hand, wincing to myself at the blue veins beneath. I wondered how I must seem to someone as young as Zoe, my life as thin as that skin and about as pretty. When I looked up again, she was still waiting for a reply.

"Do I really seem so sad, Zoe?"

"Mazie, you shouldn't ask me. Lots of people know you better than I do."

"That's why you're just the one to ask. You'll be honest with me."

"But what do you have to be sad about?"

"That is the better question, isn't it?" I sat back. "I shouldn't bother you with all my worries. It's late and you must need to get home."

"I'll let you know if I need to leave." She leaned her elbows on the table, waiting.

I took a breath, letting it out slowly. "An old love showed up out of the blue. I hadn't seen him in years but he still looked good, too good really, and I lost all my sense. So, I found out where he was staying and went to see him, and the next thing I knew he was asking me up to the bedroom for a romp, complete with mirrors and I don't know what else."

"The man at the bar?"

I nodded. "Hell Zoe, I thought he and I had a good thing once, the two of us. We even lived together. When he said he needed some time to figure out what he wanted out of life, I believed him. Then I see him years later and find out the real reason he left me was to marry his ex-girlfriend. He had been seeing her all along and I was clueless. He lied to me with a straight face and I believed him. It's humiliating.

"Running into him again made me look at myself in a way I never had before." My voice quavered. "He's rich and he has children. He thinks we live in a boring backwater. That means he thinks I'm boring too. Maybe he's right. What do I have to show for myself, Zoe? I'm not young anymore and I'm alone, mostly."

I felt my eyes tear up and I brushed them dry with the back of my hand.

"I'm alone too, you know." She put her hand to her mouth. "My parents had me late in life and are both gone now. I don't have any brothers or sisters, aunts or uncles. It scares me if I think about it too much."

"We're a fine pair."

"You do have Quit and your brother."

"Some days I wish I didn't."

"Well, men are sure to try a woman's patience sooner or later."

"That's the truth. I'm not sure I have any use for them anymore."

"Except when they're good-looking."

"Don't remind me. Why are we wasting our time talking about men, anyway?"

"I saw the way Des was looking at you."

"Zoe! You're not helping. The last thing I need is a man to worry with. My life is complicated enough as it is." I tried to sound convincing.

I felt lost. I knew I needed to get some focus back to my life and resolved right then to do what I could to help Grita. Not just the little I'd been doing but more, something that made a difference. I might be too old to change myself but I could help her get back on track. I hoped I was right.

Seventeen

After my third cup of coffee, along about noon, the fog of my hangover had just started to lift when Winston barged through the door. I winced as his steel-toed boots echoed through the small office. He marched around my desk and stood looking at me with a pained expression, but my head was pounding and I was no mood to talk so I kept staring at the company accounts and trying to ignore him.

"Sir, it's Nacho." He yelled.

I said nothing and again tried to focus on the numbers in front of me.

"Man down, sir...."

I looked up. "What are you talking about, Winston?"

"Mister Quit needs you, sir." He yelled.

"I thought you said Nacho."

"Sir, please." His face contorted with worry.

"Why can't he come up here?"

"He needs you at the barn, sir."

"Winston, in case you haven't noticed, I'm no sir."

"Yes mum, please, it's Nacho."

"I realize you were born in England, Winston but I'm not your mum either."

"It's Nacho."

"Alright, I get that it's Nacho. Tell him I'll be down there in a minute."

"Now, sir, come now. It's Nacho. He's down, sir, he's down."

The air smelled of smoke as I hurried down the rutted drive that wound across the hill to the barn. Winston had finally said the words that snapped me to consciousness and the realization that something was seriously wrong. I cursed myself for being so self-centered. As I approached the wide door, a pair of legs came into view and I quickened my steps. Rounding the doorway, I found Nacho lying next to an overturned chair, in the midst of a seizure. I knelt next to him. His eyes fluttered and spittle drooled from the side of his mouth but he was breathing. After a moment, his shaking seemed to slow. I motioned Winston over and showed him how to support Nacho's head.

"We're with you Nacho. Winston and I are right here."

"Man down, man down." Winston mumbled.

I placed my hand on his shoulder. "Just hold him like that, Winston. We don't want him to hit his head on the floor."

I heard something behind me and turned to see Quit huddled in the corner, his arms tight around his knees, rocking back and forth on his heels. I checked Nacho again and found his breathing had eased so I turned back to Quit. He faced me but his eyes stared into space, as if in a trance. I walked to the corner and sat next to him, lightly touching his arm. He jumped and his eyes slowly focused on me and then Nacho.

"What's happened here, Quit?"

"Is he dead, Mazie?" He whispered.

"No Quit, he's had a seizure."

"I thought he was dead."

"I saw my share of seizures teaching school. I think he'll be alright but I'm going to call an ambulance just to be safe."

"I thought he'd been shot." His voice shook. "I couldn't move."

"A seizure can come on suddenly. It's a shock if you haven't seen one before." I studied his face. "What's happened to you Quit?"

"He wasn't shot?"

I shook my head. "Why would you think that?"

He looked at me for a moment, his eyes wide. "Mazie, I have to leave."

"You have to leave?"

"I have to go away, Mazie. I need to be away from here."

"What is it, Quit? What's wrong?"

"I just can't stay here." He stood.

"But why?"

"I have to get away from here." He paced a circle, talking to himself. "I just sat there. I couldn't move. I couldn't help him."

"You didn't expect it, Quit."

"I have to leave. Take me away somewhere, Mazie." He pleaded. "Get me out of here."

I looked at Nacho and could see he was coming out of the seizure. Winston turned, waiting for further instructions. I stood looking from him to Quit, trying to come up with a plan of some sort. Finally, I held up my hand.

"Alright, Quit, you can come with me."

He stopped pacing. "Where are we going?"

I took him by the elbow and led him out the door and several yards up the drive. I was surprised to find his arm shaking beneath my grip.

"We're going to see someone." I nodded up the drive. "Wait for me here. I'll be back soon."

I led him beneath a tall palm. I thought he would argue but he crouched next to the trunk as if taking cover. I returned to the barn just as Cam walked through the back door carrying a pruning saw and shears. He stopped abruptly as he surveyed the scene. Nacho was trying to sit up.

"Cam, I'm so glad to see you."

"What the hell happened?" He looked up the hill. "Did Quit do something to Nacho?"

"No, Quit didn't do anything. Nacho had a seizure. Will you stay with him for a minute while I call an ambulance? Don't let him get up. Tell him he needs to sit still a while longer."

"I can do that."

By the time I walked back outside, Quit had calmed a bit although he still looked about the place as if expecting trouble. I tried to sound reassuring as I told him the ambulance would take Nacho to the hospital for tests.

Overnight rains had left the autumn grasses leaning in all directions across the drive, looking like a bad haircut. As we drove toward the gate, tattered remnants of the storm crisscrossed the sky before us while the acrid odor of burning leaves filled the air. We turned onto the street, heading south.

Quit said nothing while we drove the narrow road and it struck me that he'd had his own seizure of sorts. It was unlike him to come along without question and even now he seemed to be in some sort of shock. I again wondered what mystery lay hidden in his past.

Grita waved from the porch as if expecting us when I pulled into Caspar's drive. As I watched her hop down the stairs two at a time and hurry out to greet us, I glanced at Quit, looking for a reaction but could see nothing in his expression to tell me what he might think or do. He looked over at me.

"Why are we here?"

"I've come to tell Grita what I learned about her mother's accident."

He nodded. "Well, she should know the truth."

He watched her as she neared the car. I stared at him, puzzled by the change. I had expected him to complain but instead he showed a noticeable interest. Grita slowed as she saw him, stopping a few steps from my window and waiting. Her smile had vanished.

"Grita, I've come to tell you what Des found out about your mother."

I opened my door and stepped out. Grita kept her eyes on Quit as he did the same. He walked around the front of the car, surveying the house, not looking at her. He finally spoke.

"So, you live here?"

"I live in the apartment in back." She eyed him suspiciously and motioned toward the garage.

"Nice house."

"The best part of living here is my landlord."

As if on cue, Caspar came out the front door and limped down the stairs followed by an even slower Priddy. The old dog stopped at the last step, unwilling to go any further. Caspar ambled up to us, wincing with every move.

"We must be going to have some more of them storms if my rheumatism it tells me the truth. It sure does feel like some more rain on the way."

"Caspar, this is Quit." I nodded toward him. "I have some news for Grita and I brought some cold beer for you."

"Well, you sure don't have to be so nice to old Caspar but in my whole life I never turn down a cold beer." He turned back toward the house. "You come and sit wit me then."

I grabbed a small ice chest from the back seat and we followed him to the kitchen, each of us taking a seat around the small table. Caspar popped open a beer and handed it to me, then did the same for Quit and himself.

"I keep telling Grita this here beer is good for you but she won't believe me. I even tell her my doctor told me to drink a beer so I have some appetite for supper but she still won't take one." He turned to Quit. "I have the cancer in my back and Mazie she brings me a beer now and then. I think she wants me to get fat."

"Beer can do that." Quit nodded.

I stared at Quit. He had been so difficult to get along with the past few weeks I was finding it hard to believe he was finally being civil. Was it something in Caspar that brought out his better nature or had he had a change of heart and now wanted to impress Grita? Whatever it was, I was skeptical as to whether it would last. Lost in thought, it took me a moment to realize they were all waiting for me to tell Grita what I'd learned. I grimaced, wishing I had better news for her.

119

"Des didn't find out anything certain, just that the sheriff's office out there did a sloppy job of investigating the accident scene so it's hard to know what really happened. The troopers don't have a lot of confidence in the accident report but they said there's nothing you can do at this point."

"So, they don't know for damn sure what happened wit Grita's mama?" Caspar looked at me and then Grita.

"I'm afraid not, Caspar." I turned to Grita. "I'm sorry I can't tell you anything more definite."

"Thanks for trying." She looked dejected.

"Sometimes there are no clear answers for the bad things that happen." I wanted to say something helpful but had no idea what that might be.

"I just wanted to know the truth."

"I wish there was something more I could do, Grita."

"Why not go out there and see for yourself?" Quit sat forward looking at each of us in turn. "There's a sort of truth in being there, seeing it, feeling it, taking it all in."

"I don't know, Quit. It's such a huge and desolate place, not to mention a long way off."

"Mazie, a reason people have made pilgrimages for centuries, sometimes travelling great distances. I know it sounds hokey but making a long trip puts you fully in the place, away from everything else so you know the truth when you see it."

"You're getting a little out there, Quit." I shook my head. "Grita doesn't have time to go off on some magical mystery tour."

I stared at Quit, trying to figure out what he was up to. He had gone from basket case to guru in record time. Only a couple of hours had passed since I found him rocking in a corner of the barn. I didn't want him making it any harder on Grita than it already was and when I glanced at Caspar I could see he was worried about her too. I needed to find another way to help her past losing her mother. I decided I might be able to stall long enough for her to lose interest by

120

asking Des to try again. Before I had a chance to mention it she turned to me.

"I want to see where it happened, Mazie."

I was taken by surprise. "Grita, are you sure?"

"I need to see for myself."

I momentarily glared at Quit and turned back to her. "Quit shouldn't push his crazy ideas on you."

"No, Mazie, it's not like that. It's a good idea." She turned to Quit. "I'm not sure why you came here today but I'm glad you did."

I spoke before Quit had a chance to respond. "I don't like the idea of you going out there by yourself, Grita. It's a hard country."

"I thought we could go together. Will you take me, Mazie?" She leaned on the table. "Please take me. I know it's a long way, but I want to go."

"I don't know if it's such a good idea."

"I'll pay for the gas."

I could see in her eyes that she needed to do something, however futile, for her mother. I turned to Caspar, hoping he might try to talk her out the idea but I could see he saw the same look and would say nothing. I knew Quit would be of no help and then realized I might derail the plan by asking him to join us. Once he declined, I'd say I would only go if a man went along. I thought I was so smart.

"Alright, I'll take you but only if Quit goes along too. After all, it was his idea."

He looked at me in surprise. "It's just an idea. I didn't mean I'd be a part of it. I don't want to interfere."

"Well, we can't go if we don't have a man along. I'll just have to ask Des to dig a little deeper instead."

"Quit, won't you go with us?" Grita pleaded.

"I'm tied up with the business."

"But someone could keep an eye on it for a few days." She looked at us both. "You could have Cam do it."

"That would be asking too much." Quit interrupted.

121

"I know him. He wouldn't mind. He likes being asked to do something important."

"It's not just that. I have a lot going on." Quit fidgeted in his chair.

"Why did you come here then? Why did you say what you did?"

"I was trying to help, Grita."

"Then come with us."

"That Grita, she knows how to argue. I sure do know that by now." Caspar chuckled. "You better just go with them or you never hear the end of it."

For a moment Quit looked as if he wanted to run from the room. I had just about decided my plan had worked when he slapped the table with his palm and stood.

"Alright, I'll do it. In fact, I don't know what I was thinking. An honest-to-god pilgrimage is just what I need right now." He turned to Grita. "Thank you Grita, for inviting me. When do we leave?"

I sat there in complete disbelief. This is just what I deserve, I thought. I had said I'd be honest with Grita and I fled from that promise at the first opportunity. I had no choice but to go. I looked out the window, stalling for no good reason. I suppose I wanted to regain some sense of control over the situation. After a moment, I turned to face them.

"Grita, can you be ready to go by tomorrow morning?"

"I'm ready now."

"So am I." Quit added.

"So, we'll leave tomorrow at seven." I stood and turned toward the door, trying to hide my frustration.

Eighteen

The geology of a place is a memory of sorts, a history written in stone. The very place I live in the central part of the State was once an ocean full of prehistoric creatures that eventually became the stone beneath my feet. Looking at the landscape now, dry as it is, you would never imagine it as a broad sea. Geology tells the tale here but you have to look for it. West Texas is a different story. The bare record of time is etched into the earth clear as day. In some ancient language the land's memory is revealed like lines in an open book, marking off events one after the other, right out in the open. Immense forces turn time on its head, altering the sequence of events, thrusting the old before the new. Violence can change things that way.

The thought of violence ran through my mind as I pulled up to Caspar's house in the early morning light. Yellow leaves twisted delicate arcs in the still air as I wondered at the fate of Sephie Del Toro. It had rained again during the night, just as Caspar predicted, and a thin fog lurked among the low spots as if hiding from the sun. I pulled my jacket closer and climbed out of the car.

Quit had already passed the house on his way to Grita's apartment by the time I reached the driveway. I was about to follow him when the front door opened and Caspar motioned me inside with a wave of his hand. He stole a quick glance in Quit's direction and waved again. It was unnerving to see Caspar, always so straightforward, sneak around in his own house. Holding the door open for me, he pointed toward the hallway and began walking across the living room without a word. I followed, trying to guess what was on his mind.

We stepped into a small study containing two wooden chairs, a well-used bookshelf and a battered oak desk, the type I'd once had in my classroom. Caspar opened the top drawer, taking out a thin key. He winced as he bent to unlock the bottom drawer, then stood and turned, cradling a gray felt rag in both hands. He looked at me for a moment.

"Unwrap that cloth there, Mazie but you got to be careful."

I lifted the felt at the corners, uncovering a gleaming, black revolver. The dark metal of the pistol had a blue cast. The wooden handle, worn smooth near the base by years of handling, was stamped by the national seal of Mexico, now barely legible. Caspar held out the gun.

"This here gun, it belonged to Grita's grandfather. He was a federal policeman way down in that Mexico and he gave it to her mother. I showed Grita how to shoot but she says to keep it here in case her old boyfriend shows up and I have to run him off." His face was lined with concern. "I want you to take it wit you, Mazie. You keep my Grita safe out there in that West Texas."

"Caspar, I don't know a thing about guns."

"You just wave this pistol at somebody and they go the other way."

"I'm afraid I'll hurt someone."

He held out the gun. "I don't want not'ing happen to my Grita. You take it, Mazie."

I lifted the gun from his hands, the weight surprising in my palm, and wrapped it in the oil-stained rag. Caspar took a breath and stepped past me, wincing as he made his way toward the door. I stuffed the pistol into my purse and stood there wondering what I'd do if I ever really needed a gun. I decided I'd rather not know.

By the time I walked out the front door Quit had already loaded Grita's bag into the trunk and they stood together talking in low tones. He glanced at me and climbed into the back seat. Grita sat in front. Before I reached the car, a door slammed behind me and I turned to see Caspar hobbling down the steps. He carried a brown paper bag in one hand and a pair of binoculars in the other. I stopped beside the car and waited for him.

"I made you some biscuits and coffee in this here bag so you don't get too hungry on that long road." He handed me the bag. "Everything out there is long way off. You better take these too so you can see good."

I leaned into the car, handing the bag to Grita and the binoculars to Quit, and then climbed behind the wheel. Looking up at Caspar I could see the worry I'd noticed earlier was gone. He smiled and patted my arm.

"Mazie, I know you and Quit will take care of my Grita."

"Oh Caspar, don't say that." Grita leaned across me. "I don't need anyone to take care of me."

"Now, Grita, you let this old man worry if he wants to." He patted my arm again. "You be careful, Mazie and call Caspar if you need anyt'ing."

"Sure, Caspar."

I glanced at Quit in the rear view mirror as I pulled onto the highway, thinking of my conversation with Cam the night before. After Nacho's seizure, Quit had been easier to get along with than before but I didn't think it would last. I'd seen how he could go from charming to mean-spirited in an instant. The slightest thing could set him off and often did.

I had told Quit I would talk with Cam about taking care of things while we were gone and Quit was glad for me to do it. He hated asking anyone for help. Besides, he and Cam had been having trouble. I didn't realize just how much. I found Cam still working in the greenhouse even though it was late. He said he had already decided to do what he could to fill in for Nacho so he was glad to keep an eye on the business. He went on to say it would be a relief to have Quit out of the way because they'd come close to blows only a few days before.

Quit had taken to riding Nacho when his memory failed him. Cam said Nacho put up with it for the most part. He

125

told Cam the best way to handle Quit and keep from getting fired was to ignore him and he was determined to show Cam how it could be done. The problem was Nacho seemed to be having more and more trouble remembering, even when he wrote things down. Cam said Nacho's plan worked for a while but Quit finally went too far, getting into Nacho's face and berating him like he was a child. Cam said he couldn't stand to see Nacho treated the way his stepfather used to treat him. Before he realized what he was doing, Cam had Quit up against the wall, his arms locked behind his back. Quit struggled, yelling curses at them both until Nacho finally calmed him down. I once again wondered about Quit's past as I turned onto the highway and climbed into the Escarpment.

The pavement rose through steep hills, slipping in and out of road cuts striated with fractured limestone and cast deep in shadow. As I stared out the windshield at those gashes in the earth, I was reminded of the many ways one person can damage another. I wanted to stop seeing how Quit resembled Roddy, or how like our father Roddy could be, or the many ways I resembled our ineffectual mother. I decided I would break with that past if I could.

We headed west and the sky seemed to open, the sunlight crystalline in the clear air. Green hills gave way to flat-topped mesas dotted with cedar and mesquite, the highway stretching between them toward a horizon undisturbed and beckoning. The long stretch of road carried with it a palpable sense of relief. The place seemed without people, as if long ago abandoned and left to itself. Trees became scarce and then disappeared altogether. The land seemed empty of all but the essential. I took a long breath, feeling the sense of possibility that resides in the unwanted and forgotten.

We topped a low rise and a forest of towers appeared on the horizon, white against the hazy blue of a cloudless sky. The massive wind turbines circled slowly in the steady breeze. A nearby tin windmill seemed cartoon-like as it pumped water into a stock tank surrounded by a line of bony steers.

I realized we were running low on gas so I pulled off the highway into Fort Stockton, a dusty town known for its Texas-sized roadrunner. Quit snorted as I passed the statue and pulled into a gas station.

"Why anyone would want a giant roadrunner right in the middle of town is beyond me." He craned his neck looking back at the sand-dusted bird.

I turned off the ignition and climbed out. Quit rolled down the window, his eyebrows raised like he was waiting for an answer. I started filling the car and bent to look at Grita, ignoring him.

"What do you think of the place?"

"I like it." She turned to Quit. "You don't see giant paisanos just anywhere."

Quit snorted again. "Why not put up a longhorn or an oil well? That would make more sense. It's just an overgrown bird."

"They eat rattlesnakes."

"A scrawny bird like that can kill a rattlesnake?" Quit squinted at her.

"And eat it too. Maybe that's why they built the statue." She sat back, looking satisfied with herself.

"Quit, now that you've been set straight on the merits of the chaparral, you can make yourself useful and clean the windshield for me."

"That bird has too many names." He grumbled as he climbed out.

We continued on, the heat and barren landscape putting me in a reflective mood. We spoke to each other on occasion and even then, only briefly. After a while I turned off the interstate, taking the mountain route into Fort Davis. Past the blue-green waters of San Salomon spring, one of the few springs left in the area, we entered a short stretch of desert before climbing through a series of mountain passes formed by ancient volcanoes. Although what we were getting into worried me, the scenery was nothing short of spectacular.

Des had given me the name of a man living in Fort Davis named Lincoln Grant Sykes who had been a close friend of Sephie. People called him Linc. I figured he was where we would start.

Nineteen

The highway climbed steadily through the boulder-strewn valleys and narrow passes of the Barrilla Mountains, following the path of a shallow creek. Fingers of purple-hued stone punctured the grassy slope above us. We passed the gated entrance to Rock Rose Ranch and continued climbing between sharp crags and long-dormant volcanoes, the landscape alternating between ancient lava dykes and treeless, grass-covered hills dotted with cattle. The desert we had just passed through seemed a distant dream. As the highway followed a long arc and opened onto a broad valley, small frame houses and stucco buildings appeared on either side of the road, marking the outskirts of a town. We slowed as a blue and white Catholic Church came into view.

"This must be Fort Davis." I glanced to where Quit sat behind the wheel. "Look for a place we can get something to eat."

"It's about time." He grumbled. "But I doubt there's anything decent."

I ignored him and studied the town as it passed my window. Squat houses surrounded by Scotch pines and grassless yards lined short side streets abutting the cliffs beyond. Parents waiting to pick up their children at what seemed to be the only school in town clogged the road ahead of us. Cottonwood trees towered over the school yard, their yellow leaves flickering in the light breeze. I rolled down my window to find the air noticeably cooler than when we last stopped and laced with a hint of fall. Quit slowed and pulled into the parking lot of a small Mexican restaurant. Even though it was mid-afternoon, cars crowded the turquoise cinderblock building and spilled onto a side street. A good sign.

Grita stirred in the back seat, wiping the sleep from her eyes as Quit pulled into a parking space near the back door. We climbed out of the car, blinking in the bright sunlight, and pushed through a heavy wooden door into a large room with booths along each wall and a few tables scattered between. Black velvet paintings of bullfights and senoritas hung on the walls here and there. We squeezed into a booth next to a window, staring across the table at each other and saying nothing. Quit finally broke the silence.

"That's some long drive. We should've stopped earlier, Mazie." He craned his neck looking for a waitress. "I could eat an entire pig."

"I wanted to get some miles behind us before it got late."

"You sure as hell did it."

"Stop your grumbling, Quit. A plate of enchiladas will change your outlook, you'll see."

Quit's eyes darted about the room as if he expected trouble. I found myself worrying that *he* would be the trouble so I surveyed the restaurant trying to think of something else. Grita was still half asleep. Families and working men taking a late lunch bent over plates of tacos, fajitas and guacamole. Three ranchers sat at a table nearby, their dusty hats sitting on the floor next to their chairs. Now and then the jingle of spurs interrupted the usual restaurant din. In one corner a middle-aged man in a pressed shirt and silk tie, looking oddly out of place, talked over frozen margaritas to a buxom young woman. My gaze wandered to the other corner where two dark-haired men, one with a beard and mahogany-colored skin, the other mustachioed and pale, sat with their backs to the wall. An involuntary chill ran up my back as they stared at me, their eyes black and without expression. I tried to dismiss the thought that we were being watched but had little success. I turned to find the waitress standing over us and nearly jumped out of my seat.

"You all eatin' or just sittin'?"

"We can sit anywhere, we came here to eat." Quit barked at her.

"Alright honey, no need to get all worked up. I can see when a man needs to eat."

Quit started to say something, looked at me and changed his mind. The waitress had moved around to the head of the table and I could see that she was tall and rail-thin, with large hands stained brown by cigarettes. I tried to focus on the menu but had trouble keeping my eyes off her hair, which resembled a bright orange pile of cotton candy. With her white shirt and yellowish skin, she reminded me of the push-up fruit bars we bought from the ice cream man when we were kids. I was about to give up on the menu and just order tacos when Grita spoke.

"The green enchiladas are good here, Mazie. That's what I always get."

I nodded. "Okay, green enchiladas for you and me both."

I looked over at Quit and found him smiling at the waitress. It was not exactly a friendly smile and I knew then he was up to something.

"Do you have orange sherbet?" He suppressed a laugh, not very successfully.

"Why, we sure do, honey. It's my favorite. Is that all you want?"

He turned and looked from me to Grita, grinning as if he thought he was real cute. I nearly gave him a kick under the table but thought I might miss and hit Grita instead so I held off.

"Go ahead and order, Quit, I'm hungry." I growled.

He frowned at me. "I'll have the beef fajitas. You can save that sherbet for later."

"Anything for a good-looking man."

I held my hand up before she turned to leave. "We're in town to see someone and I was wondering if you could tell us how to get to his house. I have his address."

131

"I'm sorry but I'm new here. I'll ask the owner to come talk to you. He knows everyone from here to the border."

Less than a minute later, a dark-skinned man came out of the kitchen and ambled toward our table. His close-cropped hair and thin mustache were sprinkled with gray, although his round face looked no more than thirty-five. Beneath a white apron he was nearly as wide as he was tall. He stopped in front of the table, looking at each of us in turn.

"I am Jaime Ortiz. " He nodded. "Welcome to my restaurant. How are you today?"

"Como esta?" Quit jumped in.

"Good and you?"

I gave Quit a quick frown and turned to the man.

"I'm Mazie Goforth and this is Quit and Grita." I glanced across the table at them. "We're in town to see a man by the name of Lincoln Sykes but I'm not sure how to get to his home. I was hoping you might be able to help us."

He stared at Grita for a moment before his eyes grew wide and he jumped back with a start.

"Hola, Grita. Forgive me but I didn't recognize you."

"I've been away for a while, Mr. Ortiz." She sank into her chair.

"Aye, mija, we were very sorry to hear of your madre." He put his hands together as if in prayer. "You are too young to be without a mother."

"Thanks, Mr. Ortiz."

Grita looked despondent as she stared at the table. She worried me. I decided it would be best to get back to my question right away.

"Mr. Ortiz, can you tell us how to find Mr. Sykes? I have an address."

"Grita, don't you remember where his house is?"

"I only went there when I was little so I don't remember much."

"It is very easy to find. He lives in a stone house built by his grandfather, a Civil War hero. It is across from the courthouse." He pointed toward the front door. "It is the only house nearby with an iron fence in the front. You will find it, no problema."

"So, we follow the highway into town and we'll see the courthouse?" Quit leaned his elbows on the table.

"Yes, the courthouse is on this road across from the old bank." He took a step back. "Please forgive me but I must get back to the kitchen, the cook is out today."

He turned and left. The waitress soon returned, setting three steaming plates on the table, along with glasses and a pitcher of ice tea. Quit and I took to our plates as if we hadn't eaten in a month but Grita only picked at her meal. It was clear that seeing Mr. Ortiz had affected her. I tried to draw her out with small talk about the town but after a moment she lost interest and returned to her own thoughts. As we walked out of the restaurant, I again wondered if it had been a mistake to bring her out here.

The yellow brick and arched entrance of an abandoned bank appeared to our left just after we passed through downtown and rounded a tight curve. To the right, the white columns of the courthouse came into view and Quit slowed, turning onto a gravel side street bordering the square and kicking up a thick cloud of dust. I leaned forward to catch a glimpse of the domed bell tower sitting atop the main portion of the two-story building. Below, alternating bands of red and cream stone framed a narrow portico that somehow seemed patriotic against the cloudless sky. I turned from the courthouse and surveyed the street, spotting a stone house at the next corner surrounded by a low iron fence. I pointed but Quit was already pulling off the street in front of the small home. He cut the engine and I peered at the house, wondering if we were wasting our time. I had decided not to call ahead of time but now worried Mr. Sykes would be on vacation or otherwise unavailable and we'd be left with no plan. I turned to Grita. She had said nothing since we left the restaurant and her sad look worried me.

"Do you still want to do this?" I looked into her dark eyes.

She stared at me for a moment and then shook her head. I was about to say something when Quit climbed out of the car and bent toward the rear window, his hands braced on the roof. Based on the way he had been acting, I had no idea what he might do next so I waited, ready to step in if necessary. He looked at me through the window and then turned to Grita.

"You need to talk to this man, Grita."

I got out and stared at him across the hood. "She doesn't want to. You saw her answer."

He looked away, staring into the distance, the color drained from his face. His hands vibrated against the roof. I had seen that same look from him after Nacho had his seizure and I again wondered what preoccupied his mind in those moments. Whatever it was seemed to come on him like a chill. He took a breath and bent toward the window again.

"You came here to find something Grita. Don't give up on that."

"Leave her be." I called across the car.

He looked up. "If Grita wants to turn around and go back home, then that's what we'll do."

"Don't push her, Quit."

"She came here for a reason, Mazie. This is important."

"Don't patronize me, Quit. I know what's important and I know what's best for her."

Grita jumped out of the car and took several steps back, first facing Quit and then me.

"You're talking about me like I'm not here, the both of you."

"I just want what's best for you."

"I know but I want to hear what Quit has to say."

"You're sure?"

She nodded and faced him. Quit leaned his elbows on the roof. He glanced at me before turning to her.

"Do you remember what I called this trip?"

"A pilgrimage?"

"That's right." He nodded. "Grita, people have gone on pilgrimages for thousands of years, people of all kinds, rich and poor, the famous and the common, kings and queens. Some go to pay homage to a person or place or idea, or maybe ask for help, but many want to find an answer. They want to understand something that seems beyond understanding.

"Mr. Ortiz was right. You are young to have lost your mother. I know something about that and I know understanding is hard to find. That's why you're here Grita, to find some understanding of what has happened to you if any understanding can be found. That's why I want you to talk to Mr. Sykes. He may be able to help."

Quit's words impressed me. I never would have guessed he had it in him to talk to her like that. But I still worried we had made a mistake in bringing her to this place. She was young and seemed even younger standing there. Maybe she was too young to try such a thing. I wanted her to know she still had a choice.

"You can decide this isn't what you want. We're agreed on that."

She looked over at the small home. "I know."

"It's your decision."

She turned to face the courthouse and then continued, surveying the entire scene as if she was seeing it for the first time. When she had made a complete turn, she studied me with a somber, determined gaze.

"Do you still want to leave, Grita?"

"No, I know Quit's right. I understand why I'm here and I want to see Mr. Sykes."

"You're sure?" I prodded.

She turned and started toward the house without another word.

Twenty

I followed Grita through a creaking iron gate and up a flagstone walkway, the surface polished from years of use. Rough, irregular stones fronting the house seemed to match the reddish-brown bluff in the distance, just beyond the edge of town. Two deep-set windows caught the broken reflection of the courthouse behind us. A row of pinion pines stood to one side. We climbed the low stairs and approached the door, the porch sagging beneath our feet, and I stood waiting for Grita to ring the bell when Quit caught my attention.

"Well, are you going to blow that thing or just stand there?" He pointed to a buffalo horn that hung on a nearby wooden peg. "That is your standard West Texas doorbell."

Grita stared at him. "You're not serious."

"Sure, I'm serious." He lifted the horn by its leather strap. "Don't you want to see if it works?"

"Don't embarrass me, Quit. I used to live around here, you know."

"But that's what it's for, Grita. Just watch how it's done." He put his lips to the horn and blew, with little effect.

She rolled her eyes. "Men are so primitive. I think I'll just knock."

"Hold on, I'll get the knack of it." He blew again.

Grita banged her fist against the door and stepped back. Muffled footsteps soon followed from within the house. Quit fingered the horn as if studying a rare artifact and then put it to his lips again, blowing a mournful wail. Grita glared at him.

"The whole town heard that!" She barked. "Put that horn back where you got it."

I nodded in agreement. Grita motioned for him to hurry.

"Alright, I'll do it but only because I'm outnumbered."

Grita looked at me and shook her head and I was struck by how quickly she could go from distraught to confident. I was a little unnerved by the change until I realized I had been just as unpredictable at her age, maybe more so. In spite of her improved demeanor, I was still worrying about what might be in store for her when the rattle of a key turning a lock interrupted my thoughts.

I turned back toward the house as the door opened and out stepped a thin, angular man the color of cappuccino. A cap of silver hair framed his face. He wore a pressed shirt buttoned to the top and a pair of tattered suspenders clipped to his canvass pants. His bent hands held a thick book. He looked at each of us in a deliberate, almost graceful manner and then held out a gnarled finger and pointed.

"Why Grita, my girl, look at you now." He took her hand.

"Hello Mr. Sykes, I didn't think you'd remember me."

"Oh, my memory is the one part of me that's not so old, not yet anyway." He cocked his head to the side, studying her. "Grita, you turned out real pretty, just like your mama."

"No, Mr. Sykes." She blushed.

"Oh, yes." He turned to me, smiling. "Isn't she, though?"

"She is."

He turned back to Grita, still holding her hand.

"Grita, do you remember when you and your mama came to stay here after your house burned? You must have been eight or nine then."

She looked puzzled and then her eyes opened wide. "I had forgotten that our house burned. My horse was killed in that fire. How could I forget?"

"I'm not surprised. Forgetting is how our soul protects us from such difficulties. Those were hard times for you and your mother."

"That sounds awful." I wondered what else about her I didn't know.

He glanced at me. "Grita, I see you're not the only pretty woman come to see me today. Will you introduce me to your friends?"

Grita turned toward me. "This is Mazie Goforth."

"I'm glad to meet you, Mr. Sykes."

He took my hand. "Please, my friends call me Linc."

"Alright then, call me Mazie."

"And this is Quit." Grita pulled him closer.

"Good to meet you, sir." Quit shook his hand.

"I did serve in England during the war but I was never knighted."

Quit stared at him for a moment and then smiled. "Good to meet you, Linc."

"I see you found my doorbell." He nodded toward the horn, again hanging from its peg.

"I haven't seen a buffalo horn since I was a kid. I had to give her a try."

"Playing with animal parts is so manly." I shook my head.

"Mazie's afraid to try anything new." Quit grumbled.

"You may be wondering what an old black man with a buffalo horn is doing in this town. Well, my grandfather was stationed here in Fort Davis." He gestured toward the door. "But where are my manners? Please come inside."

I followed Grita into a living room sparsely furnished and filled with crisp light from three large windows. Thin white curtains over one window lifted and fell in the breeze as if breathing. Books of all sizes, stacked and piled in haphazard fashion amid photos and knickknacks, crammed the narrow shelves next to us and spilled out onto a side table and desk. A blackened stone fireplace filled the far wall.

"Your grandfather was a Buffalo Soldier?" Quit stared at a small picture frame.

"He was old when he had my father, as was my father when I came along, but he did serve at Fort Davis around the eighteen-eighties. He was in the Ninth Cavalry and one of thirteen awarded the Medal of Honor for his service during what they called the Indian wars. You know, it was the Indians who gave them the name of Buffalo Soldiers."

Quit picked up the photo. "Which one was he, Linc?"

Linc took the frame and pointed with a bony finger. "This one here with his cap pulled down low, holding the reins of that big bay horse."

"Did he fight in the Civil War?"

"He was just a kid but he fought in Tennessee and Kentucky before he came out west. He was here in Fort Davis until the post closed in 1891. When the army left, he decided to stay." He let out a light chuckle. "You see, he had met a pretty, young Mexican woman and they had a child. That child was my father."

"This is a long way from anywhere. Did many of the soldiers stay?"

"No, Quit, I believe he was the only one who decided to live here. Texas was part of the Confederacy during the war. Back then there were still plenty of bad feelings toward the Union and black people but over the years people out here became proud of the Buffalo Soldiers. There will always be prejudice carried by ignorant people. Still, I find that most people will respect you if you are honorable in your dealings with them."

"The Buffalo Soldiers were respected fighters in spite of their race. Did your grandfather leave you any of his cavalry equipment, like his rifle?"

"Quit, we didn't come here for a history lesson." I glared at him.

Linc set the photo back in place and turned to face Grita. She stood next to me, shifting from one foot to the other.

"Grita, I can talk on and on about my family but I think you came here for a reason."

"Yes, that's true, Mr. Sykes. I want to find out what happened to my mother. Can you help me?" She said in a near whisper.

She looked at him for a moment, her eyes dark and luminous, and I thought she might cry. Linc took her by the arm and led her to a chair, sitting next to her and patting her arm lightly. He motioned for us to take a seat. A moment later he held up a finger, stood and left the room without a word. He returned carrying a tray of iced tea, setting it on a low table and handing each of us a glass. He sat again and turned to Grita.

"Now child, tell me what it is that worries you."

"I want to understand what happened to her."

"Grita, I was saddened to hear of your mother's passing but you know she had an accident, don't you?"

"I know what they *said* happened. But she was so careful. How could she have made a mistake like that?"

"The accident happened on a dangerous part of the highway, Grita. Others have died out there."

"Could someone have done something to her, Mr. Sykes?"

"It was an accident, child."

"But our land has water on it. Maybe someone wants our land for the water, or maybe my relatives in Mexico want it back."

"Grita, I know it's a hard thing to lose your mama." He placed his hand on her arm. "But that highway is known to take people from us."

"I just want to understand." Her voice broke.

"Alright child, this old man will help you." He looked up at me and then Quit, shaking his head. "I don't know how but I will."

He stood, ran his hand across the top of his head and stepped in front of the window overlooking the courthouse, pacing a small circle and muttering to himself. I was about to ask him for directions to the site of Sephie's accident when he stopped and held up a crooked hand. He turned, walking straight to the bookshelf behind me and taking down a thick, well-used book.

140

"Plato said knowledge is the food of the soul, Grita. It can lead to understanding." He held up the book. "First, we find out what we can and then see where it takes us."

He sat beside her and opened the book, thumbing through the thin pages with care. He stopped and handed the open book to her, pointing to a spot on the page.

"Your mama and I talked of this book together many times. It is a history of the region, including the geology and land rights. This here is where your property is located and, yes, there is water under that land. Now, let me think a moment." He held up a bony hand, closing his eyes. "If I wanted to know more about that property, I'd go to the people who spend their time dealing with land. That would be Broad and Crump Nutt, twin brothers who own a land title company. They mostly work with oil companies wanting to lease a site for exploration."

"Could they help?" I leaned forward.

"Of course they can help, Mazie. That's why we're talking about them." Quit stood. "When can we get started?"

"Sit yourself down and let Linc finish what he was saying."

"We didn't come all the way out here to sit around drinking tea, Mazie. What we need is to take action, make something happen. Linc knows what I'm talking about."

"Quit, we'd be halfway to Mexico by now if it was up to you." I turned to Linc. "What can you tell us about these brothers?"

"I've known them since they were children and they're a tad odd but they'll help us if they can. They know a lot about the land out here. I think we should go talk to them."

I faced Quit. "Alright then, drink your tea and then we'll go see the Nutt brothers."

"Does this mean we're going to visit the nuthouse?" He quipped.

I looked at him and shook my head. "Why, do you need to check yourself in?"

Twenty-one

The Nutt brothers had an office on the outskirts of town and Linc directed Quit which turn to take, pointing out sights along the way. We had just come around a curve when three of the biggest pigs I had ever seen trotted across the road right in front of us. Quit slammed on the brakes just in time. An old man in a sombrero followed after them as best he could, waving a long stick above his head and cutting the air like a whip. Quit turned to Grita, who sat next to him staring at the spectacle.

"What do you do if your pigs get out?"

Grita shrugged and watched as the pigs stopped and turned to face the man, who was bent over in the middle of the road trying to catch his breath. The pigs were long-legged and seemed big as a car. All three lifted their noses in the air at once. The man reached into his pocket, pulled out a handful of corn and threw a few kernels in their direction.

"You get after them with a big switch and sooner or later they'll turn to see what you brought them."

She turned to him. "Did you figure that out all by yourself?"

"Listen now, I'm tending to your education. Pigs are exceptional animals."

"They're exceptionally smelly."

"Grita, you do know that pigs are considerably smarter than your average dog, don't you?" He gestured through the windshield. "In France those ugly noses can bring in a boatload of money by finding truffles."

"What do pigs have to do with my education?"

"I'm passing on pearls of wisdom when they come to mind. The fact that pigs are intelligent animals is useful to know."

"You must think a lot of pigs if talking about their I.Q. is one of your pearls of wisdom." She looked back at me

142

and winked. "I guess we'll have to get you one for your birthday."

"I knew a man that had a pig. He named her Pig Newton and claimed she was better company than any dog and most people."

"You know, Quit, they say people tend to resemble their pets." I leaned forward. "So, I'd say a pig is just about right for you."

"Mazie, you have no appreciation for the interesting details of life."

"Do you all go at each other like this all the time?" Linc looked from Quit to me and back.

"You're wasting Linc's time, Mazie." Quit started the car moving again.

The pigs disappeared behind a building followed by their owner as Linc directed us through a railroad crossing and into a nearby gravel parking lot. A narrow, wooden building that had once been a railway warehouse sat at the far end. Red dirt coated the yellow walls. Two pick-ups, also covered in dirt, sat outside the front door where a sign reading "Nutt Title Company" tilted in the steady wind.

Quit parked the car and we climbed a broad stairway, pushing through the outer double doors into a small foyer. Just inside a second doorway, an electric train set on a wide table raced along a curving track, tiny sparks flying at each turn. Photos of trains competed for wall space with maps of all sizes, each littered with dozens of colored pins. In spite of the train, the place seemed to be empty.

"Broad, Crump, you boys here?" Linc called out in a gravelly voice.

After a moment, a voice came from the rear of the building. "Come on back."

"The boys have a preoccupation with trains, some might say obsession, but I'd hate to see this old building burn down." Linc reached over and switched off the train.

We followed him as he hobbled along, winding our way through file cabinets and cluttered tables. Empty tins of

143

snuff and soda bottles crowded the window sills along one wall as we made our way through a short hallway that opened into a wide, sparsely furnished room. At two desks arranged back to back in the middle of the room sat the twin brothers. They looked like mirror images of one another. On the way to the office, Linc had told us they were named after a pair of longhorn steers own by a long-dead Texas writer. He said the two steers were unusually large, even by longhorn standards, and as the brothers stood I could see that the names fit them. They seemed to fill the room all at once. I struggled to rid the image of oversized bowling pins from my mind.

"Why Linc, we haven't seen your face around here in, well, how long has it been Crump?" He spit into a paper cup and handed it to his brother, who also spit and handed it back.

"Well Broad, it has been so long I can't say as that I remember how long." Crump squinted as if struggling to see something far into the distance. "I would just have to say long."

"Well, long it is then."

"Long it is."

They rubbed the tops of their bald heads and seemed quite satisfied with themselves for coming to such a conclusion. As soon as they turned their attention away from Linc to look over the rest of us, their ruddy faces turned several shades pinker. They glanced at each other and swallowed.

"Why, why, I believe you must be Sephie Del Toro's little girl." Broad stammered.

"Why, I'll be hanged if you aren't right on the money there, Broad. Why, except that she's not little anymore and she's gotten real pretty." Crump added.

"Why, she is that, brother."

"We were real sad to hear of you mother passing."

Broad lowered his eyes. "Crump said the truth right there, we were real sorry."

144

"Boys, you guessed right that this is Sephie's daughter, Grita." Linc nodded toward us. "Quit and Mazie here have brought her to Fort Davis to learn what she can about what happened to her mother, and I brought them to you."

"Why Linc, what can we tell her?" Broad turned to his brother. "What can we tell her, Crump?"

"All we know is what we read in the paper, Broad."

"What was in the paper is all we know, Linc."

"You two know more about the land around this area than anyone I know. I thought you might be able to tell her something about the property she inherited from her mama."

"Tell her about property that belonged to Sephie?" Broad turned to his brother. "Why, I believe we may know something of it."

"Why, we do know about that property. I believe we can be of some help there, Broad."

Broad nodded. "Why, I believe we can, Crump."

I moved toward them, intending to further explain Grita's concerns but both brothers took a quick step back, their eyes wide and mouths open. I stopped and looked at one and then the other, wondering what had startled them. They seemed as if they might bolt from the room at any moment. Not knowing what to do next, I turned to Linc. A faint smile crossed his lips.

"I know you boys aren't used to having a woman in your office but Mazie won't bite."

"Why, we deal with oil men mostly, don't we Crump?" He held to his chair like he might float away. "Have we ever had a female in this room?"

"Why, I can't recall a one, Broad, not one and not two, and especially not two so pretty." He turned a brighter shade of red.

I didn't know what to say so I took a nearby chair, hoping the brothers might relax a bit but they stood there paralyzed like a pair of startled bulls. Linc and Grita found chairs of their own and sat. I waited, wondering what I should do next when Quit stepped over to the wall and pointed to a nearby map.

"Is this where we are now?"

The brothers nearly fell over each other getting to where Quit stood. In tight shirts, now soaked with sweat, they looked like a couple of pale sausages but they had relaxed enough to start talking again. Quit turned to them, clearly enjoying the moment.

"So, gentlemen, we're here today asking for your help because our lovely Grita is seeking information on property that was her mother's and is now hers, property that may have some relation to the unfortunate event in question." He held up a finger. "She hopes this information will help her better understand the situation in all its many facets, at the time of her mother's accident. Is that clear, gentlemen?"

Quit leaned back, his hands clasped behind his back like some high-dollar lawyer who'd just finished closing arguments on a big case. I had to suppress a laugh. The brothers turned to each other, leaning forward as if in some silent consultation. They stood upright and turned to the map.

"Why Crump, this is the property here, is it not?" He pointed to the right. "The acreage is valuable because of this contained aquifer here, I believe."

"Why, I believe you have it right again there, Broad. It is very valuable." He held up both hands. "Why, wait, wait. I recall that we have been approached about this property three, exactly three, three times, three and no more."

Broad tilted his head to the side and squinted, nodding slowly. "Yes brother, you have it right, three and no more."

They turned, glancing at Grita and me and then facing Quit. I could see they were afraid to talk directly to either of us.

"This land is valuable for the water under it so people are interested. Why, a representative from a large oil company was the first to ask about it, last year some time. Isn't that the case, Broad?"

"Yes, yes, that is the case, Crump." He nodded. "We do a lot of work with the oil companies. We also have a lot of dealings with land developers."

"Right you are. Why, we spoke with a man some time ago who wants to put in a resort. He needs lots of water."

Linc held up his crooked hand. "Why would they come to you boys instead of a realtor?"

"Why Linc, the property is not for sale."

"Alright, Crump but did anyone that asked about it sound like they were from Mexico, possibly relatives of Grita?"

"Why, no, no one like that asked about it. We know some of her relatives and would hear about it if they had. You know how small this town is, Linc."

Linc nodded. "Yes, I do."

"Why, we hear of things that might surprise even you, Linc."

"What sort of things, Crump?"

"You were a good friend to Sephie."

"Yes, for many years but most everyone around here knows that."

"Why, yes, yes they do but they don't know how valuable Sephie's property is."

"Are you telling us that Grita is rich?" Quit interrupted.

"Why, no, we're not saying that exactly or not yet anyway. We happen to know that the land can't be sold because it's tied up in a lawsuit filed by her family."

Grita sat upright. "It's tied up in a lawsuit?"

"Why, the lawsuit hasn't been formally filed yet but we know of it because of our courthouse connections."

I wondered what that bit of news meant to Grita, confirmation of being watched or less reason to worry. I hoped it was the latter. A family going to the trouble and expense of a lawsuit seemed unlikely to try anything that might jeopardize their chances. I looked at Quit and guessed he was thinking the same.

He stepped up to the map again. "What would an oil company or developer do to get a hold of that land?"

"Why, the oil folks have lots of options. Broad, would you say they are looking for the cheapest water so they can maximize their profits?"

"I would brother. I would say that very thing." He pulled out a can of snuff and opened it. "The developers are harder to figure. Crump, is it true that we don't know them as well?"

"True, why yes, very true. They seem to come and go quickly. There have been some shady dealings in the past."

"How shady were they?" Quit interrupted. "Was anyone killed?"

"Was anyone killed?" Crump's face paled somewhat, though still pink. "Why, no, why, they just cook the books and forge paperwork is all."

"True enough Crump. You are right to the point there, books and paperwork only." Broad turned to Quit. "Do you think someone killed Sephie? We heard she had an accident out on the highway south of town."

"We're just trying to understand what happened." Quit paused to look at Grita. "She was a very careful driver."

Grita leaned forward. "You said three people asked about the property."

Before they had a chance to answer, footsteps echoed down the short hall and two men, one dark and one pale, entered the room. I recognized them from the restaurant in an instant. The pale one had a look that raised the hair on my neck. As I turned to face the brothers Broad jumped back, dropping his snuff and tripping over a chair. He just managed to grab the desktop to keep from falling. Crump looked as if he might faint.

"Wait, wait, wait. Crump, did we say three?" Broad stammered.

"Why, why no, I believe I was mistaken, Broad." He finally took his eyes off the two men. "I'm afraid that's all we can tell you. As you can see, we have a business to run and customers to see to."

"We do, yes certainly we do, Crump." Broad righted his chair. "Please, gentlemen come in. We'll be right with you."

"Why, yes, yes we will." Crump seemed to dance in place.

"Hold on a minute." Quit stepped toward Crump. "You did say you talked to three people. I'm sure of it."

"Why, as you can see, we have clients we must attend to." He backed against the wall.

"I don't care if the goddamn President himself just walked in."

"Take it easy, amigo." The dark-skinned man smiled, his silver tooth catching the light.

"I'll take it however the hell I want." Quit glared at the men.

"We're here to conduct business not listen to you argue, friend."

Quit's face darkened with anger and I stood, hoping to get his attention. He eyed the two men and I could see trouble would soon follow. Worried what he might do next, I moved toward him.

"Quit, we need to go now." I took his arm. "The brothers have told us what they know."

The two men returned Quit's stare as they moved into the office and sat next to Broad's desk. Crump turned to us and motioned toward the door. I could see he was sweating even more than before and clearly wanted us out of the way. He held his arms out and walked behind Linc as if herding sheep. We filed down the hallway in silence, wondering what had just happened. Crump's hand shook visibly as he opened the front door.

"Linc, please pardon our sudden need to conduct business."

Linc turned to him. "I hope you boys know what you're doing. I don't like the look of those two."

Crump's eyes grew large. "Why, why, yes we will be careful, Linc."

I studied Grita as we stepped into the bright light of late afternoon, wondering what we had learned, if anything at all. The brothers had mostly confirmed what we already knew other than a possible but yet to be filed lawsuit. I looked up into the cloudless sky, feeling lost.

Twenty-two

Quit eased the car up to the gate in front of Linc's house and cut the engine but no one got out. I was still thinking about how close Quit had come to getting us all into trouble. His unpredictability worried me to no end. No one had said a word after Crump ushered us out the door and here we still sat, lost in our own thoughts. I'd been trying to figure what we might do next with little success when Linc cleared his throat and turned to Quit.

"Quit, have you ever had the pleasure of a buffalo steak grilled over mesquite?"

"Those Nutt boys are up to no good." He grumbled.

"You have that right, Quit. The Nutt brothers are nice people but not real smart." Linc waved his crooked finger in the air. "My guess is they're involved in some sort of drug-running operation. Their knowledge of and access to land between here and the border would make them useful to the Mexican cartels."

"That would explain why they got so nervous when those two hombres showed up."

"Yes, especially if the third party they said contacted them about Grita's property was those two. If that is true the brothers have told us all they know about the property."

I leaned against the front seat. "So Linc, where does that leave us?"

"Well, Mazie, it takes us back to my question." He patted my arm. "We'll think better if we have a good meal."

"That's a kind offer Linc, but we need to find a place to stay for the night."

"Why not stay here? This old house has way more room than I need."

I glanced at Quit. "No, Linc, we could never impose on you like that. You've put up with us enough already."

"Mazie, don't you know this old man gets lonely knocking around that old house by himself? It would be my good fortune to have you stay and keep me company for a short while."

"I'm not sure there's even reason enough for us to stay." I was feeling discouraged.

"Mazie, you can't give up." Grita frowned at me. "We're just getting started."

I shook my head. "I can't see what there is we can do."

"We'll figure something out. Right now I'm going to stay here with Linc." Grita opened her door and got out. "You and Quit can go find a hotel if you want to."

I climbed out and faced her over the car roof. "You want to stay here? Are you sure?"

"I feel closer to my mother here. Yes, I want to stay."

"That's good enough for me." Quit called from the front seat. "Besides, we have us a buffalo to cook."

Quit and Linc made their way through the rusty gate, followed by Grita. I watched them disappear into the house and leaned against the car, studying the barren mountains in the distance as they went from blue to violet in the fading light. For the first time, I felt that bringing Grita out here might have been right. I was unsure what our next step would be but I knew we would find a direction. I could feel it. Besides, we had yet to make our pilgrimage to the site of the accident, if Grita still wanted to, and Linc was bound to have other contacts in town.

By the time I walked into the kitchen, Linc and Grita were in the midst of preparing the steaks. Quit sat in one corner drinking a beer and calling out unsolicited suggestions to Grita one after the other as if he was in charge. She tried to ignore him but I could see the hint of a smile on her lips from where I stood and knew better. Other than the porcelain sink, the kitchen seemed to be made entirely of a reddish wood scattered with knotholes, even the floor. Blackened by years of use, the cast iron stove nearly covered an entire wall while a heavy walnut table, scared and pockmarked, occupied the middle.

"Just ignore all that boss-man talk, Grita." I called over Quit's jabber.

"Was someone talking?" She glanced at me. "I hadn't noticed."

Quit hopped out of his chair. "Alright then, put me to work."

Linc disappeared out the back door and soon the acrid smell of wood smoke drifted through the open window, mixing with the fragrance of rosemary. Grita moved to the range and sautéed mushrooms while Quit and I boiled new potatoes and filled a large bowl with salad. After what seemed a short time, Linc kicked open the door, carrying a platter of grill-lined steaks. Talking little, we sat around the big table passing the food and filling our plates. I looked around the room, thinking how long it had been since I'd had a sit down family-style meal. The thought left me sad but at the same time grateful for the moment. At least until Quit finished and pushed away his plate.

"Linc that was the best steak I've ever had, without a doubt."

"Well Quit, the buffalo is extra lean but still has real flavor."

"I reckon your grandfather ate a lot of buffalo." Quit leaned back in his chair.

"No, I don't think he did. You see, the buffalo was mostly hunted out by that time except for way up north. Folks back then had little thought of wildlife conservation."

"He was probably too busy fighting savages to go off looking for buffalo."

"Quit, did you really say 'savages'?" I frowned at him. "In case you missed it, the white people in those days could be as savage as anyone."

"I can't worry about all that politically correct nonsense when I'm trying to talk man to man."

"What's with this macho talk?"

"I'm no different than always."

"That could be what's worrying me."

Linc held up his hand. "I'm not going to have to referee you two in my own house, now am I?"

Quit held up both hands. "Go ahead with what you were saying, Linc."

"As cavalry, his job was to protect settlers and shipments of supplies coming through the southwest, which meant sometimes fighting the native peoples. In truth, most of his time was spent on routine activities like building and maintaining the fort and caring for the livestock. Not exactly what you'd call exciting but still useful. He learned enough to open a dry goods store when the fort closed."

"So your family has lived here ever since then?"

"We have, more or less. My grandfather was a strong-willed man. He worked that store nearly every waking moment until the day he died. He was ninety-one years old. He catered mostly to the poorer folks that came up here from Mexico to find a better life. He felt like he had that in common with them.

"My father took over afterwards and did well until the great depression hit. He managed to hang on longer than most but the store finally went under. He never got over it. One day a few months later he went to the top of Mount Locke, not too far from where the big telescope is, and ended his life."

"Oh, Linc, that's so sad." Grita whispered.

He nodded. "Those were hard times for my family. My mother was from Mississippi and never really felt at home in this dry land. She missed her big magnolia trees and the sweet smell of her gardenias, and we had trouble making ends meet without the store. One day she decided she was going to live with her sister in Port Gibson, near the old plantation where my father's family had once been slaves. I knew my father would have had no toleration for going back to that place. He was too independent and hated being reminded of that part of his family's past. I felt it would shame his memory for me to return there so that same day I drove to Alpine and signed up with the United States Navy. That's a strange thing for a boy from this arid place to do but that's just the reason. I wanted to get as far away from here as I could get."

"Joining the Navy would do that. What sort of ship were you on?"

"Well Quit, I served as a navigator on the USS Mason, a Destroyer. We were in the north Atlantic, mostly, but after the Germans surrendered there was talk of us going to the south Pacific. I'll never forget the day in August 1945 when President Truman announced that the Japanese had surrendered and the war was over. I nearly passed out from yelling I was so happy. By that time I'd had enough death and suffering and all I wanted to do was come back here."

"Your mother hadn't sold the house?" I wondered what he had come home to.

"She might have sold it eventually but she died while I was overseas. She'd had a bad heart most of her life and it finally caught up with her."

"You were all alone when you came back here?"

"It wasn't as bad as it sounds, Grita." He reached across the table and patted her arm. "I went to college on the G.I. Bill and got a graduate degree in history, and then I taught at the college down in Alpine. That's not such a bad life for the grandson of a Buffalo Soldier, now is it?"

"No, I guess not." She sounded unconvinced.

The next morning I sat on the front porch steps watching a pair of hawks circle each other as they rose into the cloudless sky. The air, cool and clear, smelled of rosemary. I thought of our conversation the night before and the unexpected twists and turns a person's life can take, and I wondered what I would have to show for my life if I was to live as long as Linc. Angie was gone now, as was Quit's mother, and even poor Sephie. What was left of them? I would have trouble pointing out much of consequence yet I felt Angie's presence as strong as if she were standing right next to me. I realized then I wanted Grita to have that same sense of her mother, and I knew that was why we were there.

The hawks had just vanished behind the red-hued cliffs west of town when Linc appeared, handing me a cup of coffee. He sat next to me. Neither of us said a word as we sipped our coffee and watched the sunlight creep across the courthouse walls. Barn swallows crisscrossed the open field edging the town square. When I heard Grita stirring in the kitchen, I turned to Linc.

"Is there anyone else around here we could talk to about Sephie?"

"Are you married, Mazie?"

"Why, ah, no Linc, no I'm not." I stammered.

"Have you ever been married?"

"No, I never have." I managed to regain a little composure. "Why do you ask?"

"Oh, it's just a question I've had for many years. I never married. Why is it that some people marry and some don't?" He held up his finger. "For instance, you strike me as a person suited to marry."

"What makes you say that, Linc?"

"You have a sort of sadness about you, as if you've missed something."

"I was nearly married once. " I surprised myself saying it.

"What happened?"

"He found someone else, who happened to be the person he left to be with me and who had once been a good friend of mine. I found out about it not long ago."

"That must have been quite a surprise."

"Shock is the word I would use."

"A truth like that can be liberating."

I looked at him, trying to understand what he had just said. I'd felt far from liberated the last time I'd seen Len. Humiliated was more like it. I was about to ask him to explain when Quit walked out the door.

"This is some tasty coffee, Linc."

"Years ago I had a student from Guatemala in one of my classes. We shared an interest in books and would often discuss what we were reading over coffee. After she completed her degree in business, she returned home to work the family coffee farm. She has sent me a steady stream of coffee from her farm ever since."

"Well, thanks for sharing the good stuff." He leaned on the porch rail. "Do either of you have any ideas about our next move?"

"Mazie was just asking me the same question." Linc stood. "As a matter of fact, I do."

Before Linc had a chance to continue, a car rumbled up the street, disturbing the peaceful morning. I turned to see a black coupe, slowing as it approached the corner. The passenger window lowered and the pale face of the man from the Nutt brothers' office glared at us. His bearded partner, sporting a pair of bug-eyed sunglasses, sat behind the steering wheel. A chill crawled up my neck.

Before I realized what was happening, Quit had stepped off the porch and was making his way toward the gate like he meant to give chase. As the car neared the corner, he veered off the sidewalk, cutting across the lawn and jumping the iron fence. I watched in disbelief, as annoyed with him as I was alarmed by the men's sudden appearance. The pale man smirked at Quit just before the car sped off in a cloud of blue exhaust.

"Quit, get back over here." I yelled. "We don't need to go asking for trouble."

He ambled back through the gate and up the sidewalk, glancing over his shoulder before reaching the steps. I stood facing him with my hands on my hips.

"Linc, what makes a grown man go off half-cocked and start acting like a teenager?" I continued facing Quit.

"Mazie, I won't stand by and be intimidated." He stopped at the foot of the stairs. "Those two are up to no good and it involves us somehow."

"That may be but you won't help a thing if you end up in the hospital."

"I was only going to talk to them."

"I saw the friendly way you went about it too."

"They might know something."

"Why would anyone talk to you when you act like that?"

"Alright, I get the point but something here doesn't add up."

"Well, before those two showed up I was about to say we should go talk to the sheriff." Linc called as he held open the door. "Maybe he can tell us something about them. We'll go see him right after breakfast."

Twenty-three

The sheriff's office was located across the square and only a short walk from Linc's house. In spite of a cool start, the day was beginning to warm as we pushed through the outer door and into a cramped entryway. A broad-faced woman with bleached hair glanced up at us from behind a high counter and then resumed shuffling through a tall stack of papers as if we weren't there. We stood for a moment looking at each other before Quit leaned forward, laying his elbows on the counter. That got a response.

"No leaning on the counter, sir!" She barked.

Quit stepped back and she returned to her paper shuffling without another word. We stood there for a full minute longer, waiting for her to finish whatever she was doing but she continued shifting papers from one stack to the other as if she had nothing else better to do. I could hear the muffled sound of voices down a hallway to our left. Quit turned to me, raised his eyebrows and then laid his hands on the counter.

"Anyone back there who's willing to talk to us?" He yelled.

The woman jumped out of her seat and stood behind the chair. "You yelled. You can't yell in here."

"I don't intend to waste the day watching you shuffle papers." He leaned his elbows against the countertop. "We're here to see the sheriff. Be a good girl and go get him for us."

"I already asked you not to do that." She pointed to the counter.

"I believe I'll relax right here until you decide to help us. That would be your job, in case you forgot."

"It's not my job to ask questions. I'm not a detective."

"I can see that. When a person walks in that door, a detective would have sense enough to ask what they want."

159

"You're not a nice man."

Quit smiled but he looked far from friendly. I worried what he might do next. Then the sound of footsteps echoed down the hall and a young man with a shaved head and swollen eye beginning to purple walked into the room. He wore a khaki uniform and a side arm at his belt.

"Is there some problem, Verna?"

"This man here yelled." She pointed at Quit.

"I heard him." He turned to Quit. "What seems to be the problem?"

"I don't believe we have a problem anymore. I'm with Professor Sykes here and we'd like to see the sheriff."

Linc stepped forward. "I'm helping these good folks. I thought the sheriff might be able to assist us in our inquiry. It's about the Del Toro accident."

"You all want to talk to Sheriff Hudspeth?"

"Yes sir, we do."

"You know, the sheriff is a busy man. He can't go talking to everyone that walks in the door."

As he looked each of us over, his eyes lingered on Grita, clearly unconcerned what we might think. Linc stepped into his line of sight.

"Yes sir, we understand the sheriff is busy. We're hoping he'll be willing to help this young lady here." Linc nodded toward Grita.

The deputy stepped to the side and ogled Grita again as if he had the right. I could feel Quit tense as he stepped closer to the counter. The officer sat on the desk, pulled a toothpick from his shirt pocket and stuck it in his mouth.

"You married senorita?" The deputy smiled.

Grita shook her head, looking at the floor.

"Why, that's a shock pretty as you are."

Quit placed his palms of the counter. "Like we were saying deputy, we're here to see the sheriff."

He ignored Quit. "You and me would get along real good."

Quit leaned toward the man, speaking in low tones. "If you're looking for a match to your shiner, keep talking to her like that."

He jumped off the desk as if he'd been slapped.

"Wait here."

He turned and sauntered out. The bleach-haired woman hesitated for a moment and then hurried to follow him. Quit looked at me and shrugged.

"Well, I think you scared her, not that she didn't deserve it."

"We can't wait all day on people that have no sense."

"She was rude and he was creepy." Grita added.

I turned to her. "I do hope the sheriff is an improvement."

A moment later a large man in a khaki shirt and jeans walked into the room. He stepped to the counter and paused, hiking his pants up by the belt, then leaned across the counter and surveyed us.

"We don't make a habit of socializing on duty. What is it you want?"

"My name is Lincoln Sykes and I'm trying to help this young person find some information on her mother. She was killed in an auto mishap south of here."

"I know who you are, Mr. Sykes. What sort of information?"

"Anything that will help her understand would be helpful."

He stepped back. "I'll talk to her but I don't have room for all of you. Who yelled at my dispatcher?"

Quit smiled. "That would be me. I decided she was hard of hearing."

He frowned. "Everyone wants to be a comedian. Who wants to join her other than funny man here? I'll allow one more."

Linc and Quit both turned to me. I looked at Grita and then nodded to the sheriff. I could see he would be less than helpful but we were running out of ideas. He let us

161

through a nearby locked door and we followed him down the hallway and into a large office with room enough for ten. Grita looked around the room and then at me, rolling her eyes. The sheriff lowered himself into a creaking chair and rearranged several papers scattered across his desk before he spoke.

"I'm a busy man, ladies. What questions do you have? Keep it short and to the point."

I turned to Grita. "Ask your questions."

She took a breath. "My mother was Josephina Del Toro. I want to know what happened to her."

"I remember her case. I'm sure you already know she died in an accident. What about that don't you understand?"

"She was a very careful driver. She never even got a parking ticket."

"Careful people make mistakes."

"I don't think it was a mistake."

"Is it your female intuition telling you this or just your imagination?"

"Her accident doesn't make any sense."

"I'll tell you what does make sense. The facts make sense." He leaned forward and smiled. "Your mother made a mistake. She had an accident while driving a motor vehicle. She died."

Grita winced. "How do you know it was an accident? Maybe someone made her have that wreck."

"I'll say it again. She died in an accident. People like your mother die every day."

He seemed to enjoy saying it. I wanted to reach across the desk and slap him but I could see Grita was on the verge of tears, so I decided to step in.

"You don't have to talk to her like that."

He ignored me. "I don't think I can help you Miss Del Toro."

"My name is Grita Sifuentes and you don't want to help me."

He leaned back in his chair, the smile gone. "Maybe your mother wasn't who you think she was."

"What do you mean?"

"I can't prove it but I think your mother was mixed up with the drug cartels operating across the border."

She turned to me. "Mazie, how can he say that? It's not true."

I squinted at him. "If you can't prove it then it's just your opinion."

"She had known connections in Mexico." He smiled and scratched his belly.

I shook my head. "She had family in Mexico."

He dismissed my comment with a wave of his hand. "She had a prime route for transporting contraband through her property. She had been seen with several wetbacks, ah, persons of interest that we had been watching for some time and..."

"What persons? Who was she seen with?" Grita interrupted. "Are you calling my mother a wetback?"

"She was from Mexico, wasn't she?"

"What persons?"

"I'm not at liberty to say."

"You mean you won't say. You think I'm a wetback too, don't you? That's why you don't want to help me. You're against anyone who even looks like they might have come from Mexico."

He slapped the desktop. "Okay, that's enough. Remember who you're talking to. I've told you what I know."

"It's all just speculation." I stood and stepped toward the desk. "You don't know anything for certain except you don't like Mexicans."

He stood. "I know for certain that's all the time I have. I'm sure you ladies can see yourselves out."

He walked around the desk and out the door before I could think of what to say next. Grita sat staring at the floor. I placed my hand on her shoulder and she reached up, touching my fingers lightly. I felt I had failed her again.

"I'm sorry you had to hear all that, Grita. People like the sheriff don't do much for my faith in humanity."

"What really happened to my mother, Mazie? Could it be true she was mixed up with drug dealers?" Her voice broke. "I don't know what to believe."

"That sheriff is just a gossiping old fool."

"It's not right for him to talk about her like that." Her voice trailed to a whisper.

"I know this is hard for you, Grita." I bent to face her. "I wish I could do something to change that."

The office smelled of stale cigars and sweat and I had the sudden urge to get out of the building. I surveyed the room hoping to see something that might help me know what to do next when my gaze fell on a wall map of Jeff Davis County. I turned towards the door.

"Come on, let's get out of here."

The bright sunlight lifted my spirits as we walked out of the courthouse and on toward Linc's house. Across the street, he and Quit leaned against my car lost in conversation. I was determined to do something concrete for Grita if I could, something more than just talk. As we neared the car, I could see they were bent over a map spread across the hood.

"Are you two planning a picnic?" I leaned over for a look at the map.

"Linc was showing me the location of Sephie's accident." Quit pointed. "Was the sheriff any help, Mazie?"

"If you look like you're from Mexico, he thinks you're part of a drug cartel. Does that sound helpful?"

"He thinks my mom was involved with drug dealers but he said that had nothing to do with the accident. He said her accident was just an accident." Grita bent over the map. "I want to go see where it happened, Quit."

"Linc and I were just saying that's one thing we have yet to do."

I turned to Grita. "Are you sure you still want to go there? It won't be easy."

She nodded and climbed into the car without another word.

Twenty-four

A thunderstorm crowded the jagged horizon as we topped a rock-strewn basalt ridge, the remnants of a long-extinct volcano, and surveyed the scene below. Quit slowed and then began the steep descent toward a sharp bend in the highway a quarter mile beyond, the spot where Sephie Del Toro lost her life. Even in the bright sunlight, the combination of steep grade and unrelenting curve felt threatening. I glanced to where Grita sat across from me on the back seat and wondered what she must be feeling. On impulse I reached for her hand but then thought better of it and stopped myself. She stared through the windshield as if in a trance.

Quit pulled off the highway and onto a turnout near the middle of the long curve, stopping the car and setting the brake. Grita hesitated and then climbed out. I sat watching her for a moment before following. Judging by the cigarette butts scattered along the roadside, more than a few travelers liked the view. Beyond the drop-off an unobstructed expanse of broad plain stretched out below us on three sides. Violet-hued mountains cut the horizon, rippling against the rain-streaked sky. To our left, fifty yards down the sloping road, a gleaming guardrail marked the spot Sephie's car had hurtled over the edge. Lines of orange spray paint intermixed with streaks of tire rubber curving across the highway and into the dirt resembled some grotesque work of art. Below us a lone buzzard tilted one way and then the other, soaring with little effort on the steady updraft.

Quit and Linc stayed by the car while Grita ambled along the cliff face. I followed and watched from a distance, not sure what to do. When she reached the repaired section of railing she ran her hand across the shining surface as if precious metal. Down the cliff face directly below her an oval of charred shrubs and discolored stones sat squeezed between two large boulders. I had to look away. Grita reached into her purse, pulling out a tiny ring with a small roll of paper slipped into the center. She held the ring up to the light. After a moment she cradled it in her palm and turned to me, tears sparkling on her lashes.

"Mazie, why did she have to die? Why here of all places? I don't understand it."

I walked to where she stood. "It's hard to understand."

"How do I make sense of it, Mazie?"

"I don't know, Grita. I wish I did."

I had no idea what to say. I wanted to hold her, to comfort her, but something held me back. About the time I decided I'd try she turned and walked to the rail. I hesitated and then followed her.

"I don't think I'll ever know why."

"Grita, things just happen, things we don't deserve, things that are hard to comprehend."

She paced along the rail. "What do I do then? Do I just put it out of my mind? Do I act like it never happened? Tell me what I should do, Mazie."

"I don't have an answer Grita, not really." I shrugged. "If you try to avoid it, it'll never go away. I know a little something about running from your past. It doesn't work. What you can do is try to see what happened for what it is. That's not easy but it's real."

She turned back to the rail, staring out at the vast emptiness of the desert floor without a word. I stood nearby, glancing at her now and then, trying to imagine what I might say to break the uncomfortable silence. I had just about convinced myself that silence was what she needed when she turned to me.

"I think maybe that's the reason I wanted to come here."

"It is?" I couldn't believe I'd said something helpful.

"I wanted to see for myself."

"Then it's good that we're here." I hoped that was true.

"Will you help me?"

"Of course I will. What can I do?"

"I'm going to step up onto the railing. Hold my hand so I don't fall."

I hesitated. "As long as you're not planning to jump."

"Don't worry Mazie, I'm not going to jump."

I took her hand, glad for a reason to touch her as she stepped onto one of the posts supporting the guardrail. She looked down at me and then up to a broken horizon beginning to glow beneath the rained-out storm. I pointed to her other hand.

"What do you have there?"

"It's a children's ring. My mother got it for me at a flea market when I was just a kid."

"And what's the little piece of paper?"

"Just something I wanted to say to her."

She held her hand over the edge of the drop-off.

"Are you sure you don't want to keep it?"

She paused and again studied the ring.

"The ring will only rust and fall apart. The note is only paper with words on it. I'd rather leave them here, where she was last."

She held out the ring again, dropping it over the edge, and we watched it fall a winding course, carried on a stiff wind that arose at that very moment and moved on beyond us up the steep cliff face. Once the ring had disappeared Grita took a breath and squeezed my hand. She turned, steadying herself on my arm and stepping off the rail.

"Mazie, will you let me have a moment alone?"

"Of course, Grita." I kept hold of her hand. "Are you going to be alright?"

She nodded and I turned toward the car where Quit waited, leaning against the right fender. He seemed to be studying the wide plain below. Linc had crossed the highway and stood halfway up the cliff, picking through the exposed rock. I was wondering what he was up to by the time I reached the car. Before I had a chance to ask Quit, he turned to me.

"How many illegals do you think are hiding in those bushes down there?" He nodded toward the desert below us. "There are plenty of bushes and plenty of wetbacks coming across wherever they can find a spot free of the authorities."

"Quit, you're not going to start in on that redneck talk again now are you?"

"It's reality, Mazie. They're taking over this fine state of ours. They take our jobs, crowd our schools and rob us blind. They won't even learn how to speak Texan."

"It's English not Texan. Lordy Quit, where do you pick up this nonsense?" I shook my head in wonder. "Yesterday you were all chummy with the owner of the restaurant, Mr. Ortiz. Now listen to yourself."

"He owns a business and pulls his weight. He's not like them. He didn't swim across yesterday. They come over here and have babies lickety-split, like a bunch of rabbits, and then we have to feed them and send them to school and pay for their doctor bills. It's downright un-American."

"Quit, those children are guaranteed their rights under the United States Constitution same as you are. What could be more American than that?"

"That's just my point. The Constitution is wrong. It needs to be changed."

"If you think people are going to stand by while a bunch of bigots try to change the Constitution, you're dead wrong." I stepped between him and the drop-off. "What on earth made you so mean-spirited?"

He looked away. "They don't belong here."

"Does that include Grita? She was born in Mexico, you know. Do you want her sent back?"

He frowned, shook his head and looked to the horizon before turning back to face me.

"Mazie, is your life so empty you have to use a young woman like Grita to make yourself feel better?" He whispered. "You're not her mother. Stop acting like you are."

169

Before I had a chance to say anything, he turned and walked away. I was mad enough to spit but more hurt than anything. The truth is I was speechless. Although I wanted to tell him what I thought, words escaped my mouth like a breath of stale air. I wondered if I even knew. I stood still, watching as he walked to the guardrail and sat next to Grita. Was I really using Grita to satisfy my own loneliness? The thought made me ill. I began feeling lightheaded and reached for the car to steady myself.

"Mazie, I believe you need to sit down. You're looking a little pale." Linc's voice came from behind me.

He pulled open the door and I sat on the edge of the seat while he went to the trunk and pulled out a canvas satchel, reaching into it and taking out a large thermos. He poured a cup of steaming coffee into the lid and handed it to me. I sipped at the cup, trying to clear my thoughts.

"I brought coffee along because I thought Grita might be the one to fall out. I never imagined it would be you."

I looked up at him. "Why not?"

"You strike me as a strong woman, Mazie, the kind that holds a family together." He cocked his head to one side. "That's right, isn't it?"

I stared at him for a moment, nodding but unable to truly believe him. I tried to say something in return but all that came out was a gasp, and then another, and before I knew it I couldn't see a thing for the tears. I'm sure Linc was as surprised as I was. He reached down and gently patted my hand. Once I fully realized what was happening, I wiped my eyes as fast as I could. The last thing I wanted was for Quit to see me cry. I took a big gulp of coffee and tried to breathe normally.

"I'm sorry, Linc. I don't know what's wrong with me."

"It's alright to be human, Mazie." He nodded to where Quit and Grita sat. "I can see you have a lot to take care of."

"I don't know Linc, sometimes I can hardly take care of myself."

170

"We all feel that way at one time or the other. You can try to deal with what comes your way or you can run from it. Somehow, you don't strike me as the running type."

"Oh, I've done my share of running." I stared at him for a moment. "I think you're trying to tell me I'm stubborn."

"Stubbornness is also determination. It's all how you look at it."

"And I look stubborn, not to mention old." I started feeling sorry for myself.

"You want what's best for that girl, Mazie, and you're determined to see it through."

"Am I? Do I really seem like I'm helping her, Linc. Or am I just doing all this for myself?"

"Maybe she's the one who's doing the helping."

I had to think about that for a moment. "Grita is helping me?"

"You don't think you need any help but perhaps Grita can see that you do."

"I do? I just want what's best for her."

"You don't always need to be the strong one, Mazie."

"But Linc, look at her. She's so young. I don't want her to make the same mistakes I made."

"She needs to make her own mistakes, Mazie. I don't believe you really want to take that away from her."

"Maybe not. Quit thinks I'm using her to make myself feel better." I sipped the coffee. "Just because I'm old enough and then some, doesn't mean I want to be Grita's mother. I just feel bad for her. She's had it hard for someone so young."

"The better question is what makes you care enough to do this for her. I'd guess you see some of yourself in Grita." He reached into his pocket and pulled out a flat stone. "Understand Quit's words for what they say about him. He has his own reasons for being here."

"Yes, he does." I studied his face. "How do you know all this?"

"I'm old and I discovered somewhere along the way that I learn more by listening than by talking." He rubbed the stone with his thumb. "That being said, I do have something I need to tell you but I was waiting for the right time."

"What is it, Linc?"

"Sephie wasn't Grita's mother, she was her aunt."

"What?" I shook my head. "I don't think I heard you right."

"Sephie's sister, Grita's real mother, died young. Sephie never told Grita that she wasn't her mother. She was afraid to."

"Sephie wasn't Grita's real mother?"

"She did adopt Grita."

I stared at him, trying to make sense of what he had said. Then the thought struck me of Grita and Quit both thinking he's her father without either of them ever telling the other and I let out a laugh.

"You find the news humorous, Mazie?"

"Quit and Sephie were lovers when they were young. He has been thinking he could be Grita's father. I'm almost sure Grita suspects it too."

He chuckled. "Fate or God, take your pick, has a sense of humor, huh Mazie?"

I nodded as the two of us lapsed into a natural silence and when Linc turned to face the horizon I noticed he was again rubbing the flat stone between his thumb and index finger.

"What do you have there, Linc?" I pointed toward his hand.

He opened his palm and held up a flint arrowhead that had an unusual reddish-blue cast. After turning it over several times, he pointed to the cliff on the opposite side of the highway with a gnarled finger.

"A friend told me he found some native artifacts on the plateau above that cliff, so I thought some of them might

172

have washed down here. I've been meaning to come have a look for some time but never seemed to get around to it."

"It's a beautiful color."

"That's very observant of you, Mazie. This is called a Clovis point and was made by ancient peoples twelve thousand or so years ago. The color you noticed means the flint came from one of the oldest native flint quarries in the country. It's located high in the Panhandle nearly to Oklahoma."

"We're a long way from the Panhandle."

"Artifacts like these have been found from the far reaches of northern Canada to well into southern Mexico."

"They've survived for that long?"

"The past is everywhere we turn, Mazie. It surrounds us day and night. We humans are so self-centered we're unable to see the past for what it is. We talk about it as over and gone when in truth it's alive and with us, for good or bad. Our friend Quit is an unfortunate example of the bad."

"What do you mean?"

"His past follows him like a shadow."

"I suppose it's obvious. I just don't want to see it because it frightens me."

"Our past contains not only the ghosts we wish to elude but also the means to avoid making those same mistakes over again, if we let ourselves make use of it."

"That's a lesson I managed to miss."

"What's happened before me helps me understand how I came to be here. Without it I'm lost and unable to understand who I am. Take those layers of rock over there. They hold the story of age upon age, eon upon eon, and tell us how the earth, how this place where we now stand came to be. Our own past tells a similar story. We humans occupy a tiny sliver of time but we can learn from it, all the same."

"No wonder I feel so old."

173

He put his hands together and chuckled. "Forgive me, Mazie. I've been droning on like a college professor again. It's an old habit I sometimes lapse into without realizing it."

"I don't mind, Linc. In fact, I enjoyed listening to you. Lately, I've been reading a geology textbook that belongs to my brother Roddy, and I've found myself thinking about things that happened long ago. It's as if I've been trying to make sense of the geology of my life."

Thinking about time in that way calmed me some and by the time Quit and Grita returned to the car I was more or less back to my old self. Quit seemed subdued initially but came alive when Linc showed him the arrowhead. I could tell he felt bad about what he had said in the way he went out of his way to include me in their conversation. Although I was still annoyed with him, I had too much else on my mind to think about it. Linc's well-meaning comments had hit a nerve. I looked back at my life and realized I had been taking care of one or another of my family - my mother during her long illness, then Angie, and now Roddy - for as long as I could remember. Was I falling into the same role with Grita, and if so, why? It wasn't like she was ill or incapacitated. Did I know any other way to be? I felt lost in a maze as Quit and Grita walked up.

"Mazie, I asked Quit to take me to my mother's property. Is that okay?"

Quit pulled onto the highway and I looked back at the place of Sephie's death one last time. While I wanted to be sure I was doing right by Grita, I needed to concentrate on practical matters and had little idea what we would do next. I decided I would sort it out on the drive back to town if I could.

Twenty-five

We drove the highway south from town for half an hour and then turned on a grated county road, sending up a cloud of straw-colored dust that drifted in the still air. I hoped seeing the property might do Grita some good but I had my doubts. To our left, the triangular shape of Mitre Peak rose above brush-covered hills. Far to the southwest the Cuesta Del Burro range broke the horizon like the coarse teeth of a pruning saw. Juniper, yucca and catclaw acacia crowded the roadside between stands of prickly pear cactus. Even though it was still mid-morning, pale patches of shade lay thin in the crystalline light. A rusted gate appeared in the distance and then disappeared behind a low rise. Linc pointed toward it with a gnarled finger.

"That's the entrance to Sephie's property."

Before the gate disappeared from view, I noticed a brief flash of reflected sunlight behind a mound of scrub and started to say something but decided it was probably just a discarded bottle. The road dropped into a dry arroyo and in an instant became washboard rough, rattling us to pieces before Quit could slow. Dust engulfed the car.

We bumped along in a haze. In spite of the constant rattle, I could hear a low rumble sounding somewhere. I cocked my head, trying to gauge the sound's direction as we climbed toward the top of the arroyo, the deep roar gathering in my stomach like a knot. I had just leaned forward to ask Quit what it could be when a black coupe roared over the ridgeline right at us, nearly airborne. Veering into a clearing just in time, Quit managed a rough stop. I turned to watch the car vanish in a cloud of dust.

"What the hell was that?" Quit yelled to no one in particular.

"That was those hombres you were so friendly with at the Nutt brothers' place." Linc said between coughs.

"What's their goddam hurry?"

"I don't think they expected anyone to show up out here. It's a bit out of the way, if you haven't noticed."

"I'd like to catch up with those two someday." Quit mumbled.

He eased the car back into the rocky path and we rode down the hill toward the gate in silence, surveying the area for any other cars. I reached into my purse, running my hand across Grita's pistol. I had hoped the gun would reassure me but I felt as nervous as a bird in a cage. As Linc had said, we were a long way from anywhere, especially from help. In the distance a plume of dust rose into the sky like a smoke signal.

When we reached the turnoff, Grita jumped out, opened the gate and stood aside as Quit nosed the car through the narrow opening. Someone had wired a huge set of cow horns to the gatepost. Ahead, the road disappeared into a low draw. Quit drove to the edge of the ridge and then eased the car down the hill toward a low-slung house flanked by two smaller out buildings and a tin windmill rotating slowly above a dry creek. A jackrabbit appeared, zigzagged down the path ahead of us and vanished into the scrub.

"There goes one of your neighbors, Grita." Quit nodded out the windshield.

"I hope that's as close as we come to meeting up with anyone else." I yelled over the clatter.

"That's not very neighborly of you, Mazie."

"Well Quit, seeing those friends of yours took the neighborly right out of me."

"The nearest house is thirteen miles that way." Linc pointed toward the back of the car.

Grita turned to me. "I'm beginning to remember this place. I don't know why I had forgotten. I came here as a young girl with my grandparents. I wonder if the windmill still works."

"It works, Grita. In preparing to move out here your mother had it repaired."

"Did my mother often talk about this place, Linc?"

Linc nodded. "Yes, she said she thought she could start a new life here, that she could leave the past behind."

"What did she mean by that, Linc?" I said and glanced at Quit.

"Sephie wanted what we all want, to make up for past mistakes. She thought this place would give her a chance to do that."

I thought of my own past and all I'd like to forget or change. Starting over had an undeniable appeal. While a place as foreign and out of the way as this would probably do the trick, it seemed a high price to pay. I looked over at Grita, wondering what part of the past her mother had wanted to forget. An image of Len suddenly crowded my thoughts and in a flash I found myself longing for what might have been. I winced and shook off the feeling as we neared the house.

"There's the stable where my grandparents kept a horse for my mother." Grita pointed to one of the outbuildings. "Park by the corral, Quit."

Quit pulled up next to the stable. Loose fence rails lay at odd angles here and there, giving the nearby corral a gap-toothed look. The house sat to our left, its weathered siding yellowed with dust. A covered porch led to a narrow dog run that split the building in two. Further on, two broad windows stood on either side of a newly painted door partially hidden behind a rusted screen door. At the far end of the porch, a wooden swing twisted in the light breeze. Grita jumped out and climbed the steps, peering into the tall windows one by one as I slung the purse over my shoulder and stepped into the bright sunlight.

Linc and I ambled toward a low stone cistern set next to the creaking windmill. A thin stream of water poured from a narrow metal pipe into the brimming tank. I held my hand under the flow and the water ran across my palm clear and cool, glittering in the bright light. I thought again of Sephie and the mystery of her death.

"Go ahead and have a drink. You'll see why this land is worth so much." Linc dipped his fingers in the water. "That's some of the sweetest water you'll ever taste."

"We still don't know what really happened to Sephie, do we?"

"I can't say that we'll ever know for sure but she may have just had an unfortunate accident on a desolate highway."

"The truth, whatever it is, isn't likely to change things much for Grita."

"Yes, a sad fact in this life is that people die. No matter what, Grita will still have lost her mother."

At that, Linc wandered off into the high desert surrounding us and I turned back toward the house. Quit was poking around the stable. As I walked along I eyed the house warily, wondering what the men in the black coupe had been up to out here or if they had been here at all. I felt for the pistol again.

"What do you have there, Mazie?" Quit's voice came from behind me.

"What do you mean?" I turned to face him.

"In your purse, what do you keep checking on?"

"Quit, the heat must be affecting your mind. You're starting to see things that aren't there."

"You're hiding something in that bag of yours." He pointed. "Why else would you even bother with it out here in the middle of nowhere?"

"I'll have you know this is not a bag, it's a purse" I held it to my chest. "Anyway, I'm not doing anything of the sort."

"Sure you are." He took a step closer.

I put my face close to his. "Quit, you should know that what's in a woman's purse is none of a man's business."

"Is that right?" He stepped back. "Mazie, you're a poor liar."

"Watch yourself, Quit."

"Do you have a flask of tequila in there?" He sniffed the air. "How about offering me some?"

"If I had any I'd have finished it by now. Putting up with you is enough to drive any sane person to drink."

"So, then what *do* you have in there?"

I suddenly realized that it made no sense to hide the gun from Quit. In fact, Grita might be safer if both of us had access to it. I had little idea how to shoot a gun but I thought he might know enough, maybe more, having been in a war zone. I took his arm and led him into the stable, which looked to be falling apart.

I could scarcely see a thing at first, the change between light and dark so abrupt. I could tell by the scuffling sounds that Quit's eyesight was no better. I held onto him and felt my way along the wall, trying not to step on a nail or something worse. Once we were further into the room, light filtering through the cracked siding allowed us to see a little better. The room seemed bathed in a dim glow.

Three stalls with half-walls and center gates lined one side of the main room. The gate posts still held dust-covered lariats, halters and tin feed buckets on stout wooden pegs. A loft that looked like it had once held hay occupied the other side of the room, a knot-hole laced wall covering the right half. I noticed that the metal track of two large sliding doors at either end of the building gleamed as if new even in the poor light. I tried to make sense of that as I laid my purse on a work bench and lifted out the pistol. Cradling it in my palm, I turned to Quit and removed the cloth cover. He stared at the gun as if it was a rattlesnake.

"Well, aren't you going to ask where I got it?"

He stepped back and shook his head, a dazed look on his face.

"What is it, Quit?"

"Is that a pistol you're holding, Mazie?"

"You can see that it is, Quit. It's not three feet away. Why would you ask such a question?"

"No reason." He leaned forward to look at the pistol. "I'm just surprised you of all people would have a gun."

"See for yourself."

His comments were worrisome but something told me to press on. I held the pistol out to him. His hand shook as he ran his fingers across the barrel.

"Go ahead Quit, take it."

He hesitated but then lifted it out of the cloth, testing the balance and feel of the grip. He spun the cylinder and then raised the gun to eye level as if he'd done it a thousand times. His eyes still held a dazed look as he turned to me.

"What on earth are you doing with a pistol, Mazie?"

"It seems more cannon than pistol, doesn't it? Caspar asked me to bring it along. It belonged to Sephie."

"Why would Sephie need a gun?"

"I don't know. Grita asked Caspar to keep it in case her old boyfriend came around causing trouble."

"So this is what you were hiding."

"A pistol isn't something you want to wag about in broad daylight, Quit. It might get you into trouble."

"It might get you into trouble anyway. Do you have a permit?"

"I don't have to worry about details like that if I keep it in my purse, now do I?"

He was about to hand the gun back when something stirred at the other end of the building and I turned just as a man dropped from the loft and hit the dirt floor with a thump, scrambling to his feet in the shadows. He wore a white long-sleeved shirt, torn at the pocket, tattered jeans and cowboy boots. A drooping mustache covered his lower lip and trailed halfway down his chin. Even in the dim light I could see he was scared and wanted to talk but before I had a chance to speak, Quit thrust me to one side. I hit hard against the wall and fell to my knees. He slammed against the opposite corner, facing the man and holding the pistol at arm's length. The man's hands shot up just before the

180

gun filled the room with a deafening roar and a wooden slat to his right exploded in a cloud of dust.

"Aye, mi Dios!" The man yelled as he ran from the room, his hands still in the air.

It was over in an instant and in the ringing silence I was unsure what had just happened. I clambered to my feet and ran to where Quit crouched with his back against the wall, staring into space. He shook horribly and wore the same look he'd had after Nacho's seizure. I took his hand in mine, loosening each finger from the pistol one by one. Then I led him to a nearby bench and made him sit.

My ears were buzzing but I could hear Linc and Grita running across the gravel drive and calling for us. They sounded as if they were deep in a well. I heard something else too, something much closer. It was the sound of a child crying. I couldn't be sure but it seemed to come from the loft. I wrapped the gun, stuffed it in my purse and moved toward the sound just before Grita arrived at the door, breathless. I turned to her, putting my finger to my lips as I looked up into the dark space above the loft floor.

"Is someone up there?" I moved next to the ladder. "Don't worry, we won't hurt you."

I heard movement above me and after a moment a woman's face appeared from behind the knothole-covered wall. Thick braids of hair framed her round cheeks and dark eyes. She studied me and then looked about the room, unsure what to do. I held up my hands, hoping to put her at ease when I realized Grita was standing next to me.

"It's okay." She gestured to the woman with closed fingers.

The woman disappeared and returned a moment later with a young girl who looked to be about four years old. The girl stared down at us, rubbing the dampness from her eyelashes with the back of her hand. Grita stood beneath the ladder as the woman lowered the girl into Grita's arms and then followed her down the ladder. She stood next to Grita, eyeing Quit warily so I nodded toward the door.

"Grita, take them to the house while I tend to Quit."

"What happened, Mazie? Is he hurt?"

"We just had an accident and he's a little stunned. He'll be okay." I hoped I was right. "Go ahead and take these two outside, and see if you can find where Linc has gone to."

I went to Quit and sat, studying him in the half-light. He faced the dirt floor of the stable, elbows on his knees, making no effort to move or speak. His hands shook noticeably even though firmly clasped. I sat back and surveyed the room, trying to decide what to say and how best to say it. After a moment, I leaned forward and faced him.

"What just happened, Quit?"

"I don't know."

"You could have killed that poor man." I leaned closer. "What comes over you?"

"I don't know."

"Try to tell me."

"I can't."

"Try, Quit." I touched his knee lightly. "It can help to talk about it."

His entire body seemed to tense and he rocked slightly, still staring at the ground.

"I know it's hard. Try to tell me what happens."

"I remember." His voice was almost a whisper.

"You remember?"

"Things come back to me. They come on all at once, like a freight train."

"What sorts of things?"

"They come out of nowhere. I can't breathe. I feel like I'm drowning."

"What is it that you remember?"

"Something that happened, something bad, a long time ago."

"Was it when you were overseas?"

182

He seemed to fade into himself, again staring into the distance and rocking. It was as if I had left the room. I raised my hand to his shoulder and he turned to face me, his eyes eventually focusing.

"What is it that happened to you over there, Quit?"

He jerked upright, jumped to his feet and began pacing a narrow oval in the dirt, mumbling something unintelligible to himself. After several laps he stopped and faced me.

"I can't stay here. I have to go."

"Are you sure?"

"I can't do this."

He began pacing again and I reached out to stop him, waiting until he turned to face me.

"It's alright, Quit. We can leave. Let's go find Linc."

As we walked together, circling the broken down corral while I surveyed the open range beyond, I wondered what could have happened to haunt him so. I couldn't help seeing him as damaged in some way but then saw myself in that same image so I instead tried to focus on the matters at hand, the man that had run from the stables, the woman and her beautiful daughter, the way that Grita had looked at them both with a mixture of awe and envy.

In the distance a light wind tore at a plume of dust, stretching it along the jagged horizon where I caught sight of the glint of a car windshield just before it disappeared behind a low rise. The sound of footsteps caught my ear and I turned to see Linc coming around the smaller out building with the man from the stable. The man caught sight of Quit and stopped in his tracks, turning one way and then the other as if looking for an escape. Linc touched his shoulder, speaking to him for a moment before they continued toward us. Quit spotted them and held up both hands.

"No pistola." He patted his chest. "No pistolero. I won't shoot...again."

I frowned at him. "What are you playing at?"

"He's not supposed to be here." He whispered.

"Tell that to his little girl."

Linc pointed at us. "I told this good man you're not as mean as you look Quit, but to keep an eye on Mazie."

"That was considerate of you, Linc. Where are you two headed?"

"Well Mazie, Mr. Gomez has asked if we'll give his young family a ride down the road. We're on our way to get their belongings from the stable. His brother is supposed to pick them up this afternoon a few miles from here, and they're anxious to keep ahead of the authorities. We both know what the sheriff thinks of immigrants."

"We think they can go back home." Quit mumbled.

I ignored him and pointed to the east. "We'd be glad to give them a ride but they'd better hurry. I spotted a car, probably the border patrol, over that rise."

At the mention of the border patrol, the man moved toward the stable in a rush. I decided to help and followed while Quit walked the other way. By the time we loaded the car, Grita was already in the back seat next to the woman, the girl on her lap. The rest of us somehow squeezed in and Quit sped out through the gate and toward the distant highway. The car vibrated so much I imagined the fillings in my teeth falling right out but Quit managed to keep the car firmly to the road and under control. I puzzled over how he could go from basket case to redneck to normal in such short order.

Just before we dropped below the ridge, I looked behind us to see a green and white truck racing toward the small house in a cloud of dust. I hoped we had left in time. My eyes drifted to the back seat where Grita held tight to the little girl and a pang of sadness rose into my throat. I took a deep breath, turning from her to face the broken horizon. As we reached the top of another ridge, I again checked the rear window and spotted a large cloud of dust rising over the ridgeline we had passed not long before. The green and white truck soon crested the top. This time it was right behind us and coming fast. As soon as we dropped out of their sight again I leaned over and grabbed Quit by the shoulder.

"We need to stop." I whispered

"Why? We're making good time."

"A green and white truck is following us and gaining fast. We need to hide them." I nodded toward the back.

"Are you sure it's the…"

I grabbed him. "Don't say it, you'll cause a panic."

"I don't like it, Mazie. They broke the law."

"This is no time to argue. Grita will never forgive us if we let them have that little girl."

Quit glanced in the rearview mirror and then pulled to an abrupt stop. He popped open the trunk as I hopped out and threw open the back door. Mr. Gomez looked at me like I had lost my mind. Linc leaned forward and stared at me.

"What is it, Mazie?"

"It's the border patrol, Linc. I need your help."

Linc grabbed Mr. Gomez by the arm and pointed to the trunk. "Andale!"

Within moments, the Gomez's were in the trunk and we were on our way again, although at a slow pace. The road was still very rough. There had been so little room left in the trunk that Grita still held the girl in her lap. I watched as the plume of dust grew larger and then the truck crested the nearest ridge, racing toward us, lights flashing. Quit pulled to a stop.

Grita looked at me, eyes wide, and nodded toward her lap. "Mazie, what do I say if they ask about her?"

"Let me do the talking."

Two agents stepped out of the truck and one walked to Quit's window. Quit handed over his driver's license and the officer studied it a long while before leaning to look into the car. He took a second look at Grita and the girl.

"Are you a legal resident of the United States?"

"What?" Grita seemed taken by surprise.

"Please answer the question."

She held tight to the girl. "I live here."

"Please answer the question."

"What do you think I just did?" She sounded annoyed.

"Please step out of the vehicle, 'mam." He raised his voice.

"Do you mean me?" Grita slumped into the seat.

He placed his hand on the gun at his side. "Yes, you, step out of the vehicle now."

Quit seemed to appear out of thin air. I never even heard the car door open yet there he stood between the officer and Grita.

"Is there a problem?" Quit smiled.

"She needs to step out of the car, sir."

"Officer, my daughter and her little sister lost their mother only a month ago. The youngest hasn't had time to get over it. Neither of them has." He leaned toward the man and whispered. "The little one still doesn't understand where her mother has gone. You know how it is at that age."

The officer bent down to look in the window again. When he straightened to face Quit his tone had changed noticeably.

"Yes sir, my wife and I have a son who'll be three soon." He took his hand off his pistol. "Where are you going, sir?"

"We were at the place back down the road that has a rusty gate with a set of longhorns on the post. My wife inherited it not long before she died."

"Do you come here often, sir?"

"We went to see the Sheriff Hudspeth before we came out. I thought it would be a good idea to bring the family to look over the property, see what kind of shape it's in, that kind of thing. I'd never been there before today."

"That may not be such a good idea right now, sir. There are drug runners known to be working this area. I'm surprised the sheriff didn't warn you. It's also used by human traffickers smuggling illegals into the country. The men involved in trafficking can be more dangerous than the drug smugglers. Either way, it's no place for a family, if you know what I mean."

"That's good to know, officer. We'll take particular care in the future."

"Please give us a call if you plan to come out here again. We can keep an eye on things while you're making a visit."

"I appreciate the offer. We'll be sure to contact you." Quit looked down the road. "We probably should get moving. The little one has had a long day. You know how they can get when they're tired out."

"Yes sir, I do. You folks take care now."

Quit got back into the car without another word and we crept along for what seemed a long while. I was finally able to breathe again when the green and white truck disappeared over a distant hill. Quit stopped at a crossroads, popped open the trunk and we helped the Gomez's back into the car. A short time later a rusted Ford pickup appeared, driving toward us as Quit pulled behind a grove of stunted trees and Mr. Gomez got out, motioning for his brother to join us. We stood by as Grita hugged the girl, and then we all said our good-byes before the family climbed into the truck and sped off in a cloud of white dust.

Twenty-six

As we neared the courthouse and turned left toward Linc's house, an inexplicable feeling of apprehension passed through me like a chill. A few drops of rain spattered the windshield, trailing downward in quicksilver arcs. I leaned forward in my seat, peering through the window at the road ahead while Quit pulled past the row of pine trees standing at the eastern edge of Linc's property. The house came into view yet all seemed to be in order. I walked through the iron gateway wondering what I'd expected and where the feeling had come from. As I climbed the porch steps, I noticed Linc had stopped before the door. He held up a gnarled hand and we all stopped, looking at each other without a word and waiting for his next move. He half-turned toward us, speaking in a near whisper.

"The door has been jimmied. Quit, you go around back and come in through that door. Mazie, you and Grita stay here."

Linc waited while Quit vanished around the side of the house and then he stepped through the door. As I watched him disappear into the dark interior, a flurry of footsteps caught my attention and I turned to see Grita hurrying away from the house. I started to call out to her when a loud thump came from inside the house. Without thinking, I eased back down the steps and around to the side of the house, stopping beneath the living room windows, straining to listen. Linc should have reappeared or at least called to us but there was no sound except a low murmur I couldn't quite make out.

I leaned against the house and inched my eyes to window level. The two men we had seen at the Nutt brothers' office stood before me with their backs to the kitchen. The pale one cradled a pistol in his hand as if it was a small, black bird. The bearded man held a blackjack. Linc sat opposite them, pressing a cloth to Quit's forehead. In spite of the blood on his cheek, Quit looked like he might lunge at the men at any moment.

I took a breath, trying to think what I should do. The sheriff's office was two hundred yards away but the thought of leaving Quit and Linc was more than I could bear, especially in view of Quit's defiant expression. There was no telling what he might do and no time to lose trying to convince the sheriff to help. I had my doubts whether the sheriff would believe me anyway.

Crouching as low as I could, I moved to the back porch, entering through the open door. I stopped and pulled Sephie's big pistol from my purse with a shaking hand, wrapping my hands around the wooden handle and threading a finger across the trigger. While I crept across the kitchen, Linc's voice echoed through the doorway, calm and rational, as if lecturing a favorite student on the finer points of history. I realized it was his way of stalling for time.

As I rounded the doorway, I could see Quit standing next to Linc, the bloody cloth trailing from his hand. He looked even angrier than before. The two men came into view next, their backs still to me, the floor around them littered with books, broken glass and paper. I was wondering whether they had found what they were looking for when the pale one spoke.

"We know it's here somewhere. We've looked everywhere else. You spent time with her. She could have left it with you."

"I can't believe Sephie would have gotten herself involved in drugs."

"Drugs? We didn't say anything about drugs, old man. This is about mineral rights, water rights to be exact. She agreed to sign over the mineral rights to her property but not to the land itself, which she wanted to go to her daughter."

"Where is that sweet young thing?" The bearded man licked his lips.

"You leave her out of this." Quit threw the rag to the floor.

"Before the original documents were officially filed, she changed her mind and drew up papers rescinding the agreement. The oil execs want to be sure the agreement stands and the papers rescinding them never get filed. That's why we're here. Hand them over and we'll forget all about this unfortunate incident."

"If I knew where they were I wouldn't tell you but the truth is Sephie never mentioned the papers or the agreement." Linc shook his head. "This is the first I've heard of it."

"A shattered kneecap might improve your memory but we'd rather avoid such primitive measures. All you have to do is hand over the papers and we'll leave you macho men alone."

"If you leave, what's to keep us from going to the sheriff?"

"Knock yourself out. We'll be long gone by then. You forget these oil companies are multinational corporations with offices all over the world. They can find a lucrative position for us elsewhere with ease. Besides, do you really think anyone will go to the trouble of tracking us down on another continent over a few broken knickknacks and a sore head?

"I call it aggravated assault. There's prison time in that." Quit took a step and Linc grabbed him.

"Like I said, no one will care. Now, are you sure you want to say goodbye to your kneecap old man?"

"It's just like cracking walnuts." The bearded man smiled.

"You're a sick bastard." Quit leaned against Linc's grip.

"Maybe we'll include you in on the fun."

In the silence of that moment, I stepped into the room unseen by the two men, cocking back the hammer on the big gun. The men both stiffened and turned to face me, the whites of the bearded man's eyes growing large as he stared into the impossibly large bore of the pistol. The pale man still cradled the small gun in his palm and he extended his arm without hesitation. Quit leapt forward, grabbing the gun and whipping it across the man's cheek in a flash.

"Quit, stop it!"

Just as Linc grabbed his arm, pulling him away, the front door swung open and the sheriff strolled in as if it was his own house, followed by the deputy with his gun drawn. Grita peeked around the door and then followed at a distance. The sheriff hitched up his pants, surveyed the room and then turned his gaze to me.

"You got a permit for that firearm?"

"It belongs to Grita. The permit is in her mother's name."

He nodded toward Grita. "I'll let it go under the circumstances but you need to remedy that."

"Is that all you have to say?"

"I take it you want me to take these two off your hands?"

I nodded, the big pistol shaking in my hand.

"I'll need you to lower that big gun. I don't aim to get shot."

"That pistol could bring down an elephant." The deputy puffed out his cheeks.

"What are you saying, Hiram?"

"Oh, sheriff...I, uh...I didn't mean that you...I mean, I didn't intend...I wasn't referring to..."

"Get them out of here, Hiram."

"Yes sir, right away."

The deputy disappeared through the door, followed by the sheriff, and I nearly collapsed with relief.

The next morning I sat on the porch steps, staring off toward the auburn hills beyond the town limits, trying to understand what had happened the day before. I'd never even pointed a gun before, much less at two criminals, yet I had somehow done both. Grita hadn't said much since then but I hoped the new information helped her understand what had happened to her mother, at least a little. The sheriff said he had verified the men were in another state at the time of Sephie's accident. It was just a sad, unfortunate accident after all.

Grita walked out the door and stood at the top of the stairs, her face pale and drawn, the usual rose color missing from her cheeks. All at once she began swaying as if she might collapse. I jumped up, grabbing her arm and lowering her to the step. I sat next to her.

"What's come over you, Grita?" I fanned her with my hand while I studied her face. "You nearly passed out."

"It's so dry out here. I think I'm a little dehydrated."

"I'll go get you some water."

She grabbed my hand. "Mazie, stay here. I'm just fooling myself. I'm not dehydrated, I'm pregnant."

I gasped. "Lordy Grita, are you sure?"

"I'm sure. I have all the usual signs."

"Oh mercy, that's a complication."

"I know, Mazie. I'm so mad at myself." She pounded the step with her fist. "And I'm so emotional. I cry at the drop of a hat."

"I wish I had that excuse." I sat thinking about what I'd just said. "Well, not that excuse exactly. Can you imagine me pregnant? Now *that* would be a nightmare."

"Why do you say that, Mazie? You don't seem unhappy."

"Oh, I don't know. I suppose I have been more often than I'd like to admit."

"You seem like you have everything so under control."

"I'm not sure what, if anything, I have under control. It's just that I'm going through a strange time and I don't know what to make of it." I looked at her and held up my hand. "Nice try, Grita. We need to talk about you, not me."

"Getting pregnant was a surprise."

I studied her face. "So, that explains why you've been picking at your food."

"My appetite is all out of whack. Sometimes I can't look at food, other times I can't get enough." She looked at me, eyes wide. "You can't tell anyone, Mazie."

"Of course I won't tell anyone. I'll leave that to you."

"Do you think Quit knows?" She glanced into the house.

"Are you kidding? He's as clueless as any man." I leaned over to look her in the eyes. "Have you told Cam?"

She shook her head. "He's not the father."

"What?" I nearly yelled.

"Mazie, don't make this any harder that it is."

"I'm sorry, Grita. I'm just surprised, that's all. Who is it, then?"

"I had a boyfriend but I broke it off. We met when I lived out here and then he followed us after we moved. He was big trouble."

"What kind of trouble?"

"After mom died he started acting like he owned me. When I wouldn't do like he wanted, he hit me. The first time I convinced myself it was a mistake but the second time I knew better. After I broke it off, he harassed and threatened me. I finally told Caspar and he talked to the sheriff. That stopped it. At least, I think it did."

In light of Grita's violent boyfriend, her fear of being followed began to make more sense. I studied her profile, wondering how the experience had influenced her view of Sephie's death. As she turned to me, a silken strand of hair fell across her face and she brushed it away with a wave of her hand. She looked at me in expectation.

"I don't know how I've made such a mess of my life, Mazie. What do I do now?"

"You're going to have the baby, aren't you?"

I'd surprised myself even before I finished the sentence and I struggled to understand why I would say such a thing. I'd always believed that the only person who can make that decision is the one who is pregnant. Why would I want to take that away from her? I again thought of Quit standing at the site of Sephie's accident, telling me to stop acting like Grita's mother. Maybe he was right to say it.

"Do you think I should, Mazie? I had almost decided not to. The father wants me to but I hate him. I don't want anything to do with him or anything that will remind me of him."

"Grita, it's not for me to decide." I shook my head. "I don't know why I said what I did. Please try to forget it."

"But I want to know what you think. Should I have the baby? Should I have an abortion?"

"I was out of line saying what I said. I'm not your mother. Whatever you do, it's not for me to decide."

"I'm only a teenager. How can I take care of a baby?"

"Then don't have it."

"Then you think I should have an abortion?"

"It's none of my business."

"But I want it to be your business. I don't want to go through it alone. Will you help me, Mazie?"

Before I could answer Quit came out the door and sat on the step next to Grita. I stared at him, grateful for a chance to change the subject.

"What's wrong with you, Grita? You don't look so good."

"I'm feeling a little light-headed. Mazie thinks I'm dehydrated."

"Well why didn't you get her some water?"

"I didn't want to leave her here in case she passed out."

"Oh, right. I'll be back in a minute."

He vanished into the house and I turned to Grita.

"Now, I don't want to make things any more complicated than they already are, Grita so… The sound of approaching footsteps stopped me from saying another word. A moment later Linc appeared at the door.

"Everything alright out here?" Linc stood over us.

194

I stared at Grita waiting for her to speak. Before either of us could answer, Quit returned with a tray of cheese, crackers and chocolate chip cookies. He sat on the step next to Grita and set the tray between them. I stared at the tray.

"I was wondering what took you so long, Quit. Now I know."

He ignored me. "Grita, darlin', how are you feeling? Have some of this sharp cheddar cheese. It'll put the color back in your face."

I snorted. "Quit you sound like some old granny."

"Mazie, you sure are hard-hearted for a woman." He stuffed some cheese into his mouth and kept talking. "Grita gave me a start when I saw her. She looked half-dead."

"Half-dead? Do I really look that bad?"

"No, you don't and there's no need to make such a fuss about it."

"I'm only trying to revive her like anyone would, Mazie. Anyone with any sense, that is."

"Well, you forgot the water."

He jumped up. "Oh hell, I'm sorry Grita. I'll go get some."

"No, this is fine."

"Good thing she wasn't thirsty." I sneered.

"At least I tried to help." Quit grumbled as he turned toward the door.

Grita grabbed his wrist and frowned at each of us in turn. "If you really want to help, try getting along."

I stared at Quit, barely hiding my irritation. Grita's pregnancy had stirred something inside me I wanted to avoid. And the things Quit had said at the accident site still stung. I was in no mood for forgiveness but a familiar rumbling caught my attention and I turned to see our old truck rattling up the street, Des behind the wheel, Nacho next to him. Nacho climbed out and stood at the street, his face unsmiling in the shadow of his cap. Des stepped next to him. I stood and hurried down the stone walkway, looking from Des to Nacho and back, trying to make sense of their appearance. My mind raced in all directions. Des held up a hand as if to slow my running thoughts.

"Take a breath Mazie. Before you start in with your questions, let me tell you what's happened."

"Why are you here, Des? Nacho, what's wrong?"

"He wouldn't let me come alone." Nacho nodded toward Des.

"He would have come anyway but the doctor said he's not supposed to drive so soon after the seizure."

"But why are you here?" I heard my voice raise an octave.

"It's Roddy. His cancer has returned."

Quit stepped off the porch. "Why didn't you call us?"

"We tried but the phone service out here is poor." Nacho shook his head.

"Linc doesn't have a phone and the sheriff refused to help." Des added.

"You don't have a phone?"

"I'm sorry, Mazie. I gave it up long ago." Linc patted my arm. "This is the only time I've regretted it."

"Wait!" I held up my hand.

I felt like the world was closing in around me. I climbed back up the stairs and found the nearest chair, sitting down hard. Des followed and I reached out to take his hand.

"It was good of you to come all the way out here to tell us. This isn't your responsibility."

His smile had a hint of sadness to it. "Do you want to hear more?"

"Yes, please tell me."

"Nacho better fill you in. He was there."

Nacho sat on the top stair and took off his hat. The crescent-shaped scar showed briefly beneath his black hair and I thought how strange it was that two of the men in my life would have similar afflictions.

"Roddy collapsed in the middle of a chess game late last yesterday." Nacho fingered the bill of his cap. "Cam came

196

to find me when he couldn't get him to respond and then we called for an ambulance. Cam said he seemed fine right up until it happened. It was like Roddy just fell asleep. Cam said he might not have noticed if they hadn't been in the middle of a game."

Quit sat on the step next to him. "How is he now, Nacho?"

"The same. They're running tests but it doesn't look good."

"Poor Roddy." Grita whispered.

"We should leave right away then."

"You best have something to eat before you get back on the road." Linc disappeared through the door.

Grita helped Linc bring sandwiches and coffee to the porch and we picked at our plates for a while, saying little. Grita barely touched her food. I figured we were all anxious to get home. We finally gave up on lunch and began loading the car as Nacho and Des climbed into the creaking pickup, pulling away with a low rumble.

Quit and Grita were still packing as I stood in front of the house next to Linc, watching the remains of a small storm move across the spiked ridge that rose above the west side of town. Linc reached out a bony arm, pointing toward the horizon.

"See that rain trailing off the storm there, Mazie? The reason it seems to disappear is because it's evaporating before it ever hits the earth. They call it virga and it shows just how dry it is in this place. Water is precious out here. It sometimes marks the line between life and death. Those folks we found at Grita's place could easily have died of thirst on their trip out of Mexico. It happens all too often."

"That's a scary thought when I think of their pretty little girl."

"This land can be hard but it makes you appreciate what you have and what sometimes will come along." He reached over and lightly touched my arm. "I appreciate the chance to know Grita and Quit, and especially you, Mazie. You're an exceptional woman."

"Roddy would say exceptionally stubborn."

"There you go again making light of yourself. You have a big heart, Mazie but you don't let people see who you really are. You don't need hide it."

I shook my head. "I don't know how else to be."

"When you get to be my age you come to realize all that you failed to say, all that you could have said when you had the chance. Life goes by and eventually you learn you have only so many opportunities to voice what you truly mean." He ran his hand across his face. "You also have only so many chances to be yourself, who you really are. Take hold of those chances while you can, Mazie."

"Sometimes I feel my life passing by and I want to grab hold of something to slow it down but I don't know how. When I look at Quit and Grita, I feel that way."

"The young can do that to us. Let them know you, Mazie." He turned to the house. "I'd better see how they're getting along."

I reached out to him but he had already started moving away.

"Thank you Linc, for everything." I called after him.

Twenty-seven

On the trip back home I tried to think through what needed doing but my mind kept slipping into the past, to the weeks after Len left. At the time, I was so lonely and distraught about the break-up that I dropped out of school and went to live with my aunt in Houston. Aunt Betty Belle had been born in Birmingham, Alabama and in some ways never left that part of the world. She called her husband Uncle Mister just as her sister, Carolina, called her husband Uncle Doctor. I never heard Betty Belle or Carolina use a first name for either of them.

Betty Belle and Uncle Mister lived in an older part of town that resembled the Deep South more than rest of the city or even the State. In their neighborhood, hundred-year-old live oaks buckled sidewalks and stretched over entire streets to form shady tunnels of green. Their two-story frame house stood back from the road, much of it hidden behind an overgrown wall of azalea and crepe myrtle. White shiplap siding peeked through the foliage here and there on either side of a deep wrap-around porch whose thick pillars seemed to overwhelm the house behind them. An ornate wooden railing, painted sky blue and gold, connected the pillars. Porch swings hung at each end.

I had lived with Aunt Betty Belle and Uncle Mister off and on since I was sixteen. They took me in not long after my mother died. Years of smoking unfiltered cigarettes finally caught up with mother and, in a way, with me too. She was the first person I would watch die. Quit's mother was the second. Although I was raised to call Betty Belle my aunt, she was in truth unrelated to me or my mother. Mother and Betty Belle had been close for most of their lives and decided early on that their friendship outweighed any technicalities regarding kinship, so they deemed themselves as good as sisters and that was that. I learned the truth only after my mother was dead and there were legal reasons for bringing it up. In Betty Belle's view, it was as natural as the sun rising each day and there never had been cause to mention it before then.

The second time I arrived at Betty Belle's home, after getting dumped by Len and abandoning my life in Austin with no job and no prospects, she and Uncle Mister took me in without question. I could see by the concern on their faces I was a pitiful sight. Len's leaving had left me feeling shamed and ashamed. I had failed at love, the one thing most people I knew believed really mattered. Before I met Len, I'd been independent and confident. I saw marriage as something I could take or leave and I had little concern with what the future might bring. Somehow over time I changed and also came to believe that getting married was all that mattered.

Rather than return to my old room, which had been converted into a smoking parlor for Uncle Mister and Uncle Doctor, Betty Belle set aside a room for me in the upstairs garage apartment behind the main house. Not needing the income it provided, they had long ago stopped renting it. The apartment had a separate entrance that opened onto a narrow alleyway bisecting the block from end to end so I could come and go as I pleased, not that I had anywhere to go. I'd lost touch with most of the people in town I once knew and the rest were away at college or a new career.

The apartment consisted of two small rooms and a tiny kitchen, and as the garage was unused, the place was quiet and comfortable. Outside, a set of red wooden stairs on one corner led from the alley to a small landing overlooking the neighbor's palm grove. A mass of broad fronds crowding the little porch bathed the entrance in a green glow. Just inside the door, a shallow alcove holding a small table and two chairs faced the sparsely furnished main living area. Across the room a faded couch sat beneath two windows that divided the far wall. The adjoining bedroom had space enough for a large four-poster bed but not much else. Lively paintings Betty Belle had picked up on her many travels to the Caribbean brightened the plain walls.

Once I settled in, the weeks slipped by in a blur of unplanned but self-imposed seclusion until the day Uncle Mister found a job for me as cashier for a nearby corner grocery. The store was a small, family-run place that largely catered to the neighborhood and surrounding area. Most of the customers were an odd mix of students from the local Catholic university and elderly widows constantly on the lookout for eligible unmarried men, at least according to Uncle Mister. One morning before I started working there, Uncle Mister complained to Betty Belle that the widows were so plentiful he would surely be accosted if he entered the store, thinking the excuse would relieve him of his shopping duties. Wise to his plan, Betty Belle simply said a gentleman should be honored by such attention, which was all the more reason for him to continue with the shopping.

"But Betty Belle, what if I should succumb to their advances?"

Uncle Mister's drawl moved like cold molasses. Tall and scholarly with a thin angular face, Mister's bushy eyebrows matched the gray hair that fell across his forehead in a clean line. When he smiled his otherwise pale cheeks held dimples the size and color of small apples. He turned to me for support but I shrugged and shook my head, not wanting to take sides.

Uncle Mister and I were sitting at the kitchen table snapping green beans while Betty Belle prepared to roast a chicken. With a high-ceiling and windows on two sides, the light and airy kitchen held a hopeful feel of morning at any time of day. A broad walnut table in the center of the room was my favorite spot in the house and we seemed to spend most of our time there, the smell of roasting, frying or baking often filling the air. I had told them little of what happened before my arrival but enough that their efforts to give me hope for the future were more than obvious.

"They're very persistent." He added.

"Mister, you better find yourself a good hiding place if you should stray because you know the kind of trouble you'd find yourself in. One can never underestimate the wrath of a woman." She winked at me. "Isn't that right, Mazie?"

Betty Belle looked like a bowling pin next to the broomstick shape of Mister. Her salt and pepper hair twisted around her face in loose curls that hung to just above her shoulders and framed her hazel eyes. Her strawberry-colored skin still held a youthful beauty that few women her age could match.

Every now and then I would catch Mister admiring her from a distance. When Betty Belle was in the room, Mister seemed a different person than his usual lawyerly self. Reserved and to the point, Mister the Lawyer would fix his penetrating gaze on you and make you focus on every word to ensure its accuracy. Yet when Betty Belle walked into the room his hard edges and exacting demeanor softened and Mister the Husband puttered about the room just for a chance to be beside her. It did me good to see that two people could still enjoy each other's company after so many years.

"I don't know much about women's wrath, Aunt Betty Belle." I offered.

"Oh well, a sweet young thing like you wouldn't understand. After you've lived as long as Uncle Mister and seen all the mischief men can create, then you'll know a woman's ire is the one thing in God's wide world a man with any sense wants to avoid."

"Now Mazie, don't you start believing all men are as underhanded as your aunt makes them out to be." He patted my knee. "There are still plenty of good men left in this world."

Betty Belle snorted. "Here comes one that fails to meet even that rather mediocre standard."

Uncle Doctor sauntered into the kitchen wearing a white summer suit, white shirt and red silk tie, with a thick, unlit cigar clamped between his teeth. The tips of two more cigars peeked from his chest pocket. Once he spotted me, he smoothed his beard with a stroke of one hand while raking back his longish hair with the other. Uncle Doctor had always favored women. While he was not a medical doctor he let people, especially women, believe that he was more often than not. He had been a large animal vet in Birmingham until his retirement several years after Aunt Carolina's death, when he purchased a house down the street from Betty Belle and Mister's home. He smiled at me and took the cigar from his mouth, slipping it into his pocket beside the others.

"Why, Mazie Goforth, I would not have thought it possible you could be even prettier than you were the last time I saw you but here you sit as proof to my foolishness." He sat across from me and took my hand.

"Foolishness is your most memorable trait, Doctor." Betty Belle wrestled with the oily chicken. "Remember what I was saying about the coarser sex, Mazie? Well, Doctor here could write a book on that subject based solely on his own personal experience."

Doctor's eyes lit up. "Yes Mazie, I've long fancied that I could be an author of note. As a man of much experience, I'm just the right age to start a new career. Regrettably, I was far too young and full of life to retire when I did. I can't imagine what got into me."

Betty Belle snorted again. "Whiskey and cigars is what got into you, Doctor."

"More whiskey than cigars." Mister added.

"Ah, but the nectar of the gods makes life worth living, Betty Belle. It's the very reason your Mister lives life with such élan." He waved his hand in the air.

Betty Belle looked up from the chicken. "Mister has had a cough lately. Is that what you doctors call it?"

He ignored her and pulled the partially chewed cigar from his pocket. "Shall we make our way to the smoking room, Mister?"

Mister dropped two snapped beans into the bowl and turned to Betty Belle with a questioning look. She nodded her approval. Doctor stood, kissed my hand with much ceremony and then walked to the door, followed by Mister. Doctor stopped at the doorway.

"I regret I must leave you, Mazie, but I'm sure you ladies have important news to discuss outside the company of men."

"Doctor thinks what we're having for dinner is important news, Mazie."

"Betty Belle, I'll leave you with the words of the Greek philosopher Epicurus, who said our greatest happiness resides in simple pleasures, like a perfectly roasted chicken."

With that he turned and left.

"We don't have enough dinner for you, Doctor." Betty Belle called after him.

"Don't be too hard on him, Betty Belle."

"Oh, don't worry, Mazie. Ever since Carolina passed he's acted like a reincarnation of Mark Twain. I'm just bringing him back to earth so he doesn't start believing it too much. I figure I'm doing him a favor."

"He does have a taste for summer suits and cigars."

"Not to mention whiskey. Mister is no better." She tossed the chicken into the oven and slammed the door. "I must say I find these men tiresome."

The days seemed to blend together in a mix of work and the on-going business of living, fixing dinner, washing dishes, taking care of household chores. I insisted on helping Betty Belle with cooking, cleaning house and tending the garden in exchange for rent, but I still had time most evenings for a walk along the shady, broken sidewalks. The weather was warm and the sound of voices often drifted to the street, leaving me entertained but strangely sad at times.

One evening I noticed a young man coming toward me carrying an armload of books and leading a large dog on a heavy leash. As he neared I could see that the leash was actually a coarse rope tied to the dog's collar in a thick knot. Every few steps the dog, a mix of some sort, would stop and toss her head back, biting at the rope and trying to shake free. Just before they reached me the dog took the rope in her teeth, gave it a shake and in an instant the books were tumbling along the sidewalk and the dog was free. She bounded toward me in a tail wagging blur.

"Dogberry!" The owner yelled, chasing behind.

As I knelt and called the dog to me, I wondered who on earth would give their pet such a name. The dog reached me and sat as if expecting a treat, so I patted her thick coat while the man gathered up his books and found the end of the rope. He pulled at the dog's collar.

"I'm sorry Dogberry bothered you. Her leash is missing so I improvised, just not very well."

"Dogberry? Is that really her name?"

"She belongs to Norvis Nagel, a professor at the university. He likes to name his pets after characters in Shakespeare's plays, and the Bard came up with some odd names if you ask me. Professor Nagel has two cats named Goneril and Regan, and a parrot he calls Iago." He stood with a start. "You're not named something like Ophelia or Desdemona are you?"

"No, but my name isn't any less strange." I held out my hand. "I'm Mazie Goforth."

"I'm Arnet Almond. Some of the guys call me "Double A" or "A Squared" but you can call me Arne."

He gave my hand a light shake. Arne was cute but not handsome, with an attractive athletic build. His thick hair fell around his face in tight curls the color of straw, setting

205

off his blue eyes. He had a thin beard and the longest eyelashes I'd ever seen on a man. I found myself wondering if he was involved with anyone.

"Has your professor read those plays? Those are not the most likeable characters."

"He's a Shakespeare scholar. He likes the names because they're offbeat. He goes for anything out of the ordinary."

"Dogberry is offbeat alright. Why are you walking her instead of the professor doing it?"

"I'm a student at the university. I do research for him and house-sit when he's away."

"I've always liked Shakespeare, although the language can be hard to follow. And I don't much like it when everyone dies at the end."

"The university is putting on *Much Ado About Nothing* this week. Nobody dies in that one. I can get free tickets if you'd like to go."

I was so surprised by his offer that I just stood there looking at him, my mouth half open. A whole boatload of thoughts raced through my head, making me feel a little dizzy. I must have looked less than happy about the offer because he began to backpedal right away.

"Oh, wait, that didn't sound right. You probably think I'm bold to ask you out right off the bat. I didn't mean for it to sound like a date. It's just that I can get free tickets." He barely took a breath. "Of course, if you want it to be a date, it could be a date. That is, if you wanted to go out with me and didn't mind that we just met. But I understand if you don't. We hardly know each other. How could we since we just met?"

I held up my hand. Being dumped by Len had left me standoffish and suspicious when it came to men but Arne's unassuming approach set me at ease. Standing there listening to him babble, I realized it was time for me to try something new. Besides, the more I watched him the more I liked him. I dropped my hand and, most surprising of all, smiled. It hit me right then how seldom I had smiled in the last few months.

"Arne, I have something to say if you can stop talking for one second."

"Oh, sorry, I have a habit of talking really fast when I get excited."

"So that's why you're carrying on so." I tried to sound puzzled. "What is it that you're excited about?"

"It's just that I love going to plays but I don't like going alone."

"So then, Arne, who are you going to go with?"

He stared at me with a bewildered look. "Well Mazie, I thought maybe you might possibly consider whether you would perhaps want to go with me to see the play."

"That sounds a bit tentative, Arne." I gave my best impression of Betty Belle. "A woman wants to know where she stands before deciding anything, especially when it concerns a night at the theater, so are you asking me to go with you or not?"

"Does that mean you want to go to the play with me, Mazie?" His face was a mixture of hope and fear.

"It depends on if you're asking."

"What have we been talking about then? I have to admit I'm completely lost."

Although it had been a long time since I'd felt confident enough to talk to a man like that I decided my game had gone on long enough.

"I'm just kidding with you, Arne. I'd love to go see the play. When is it?"

"How about Thursday night at eight?"

"Thursday night it is."

"Thursday it is." he repeated.

"That's tomorrow, Arne."

"Okay, great, we're on for tomorrow." He seemed to bounce in place. "I'll come pick you up then."

He took up the leash, pulled Dogberry to him and turned to leave. I stood watching, trying not to laugh.

"Uh, Arne, aren't you forgetting something?"

He turned. "I've got the dog and the collar and the leash. Did I drop something?"

"Your books."

"Oh, right." He gathered the books in one arm.

"There's something else."

He turned a circle looking at the ground. I stifled another laugh.

"I don't see anything else."

"So Arne, where will you pick me up? Here?"

"Here?" He looked across the road. "Why would I pick you up here?"

"Where then?"

"At your house."

"Which is located where?"

"Don't you know?"

"Yes Arne, I know where I live."

He looked down the street one way and then the other as if the answer would soon come to him. I waited until he turned back to me.

"Oh, right, I need to know where to pick you up."

"Are you a little forgetful, Arne?"

"Everyone tells me I'll make a great absent-minded professor someday."

"I can believe that." I pulled a pen out of my purse. "Hold out your hand. I know a cure for absent-mindedness."

I took his hand and scribbled my phone number on his palm. When I'd finished he held up his hand and stared at it in amazement. I handed him the pen and held out my hand.

"Just in case you forget."

Smiling like a kid, he scrawled an almost unreadable set of numbers across my palm and then turned to leave.

"Some things I don't forget." He called over his shoulder.

On the way back to my apartment, I realized the fog that had settled on me long before had vanished, leaving a crystal clarity. Palms lining the street rustled in gentle waves, throwing spiked shadows across sidewalks and yards. Silver mats of cloud drifted across the darkening sky. Golden light from living room windows no longer seemed depressing and instead fell across my path as if showing the way home. An image of Arne's square shoulders floated through my mind, stirring me in a way I'd almost forgotten. I realized with a start how long it had been since I'd looked forward to spending time with a man.

Twenty-eight

I sat at the kitchen table, watching the steam rise off a large bowl of oatmeal while fending off a wave of nausea. The air felt warm and hard to breathe. I glanced at Betty Belle as she paced the floor in front of the stove like a nervous cat, sipping tea and casting worried glances my way while refilling Mister's coffee or checking on the rice pudding she'd planned for her book club that afternoon. Now and then I could feel her hovering at my back as if reading over my shoulder.

On and off for weeks I'd felt sickly but gave it little thought, figuring the queasiness and pain in my side was just a lingering bug or maybe too much of Betty Belle's rich cooking. About the time I'd start to think I should go see a doctor I'd begin feeling better again. That made it easy to ignore. I picked up my spoon, dipped into the bowl and scooped out a mouthful of sticky oatmeal. I hoped to lull Betty Belle into thinking I was planning to eat. Before taking a bite, I looked over the spoon and across the table at Mister, his face hidden behind the morning paper.

"Mister, do you still lawyer for any professors?"

Mister had been a lawyer for years and still maintained a few long-term clients on retainer. He had always based his practice at home, working out of a window-covered alcove adjacent to the living room that resembled a tiny courtroom. The dark paneled space, packed with leather chairs and glass-fronted oak file cabinets, held what seemed to be an entire library of legal texts. Betty Belle had always had a liking for the university, regularly attending concerts and lectures, so I hoped the question might provide a diversion from my oatmeal. Mister lowered the paper and squinted at me. His habit of looking over the top of his glasses and down his nose made him seem more than a little judge-like. He looked over at Betty Belle and then back at me.

"I have to ask myself why you would ask such a question, Mazie? My work has never much interested you."

"You sound like a lawyer instead of an uncle."

"Now that you mention it, I've been a lawyer longer than I've been your uncle so it follows I would sound like one, especially when I suspect subterfuge."

"Why Mister, I'm shocked that you would accuse Mazie of such a thing." Betty Belle sat next to me.

I decided my plan was working and did my best to look offended.

"You've never before accused me of being dishonest."

"Not true, Mazie. You do remember when you had that party while we were out of town and then tried to act like the neighbors made it all up once you were found out?"

"It was a gathering of friends not a party. It's upsetting to be falsely accused, especially by your own family." I set my spoon back in the bowl. "Besides, the so-called party you're referring to was a long time ago."

"Not so long that I'd forgotten."

I frowned and laid my hand across my stomach. "Nothing was broken."

"Now see what you've done, Mister." Betty Belle patted my arm. "Mazie has lost her appetite because of your careless remarks."

Mister stared across the table at us. "Why did you ask, then?"

"I met someone that works for a Professor Nagel."

"You know someone that works for Norvis Nagel?" He chuckled.

"Do you know the professor?"

"Norvis Nagel is a walking definition of the word 'eccentric'. He wears orange pants and purple shirts – at the same time. He spouts off Italian poetry and Greek philosophy like he's talking about the weather." He peered at me again. "Who is this someone?"

211

"I met him last night while I was out walking."

"You've met a boy?" Betty Belle nearly yelled.

"He's not a boy, Betty Belle. He's a man that happens to be attending the university."

"Are you saying he's an older gentleman?"

"No, he's more or less my age."

"Isn't that what I said, Mazie?"

"No, you made it sound like he was twelve years old. He's a university student, after all."

"Tell us about him, then." She moved her chair a bit closer.

"There's not much to tell other than what I've already said. I've only just met him. We're going to the theater tonight."

"He's taking you to the theater?" She turned to Mister. "Did you hear that, Mister? Some boy has asked Mazie out on a date to the theater. It sounds so romantic."

Mister was hidden behind the newspaper again. "The boy's suspect if he works for Norvis."

"Mister, Betty Belle, please stop. He's just someone I met and we're going to see a play over at the university. He gets free tickets and wanted company, that's all."

"I'll bet he gets his tickets from Norvis." Mister lowered the paper and snorted. "Does he wear orange pants too?"

"Just because he works for a professor doesn't mean he wants to be like him." I tried to recall what color pants Arne was wearing last night.

Betty Belle touched my arm. "What's his name, Mazie? We must know the name of the boy you're dating."

"I'm not dating anyone." I frowned at her. "I'm going to a play because someone I met, a *man,* has free tickets. We may not even sit together."

"Does this someone have a name?"

"Yes, Betty Belle, he does. His name is Arne Almond."

"And he works for a nutty professor." Mister set the paper on the table. "The first time I met Norvis I was attending a fundraiser for the university's fine arts program. He was wearing plaid pants and a matching purple scarf, and he had a purse or some sort of bag over his shoulder. After he introduced himself, the bag started moving and the next thing I knew a dog, one of those little ones that look more like rats than dogs, popped his head out the opening. Norvis reached into his pocket, pulled out a cookie he had pilfered from the dessert tray and fed it to the dog. Then he pushed the mangy thing back into the bag. He kept talking the entire time as if having a dog hidden in your purse was as normal as chicken soup."

"Mister, don't you have some work to do?" Betty Belle frowned across the table at him.

"Yes, I suppose I do but if you want to talk in private just say so."

As I watched him walk through the door I wondered if Betty Belle was going to get onto me again about eating. I glanced at her and could see she was working up to something less than pleasant. She looked as if she'd just eaten a bad prune.

"Mazie, how have you been feeling these past few weeks?"

"I've felt just fine, Betty Belle." I lied.

"I can't help but notice that you don't seem to have much of an appetite for breakfast anymore. I hope my cooking still agrees with you."

"Oh yes, Betty Belle, your cooking is as good as ever."

"Well, I must admit that some days your appetite can be rather robust by dinnertime. In fact, I noticed just yesterday that you have filled out some, especially in your face, although you're looking a little pale right now." She shook her head. "You were a gaunt little thing when you first arrived here."

When I thought about it I realized she was right. I'd been so busy with the new job and apartment I hadn't noticed the comings and goings of my own appetite or the change in my appearance. Overall, when I looked back I seemed to remember the queasiness more than anything. I suppose she could see the confused look on my face so she continued with her line of thought.

"You know that Mister and I never had children ourselves. It wasn't that we didn't want children but I just wasn't able to have any. That's one reason it meant so much when you came to live here with us."

She paused and raised her eyebrows as if she expected a response while I shifted in my chair and puzzled over the strange turn in the conversation. I had started out confused but now felt completely lost. I had no idea what I should say next. I looked around the room for a moment to stall when an idea came to me out of nowhere, so I turned to face her.

"Betty Belle, I'm glad to be back with you and Mister in spite of the reason. Did you know that this is my favorite room in the whole world? It always has been." I felt like I was getting somewhere. "I always feel at home right here, at this table, in one of these chairs. In fact..."

Betty Belle put her hand on my arm and squeezed until I stopped talking. Her frown seemed even more intense than before and it was clear she wanted to say something else but was struggling with how to go about it. Betty Belle had never had any trouble speaking her mind and seeing her nearly speechless disconcerted me even more than her odd manner. She squinted at me and swallowed hard.

"Mazie, are you pregnant?" she blurted out.

"What?" I thought I'd misunderstood her.

"The signs are there, Mazie. As much as I'd like to join you in ignoring them, I just can't let day after day pass by without saying something." She slapped the table. "A pregnancy is nothing to toy with and I don't intend to stand by while you let yourself go."

"You think I'm pregnant?" It was all I could manage.

"You don't think so?"

"Why would I think so?"

214

"How long has it been since your last, you know, spell?"

"My last spell?"

"Yes, Mazie, don't play dumb with me."

"You mean my last period?"

She nodded. "How long has it been? Be honest now, this is serious."

Right at that very moment the picture Betty Belle had painted for me in her roundabout way appeared in my mind clear as day and the room began to move about me in a swirl. I had to grab hold of my chair to keep from falling out. I shut my eyes and the past weeks flew before me in a blur but nowhere could I find hide nor hair of my period. My heart sank as I quickly figured I should have had not one but nearly two. How I could have failed to realize it was beyond me. I opened my eyes, faced Betty Belle and shook my head.

"Sometimes I miss but never for this long." I whispered.

She patted my knee. "I'm not surprised but don't you worry, Mazie. Betty Belle will help you take control of the situation. We live in the twentieth century after all and we women have come a long way."

"What should I do, Betty Belle?"

"Surely you know other girls who had a pregnancy taken care of?"

"You mean an abortion?"

"You are in control of your body, Mazie. Don't you let some man tell you otherwise."

"You think I should have an abortion, Betty Belle?"

She sat back and shook her head. "Good heavens, child, I just want you to know you have a choice in the matter. This is not nineteen-forty."

"The choices don't seem much like choices."

She touched my arm. "There's no hope that the father might come back to you then?"

I stared at the floor and shook my head. "I can't imagine having anyone's child, especially his."

215

"Yes, it's still true that having a child at your age and unmarried would be a struggle. On the other hand, you would always have your Aunt Betty Belle and Uncle Mister around to help, not that Mister would be of much help. He can barely care for himself as it is."

"It's too much to think about. I don't know what to do."

"First thing we need to do is get you to a doctor so we can be sure. It might be something else, you know, like bad ovaries or some such condition."

"Bad ovaries?" I nearly choked on the words.

She had meant to reassure me but I must have turned a new shade of pale because she took my hand between her palms and squeezed lightly.

"Don't pay attention to your poor old aunt, Mazie. You're going to be just fine. Now go get ready for work or you'll be late. I'll have that appointment set before you can sneeze twice."

As I walked up the stairs to my apartment a heavy drizzle pattered on the rail and dripped in thin lines from the eaves. My legs felt heavy. Palm fronds from the grove next door drooped over the landing in a green mass, weighed down by the rain collected in their shaggy creases. Globs of water splashed from them onto the landing with each gust of wind while in the distance gray clouds scudded above roofs and treetops in ragged lines. Like the rain, memories of Len seemed to flow out of me in a blur that I made no effort to catch.

Twenty-Nine

At three o'clock I stood next to the cash register sipping a soft drink and wishing I would start feeling better. The queasiness was usually gone by lunchtime but here it was mid-afternoon and I felt no better, maybe worse. The pain in my side was still there too. I wondered if the feelings were in my head since I knew I might be pregnant. Part of me wanted to find a hole somewhere to crawl into.

For some reason people seemed to have little interest in grocery shopping that afternoon. The store was nearly empty. One or two customers at a time straggled in, making the time drag by and leaving me nothing to do but think about cancelling my date with Arne when I should've been looking forward to it. Instead, I just wanted to crawl into bed. I started feeling sorry for myself until the store owner's son wandered up to the checkout stand and gave me something else to think about. He stopped and stood behind me without a word.

Carnivorous Jones was tall and thin with a burr haircut and a high forehead mapped with pimples, and so pale that in his white shirt and apron seemed as if he might fade into the air at any moment. His father believed if he gave his son a name no one would forget he would make something of himself but it seemed to have had the opposite effect. Carne could be standing next to you for a whole minute before you'd even realize he was there. To his father's dismay Carne up and decided he was a vegetarian, only adding to his thin paleness.

One afternoon after he'd snuck up on me yet again, I told him he would make a good detective someday and he took to the idea. He began carrying a paperback mystery in his apron pocket most days and I'd often catch him with his nose in it during breaks or when business was slow. He never said much but if I asked about the book he was reading he would go on and on until I was sorry I'd asked. Unlike the other clerks, he never had visitors coming in to see him so I wondered if he had any friends at all. Then again, no one came in to see me either.

We were standing at the register when a man I had never seen before pushed through the glass doors. Short and hunched over, he limped past me with his hands in his pockets and then paused to look down the aisles one by one as he ambled through the store. Short spikes of hair stuck out from beneath his frayed baseball cap. Something about him struck me as odd and I'd decided to keep an eye on him when Mr. Queed walked up to the checkout stand and set his basket on the counter. Mr. Queed was my least favorite customer. He had bad breath and a reputation among the female cashiers for trying to look down their blouses as they leaned over the counter. I had caught him ogling me more than once. Most of the time I'd stare him down when his eyes got to wandering but that day I was trying to look past him at the stranger walking the aisles. Mr. Queed kept turning around to see what I was looking at, which annoyed me even more than his usual disgusting habits. I tallied his groceries as fast as I could and nearly threw them at Carne. As usual, he was in no hurry to bag them up so I sighed and turned to help.

When I turned back to the register the man in the cap was standing in front of me, hunched over a bag of potato chips he had already opened. He crammed a handful of chips into his mouth and tossed the bag on the counter without looking up, so I swept the crumbs away and rang up the total.

"That's one twenty-nine." I tried not to show my irritation.

I struggled to get a look at his face but he kept his eyes to the floor as he fished out two one dollar bills, throwing them at me. I picked up the bills and turned but then hesitated. A faint voice in the back of my mind told me to wait, so I stood there with my hand poised over the register.

"What's the matter?" His voice came from beneath the cap. "Aren't you going to open the drawer?"

I stood without moving or speaking as the man shifted from foot to foot, still hunched over the counter. Behind me Carne rustled a paper bag. The store still seemed empty and I heard no sound other than the man's ragged breathing. He glanced up at me and then thrust his hand in his jacket, pulling out a small pistol and waving it in the air like a flag. Yellow sunlight slanting in through the glass doors glinted off the blue metal. I stared at the gun, unable to move my eyes.

"Open the drawer and give me what you got." he spoke in a near whisper.

"There's hardly anything in there. You can look around and see how slow it is today."

"I don't give a rat's ass how slow it is. Open the goddam drawer." he hissed.

That got my attention. I lifted my eyes from the gun and looked at him. Something was tugging at the back of my mind again but the anger rose up inside me like a wave and suddenly I felt as if I might reach across the counter and slap him in the face. He looked away. Dropping out of school, getting dumped by Len, retreating back to Houston, all the disappointments of the last few months flooded my mind. At that moment I must have gone half-crazy because I turned to face him squarely, staring at him without a word as if my defiance could bring some sense of control back into my life.

Something pulled my gaze back to the pistol and in an instant I realized what had been nagging at the edge of my mind. I could clearly see all five of his fingers wrapped tight around the pistol grip, nowhere near the trigger. He had no idea what he was doing. Without a second thought I reached out, grabbing his wrist with one hand and twisting the gun free with the other. It was as easy and effortless as

219

picking apples. The man stumbled back, looking around with a dazed, bewildered expression. I pointed behind me.

"This here is Carnivorous Jones." I nodded toward Carne. "He's a part-time deputy with the sheriff's office and he's going to take you in."

"Carnivorous?" The man shook his head. "Sheriff?"

I held up the pistol to get his attention and he pivoted, dashing out the door, the limp gone. I turned to see Carne standing with his back against the wall, his pale skin nearly transparent and his blue eyes wide.

"Go after him, Carne!" I pointed the gun at the door.

To my surprise he was out the door so fast I had no time to add I meant only to get a description of the getaway car. I didn't want Carne to get hurt. He returned a minute later with both a description of the car and a license plate number, clearly pleased with himself. He stood there staring at me like I'd saved the world until I got so uncomfortable I told him to look the other way.

I called the police and told Carne to call his father. Once Mr. Jones had finished scolding me for taking such a chance, everyone got a laugh out of my bold actions. The police had just finished taking our information when it dawned on me that I was feeling better. Not only that, I was famished. I thought of Arne and the new blue dress I planned to wear as I rushed home to get ready for the play.

Thirty

In 1927 a German scientist named Werner Heisenberg discovered that, at least at the level of atoms, there is a limit to what we can predict with certainty. He called this inescapable feature of our world the uncertainty principal. In other words, not only is the future beyond prediction, even the present moment is suspect. Add human nature to the mix and there's no telling what might happen. I was thinking of Heisenberg when I climbed into Arne's car.

He drove his blue Skylark along shaded streets scattered with wet leaves and shimmering puddles of rainwater. I noticed right away he had a strange habit of shifting from first directly to third gear, skipping second gear altogether. He would lean back with a satisfied smile as the car shuddered and then crept up to normal speed. Although November had arrived the weather that night was warm and balmy, the thick air smelling of late season flowers and wet earth. Overhead the planet Jupiter winked between patchy evening clouds that still reflected a hint of sunset. A symphony I'd never heard before drifted in through the window from somewhere.

Arne slowed to check street signs as we neared the broad grounds fronting one of the local churches and I turned to see dozens of white crosses stretching across the church lawn beneath a billboard that read "Pregnant? Alone? Need help?" Below in large red letters was the warning "Abortion is murder. Save yourself!" I sank into my seat wondering how I had somehow brought on this curse. Arne noticed the crosses and chuckled.

"That'll make the feminists twitch."

"Does that mean you're against feminists or abortion or both?"

"The church says abortion is wrong."

"It's never that simple, Arne."

"It is if you believe in the Bible."

I sat up. "The Bible doesn't say anything about abortion. Besides, a woman has a right to control what happens to her own body."

"Then she shouldn't get pregnant in the first place."

"How can you talk like that, Arne?" I could hear the anger rising in my voice. "You have no idea what it's like to be a woman."

"It's what I was taught." he glanced at me with a worried look.

"You learned that in school?"

"No, from my father."

"And you believe him?"

He cringed. "He's my father so I believe what he says."

"I'm not surprised. Men don't have a clue what women have to deal with." I growled. "But you should know better than to just believe whatever your parents say. Make up your own mind, Arne."

"You sound annoyed." He glanced at me. "Are you angry, Mazie?"

"We don't agree."

"Please, let's not argue, Mazie." he pleaded. "My old girlfriend said all I ever did was to argue. I don't want to do that with you."

His pitiful tone took the fight out of me. "Don't worry, Arne."

"You're not angry, then?"

"It's okay." I lied.

I realized at that moment I would have an abortion before I'd ever let someone talk me into having a baby, especially Len's baby. I was nowhere near ready to have children. No one could make that decision for me and I wasn't about to let go of my freedom. The people who put up those crosses, whoever they were, would never intimidate me into giving up control of my body. Being pregnant was hard enough without religion coming into it. I stared at the crosses and struggled to separate my feelings

222

for Arne from my anger at what was happening in my life. It was not his fault.

I took a breath, trying to calm myself and return to that instant when I realized I was glad to be on a date with a good-looking man. I wanted that feeling again. I looked over at Arne, trying to focus on where I was right then and nothing else and then I sat back in the seat, letting the houses pass by in a blur.

We turned on a wide boulevard lined with older homes, most with weathered shingle exteriors. Across the street two small art museums sat on opposite ends of an open park area. Warm light from the museum windows cast rectangular shadows across the lawn as Arne pulled in behind a line of cars parked along the curb fronting Professor Nagle's house. He was hosting a pre-play gathering.

I turned to Arne, trying to sound friendly. "Why don't you have to be at the theater helping out?"

"Dr. Nagle teaches literature in addition to drama. I assist with the literature, another research assistant helps with drama." His broad smile glowed in the dim light. "And I still get free tickets."

I opened the car door and a warm breeze passed through my hair, pulling me into the night and away from my previous thoughts. A light thump of music danced across the lawn. Through half open windows, smiling figures came and went in the dim yellow glow. Someone laughed deeply and I decided I was going to have fun.

"You're not proud of yourself or anything, huh, Arne?"

"How many people around here do you know with free tickets to Shakespeare?"

"I don't know any people around here."

He frowned. "You know me."

"Well, that depends on what you mean by the word 'know'. In the Bible it means sex."

"Sex?" His face turned a bright pink.

"Yeah, that's what they mean when they say 'to know a person in the biblical sense'."

He frowned. "Not everyone agrees with that interpretation. Some scholars believe it refers to love, not sex."

I snorted. "What do a bunch of musty old Puritans know about it? Do they even have sex?"

"Scholars aren't Puritans." He had a hurt look. "I hope to be one someday."

"Which one, a scholar or a Puritan?"

He stared at me with his mouth open, unable to speak. I had no idea why I was being so horsy but I could tell I was close to offending him. I held up my hands.

"Okay Arne, I'll stop." I gave him a quick smile. "I'm only playing around because I like you."

"You do?" His eyes sparkled. "You're not mad about the comments I made?"

"What comments were those? I don't remember."

"I can't tell when you're serious and when you're not."

"Well, tonight I'm not so let's go have some fun."

Norvis Nagle lived in a small stone house with sharp gables and a sloping roof that gave the place an alpine look, a bit disconcerting on such a warm night. Scotch pines on either side of the door only added to the feel. We stepped through the door and into the living room just as a country and western band started in on a song by Merle Haggard. I followed as Arne squeezed through a crowd of students and what looked to be a few scattered faculty members. Other than Arne most of the men had long hair, several with ponytails. I could see none without a beard of some sort. The overall impression was an abundance of hair.

Arne poured two beers from a keg as we passed through the kitchen and we moved out the back door and into a lush garden. A narrow paved walkway led through a towering stand of bamboo fronted by low palms and scatterings of thick grass. Benches were tucked here and there in hidden

224

nooks along the walkway, giving the place an intimate feel. We came around a sharp bend and stumbled on Norvis Nagle whispering in animated fashion to a young woman that I guessed was one of his students. She looked at us, eyes wide, turned and left without a word. The professor looked after her and sighed before turning to us.

"Arne, you're a hell of a researcher but I can't say much for your timing." he shifted his gaze to me. "Oh, and who's this?"

Norvis Nagle looked me over and smiled as if he had just found dessert. Although short and thin there was nothing small about his appearance. Red hair stood above his face in a tussled mound, fading to mere stubble above his ears. Between his angular cheeks, a bulbous nose leaned to one side as if about to slide off altogether. He wore a purple blazer over a lime-green shirt and pink tie. Trying not to stare, I glanced down to see pants a brilliant shade of orange. He straightened his shirt cuffs in dramatic fashion with his small but graceful fingers, clearly enjoying the attention. In spite of his unusual features he was almost attractive in an off-beat way. Arne seemed as mesmerized as me.

The professor peered at Arne. "Earth to Arnet, are you there?"

Arne jumped. "What? Oh, right. Dr. Nagle, this is Mazie."

"Please call me Norvis." He kissed my hand.

"Does that mean I should call you Norvis?" Arne leaned towards him, eyebrows raised in expectation.

"Of course not." He gave Arne a disdainful glance. "All my students call me doctor or professor. Anything less is disrespectful."

"Oh yes, right, Dr. Norvis, uh…I mean Nagle. I understand perfectly."

"Speaking of perfection, the use of formality with a woman in a stunning blue dress with whom I feel such an intimate connection would be a shame." He continued holding my hand. "Don't you agree, Ms. Goforth?"

I pulled my hand free. "I prefer Mazie."

"Oh, and so do I, Mazie, so do I." He put one hand on his hip and raised his red eyebrows. "What do you do, Mazie?"

That particular question always irritated me but even more so at that moment. I squinted at him trying to show my annoyance but could tell it had little effect. He looked like he was about to drool.

"I'm taking care of an elderly aunt." I lied.

"You do look like the comforting type, Mazie Goforth. The life of a university professor can be quite trying. I feel I could use some comforting myself at times."

He leered at me waiting for a response. I turned to Arne, trying to avoid saying something I'd regret as I took his hand. He looked down at my hand in his as if he had no idea who it belonged to.

"Arne, you promised me a dance."

"I did?"

"Yes Arne, and I'm still waiting."

"You are?"

"Mazie, you're not going to leave just as we were getting to know each other, are you?" Norvis put his hand on my shoulder and squeezed it.

I nodded toward the house, pulling on Arne's hand. "The band is in there, remember?"

"There's a private party after the play. Will you come, please?" Norvis pleaded.

I moved away from his clammy hand and turned, no longer concerned about what I might say but before I opened my mouth a young woman with purple streaked hair appeared out of nowhere. She whispered into Norvis' ear and then vanished into the dark. Norvis tilted his head to one side, frowned and clasped his hands as if about to pray.

"Oh drat, I've been called away. There's some sort of emergency at the theater and, well that's my bad luck." He held up his thumb and index finger nearly touching. "I was that close wasn't I, Mazie Goforth?"

I looked at him and shook my head, not wanting to give him the satisfaction of an answer, and then I turned and walked toward the house. I hoped Arne would follow. By the time I reached the back door, I could hear Arne hustling up behind me. He took my hand, leading me back through the kitchen and onto the makeshift wooden dance floor of the living room just as the band started in on a rousing version of *Okie From Muskogee*. Arne twirled me around the floor with surprising grace and I soon found myself lost in his blue eyes. It was wonderful. By the time I had worked up a pretty good sweat and was ready for a rest, the band began the first few bars of *Silver Wings*, one of my all-time favorites. I gulped the rest of my beer and grabbed Arne's wrist, pulling him back onto the floor.

We had only made a few rounds when suddenly I felt faint. At first I thought it was the twirling but realized the pain in my side had returned as well, this time with a vengeance. I stopped, trying to catch my breath and an instant later I was doubled over with pain. If Arne hadn't taken hold of me I would have hit the floor right then. I stood still, trying to figure out what was wrong and hoping I'd soon feel better but the moment I tried to straighten up the world went white. Then there was nothing.

The next thing I knew someone in a mask was leaning over me mumbling incoherently. I tried to speak as the world went white again and I floated up and over the house, watching the party-goers twirl out onto the lawn to the tune of a song only they could hear. I watched Arne wander the thick garden as if looking for me, so I called to him but the rushing wind drowned out any hint of my voice. I cried to see him so forlorn and alone.

When I came to the second time a deep ache held me like a vice, squeezing my breath to a whisper. I tried to speak and the white descended again. I awoke for a third time and realized the vice had loosened and I could breathe again. I lay flat on my back, metal rails to my left and right, blinking lights all around. I tried to speak and the vice returned but I stayed conscious this time so I kept still, hoping to keep the pain at bay.

I lay there for what seemed a long time, trying to think what I should do next, when Uncle Doctor's face appeared over me. He seemed to have a halo around his head, which seemed odd for a man of his habits. When my vision cleared I could see he was looking at me in a way he never had before. The mischievous sparkle of his pale blue eyes had been replaced by a dark sadness. He took my hand in his and gave it a gentle squeeze. I made a weak attempt to speak, wincing at the pain.

"Don't try to talk just now, Mazie. I'll do the talking for both of us. You just tell me when you need a rest and I'll back to my corner." He pointed across the room.

I nodded in agreement.

"Did I ever mention how much you remind me of my Carolina when she was your young age? Looking at you is almost like having her back for a brief moment."

I nodded, trying to manage a smile as he paused, lost in some memory. I wanted to know where I was and what had happened to me but at the same time I was afraid to know. I could see Doctor was in no hurry to say anything about it. I had no idea why. After a moment, he checked his watch and turned to face me.

"When I first met Carolina she was working as a nurse at the university infirmary and I was in vet school. You may not know this but I once considered going into medicine. Back then it was easier to get into medical school than into a veterinary program. My grand plans fell apart once I realized I had no patience for all the complaining people are prone to. Horses and cattle never talk back but people are another matter altogether."

He checked his watch again and craned his neck toward the door. I turned and tried to follow his gaze but fell back, too weak to move.

"I know you're wondering what has happened but I'd like Betty Belle to be the one to talk with you. I can't imagine what has held her up."

As if on cue, Betty Belle hurried into the room loaded down with flowers, books and an overstuffed cloth bag. As soon as he spotted her Doctor hopped away from the bed and stood near the door. He looked as if he might bolt at any second. Betty Belle glanced over at me while she filled a cut glass vase with water and set the flowers on the window sill. She stepped to the side of the bed and brushed the hair from my eyes.

"How are you feeling, sweetheart?"

"Better now." I managed in a hoarse whisper.

"She only woke up a minute ago." Doctor volunteered from the doorway. "She's yet to get her voice back."

Betty Belle looked up at him. "I think Mazie and I will talk now, Doctor."

He nodded. "I'll be down the hall if you need me."

"Mister needs your company more than I do at this moment. You know how he hates hospitals."

"Has he started talking to himself yet?"

"Yes, so you'd better take him out for a walk. Mazie and I can take care of things here for a little while."

"I have some courage here if he should need it." He patted his coat pocket.

She rolled her eyes at me. "Doctor, I see you came prepared for any eventuality. Why am I not surprised?"

"The Roman Stoic Marcus Aurelius wrote that where a man can live, he can also live well. I do my best each and every day to follow that wise advice."

"Why Doctor, I thought you were a follower of the American philosopher, Jack Daniels."

"I must admit I've not heard of the gentleman."

"I believe he resides in your house."

He dismissed her comment with a wave of his hand. "I will return with Mister in due time so Mazie, until then."

Betty Belle's face clouded over as she turned from the door and looked down at me. She took a breath and again brushed back my hair, for a moment leaving her hand on my cheek. I didn't need to ask if the news was bad.

"I'm not going to beat around the bush Mazie, much as I'd like to. You're here in the hospital because you had an ectopic pregnancy that ruptured and very nearly killed you." her voice broke.

"I'll be okay?" I squeaked.

"Yes and no."

"Why no?"

She held up her hand. "Don't worry, sweetheart, the worst is over. It will take some time but you're going to recover."

"But?"

"There were complications, Mazie. The doctor did what he could but the bleeding was too severe." she paused, her eyes brimming. "Sweetheart, you won't be able to have children."

"Not ever?"

"No, Mazie, not ever."

My eyes filled, melting the ceiling into a hazy blur. I tried to catch my breath as I struggled to stifle something that ricocheted inside my chest while my head spun with all that had happened. How could I feel glad to be alive when I had just learned I would never have children of my own? I was in for a long and probably painful recovery yet, as strange as it sounds I felt relieved to no longer be pregnant. I finally had a date and it ended in a hospital emergency room. What did I do to deserve such a life? I suddenly found myself wanting to see Len, which only added to my confusion.

I would have continued feeling sorry for myself but I heard a knock and turned to see Roddy standing in the doorway. Now that was a shock. We'd lost touch when he left for school so it had been years since I'd spoken to him much less seen him in person. He walked to the bedside and patted the metal rail with his palm.

"Well Mazie, look at you lazing around as usual."

Betty Belle dabbed her eyes with a handkerchief. "I called Roddy once they took you into the operating room, sweetheart. I thought he should know."

I nodded, although I had trouble sorting through my feelings about his appearance. We had never been what you might call close. On the other hand, we had shared a family and more than a few important memories; important to me, at least. A good bit older than me, Roddy had left home when I was still a girl and was never one for showing affection or, for that matter, emotion of any sort. Still, he was my brother.

Betty Belle stood. "Well then, I'll let you two talk."

She swept out of the room without another word. Roddy reached over the rail and touched my arm, studying at me with an odd mix of concern and disapproval.

"I'm glad to hear you're going to be alright."

I nodded.

"You had a close call, Mazie."

"I know."

"You gave everyone a real scare."

"I know." I mumbled.

He paced the floor beside the bed doing his own share of mumbling. I wondered what had compelled him to come see me and decided it had more to do with him than me. He had always been the center of his own world. He stopped and again turned to me.

"When Betty Belle called she was beside herself with worry." He frowned. "Do you know what it would've done to her if you hadn't made it through the surgery?"

"Yes."

"She feels responsible for you and then you end up like this."

I shook my head in frustration. "I didn't mean to."

"You got yourself pregnant, Mazie. That was your decision."

In spite of the pain I turned to face him. "It just happened."

"It doesn't just happen. It happens to women who sleep around." He slapped the metal rail. "How could you be so irresponsible?"

"It's not like that." I growled.

"Well, it's clear you can't take care of yourself."

"Why did you come here?" I somehow found my voice. "I don't hear from you for years and then you show up thinking you can lecture me. You love it when you can feel sorry for someone, then you can be your usual superior self. Well, I don't need your pity."

"You need someone to keep you in line."

"I can take care of myself." I rose up on one elbow, the pain ebbing beneath my anger.

"You're going to come live with me."

"Are you crazy? I'm a grown woman!"

"Then act like it!" He gestured around the room. "Until then you need to be where I can ride herd on you."

"I don't need you to tell me how to live my life."

"Are you sure? You brought this on yourself."

"That's not fair!" I slapped the mattress, feeling the tears rise into my eyes.

"Who told you life was fair?" He smirked.

"Get out." I wiped my eyes with the back of my hand.

"Betty Belle didn't sign on for this."

"Get out, now!" I yelled and fell back onto the bed.

I turned away from him and stared out the window, wishing I could stand up right then and walk out of that room, away from all that had happened. A hurtful anger filled my throat and spilled into my eyes, anger at Roddy, anger at myself, anger at Len. Somewhere deep down I knew Roddy's self-righteous and patronizing manner was just his way of trying to do what he thought right but at that moment I had no toleration for it. We had grown too far apart. I knew then it was up to me to get my life in order and no one, not Roddy, not Betty Belle, not even Len could do it for me. In this I was alone.

Thirty-one

Gaze into the night sky and you look into the past. The starlight casting dim shadows at your feet is years old, sometimes hundreds or even thousands of years. It is what once was, still visible. The present is somewhere in the future. My thoughts bounced through time like wayward neutrons, now present, now past, until I found myself back in Houston, face to face with Betty Belle.

She fixed me with her intent gaze while Mister and Doctor stood behind, looking as if they had just smoked their last cigar. I'd never seen them so sad. I told myself I wouldn't cry and in truth I felt anything but sad. In fact, I felt surprisingly good, considering all that had happened.

"Are you sure you're strong enough to travel, Mazie?" Betty Belle took my hand, cradling it in hers. "You've only been out of the hospital a short while."

"Betty Belle, it's been nearly a month."

"Sweetheart, we almost lost you."

"This job is a good opportunity and it'll give me a chance to finish up my degree."

"I understand dear but I can't help but worry after what you've been through."

"I know it has been hard on you all."

Doctor held up his hand. "Now Mazie, you're too young to be worrying about a bunch of old people like us. You have your own life to live."

"The only old person I see in here is you, Doctor." Betty Belle gave him a dismissive wave of her hand. "You'd live twice as long if you gave up whiskey and those nasty cigars."

"What would be the point in living then, Betty Belle?"

"Mazie needs to be leaving if she's to arrive before dark." Mister stepped around Betty Belle and took both my hands. "Call us when you get there."

"Oh Mister, how can you be so matter of fact about Mazie leaving us?" She sighed and took my hand once again. "Don't let this time you've had sour you on love, Mazie. You're a beautiful woman and some man will see that, you'll see."

Betty Belle looked like she might cry. That was the last thing I wanted to see because I knew I'd be next. I gave her a quick hug and did the same with Mister and Doctor, and soon I was driving through the shady streets of Houston, a cool late autumn wind blowing through my hair. A mixture of sadness and excitement coursed through me and I hesitated, wondering if I had made the right decision. I had little reason to trust myself.

Before I had gone more than a few blocks I decided to see Arne one last time if I could. I turned the car around and headed for his apartment. Parking well short of his address, I sat in my car as if waiting for someone. If asked, I'd have had no reason as to why I hesitated. I suppose I was unsure how he would react if I showed up out of the blue but before I had a chance to change my mind, he walked out the front door of the duplex and headed for the curbside mailbox. I climbed from behind the steering wheel, reaching him before he had finished retrieving his mail.

"Hello Arne." I called from across the street.

He turned and stared as if I was a stranger. There was nothing left to do but act like he was glad to see me so I crossed the street, doing my best to smile.

"Mazie, where did you come from?" He looked up and down the street.

"I was passing by and saw you, so I thought I'd stop and say hello." I lied.

"Why are you here?"

"I've wondered where you'd vanished to."

"I haven't seen you since the party."

"That's right, the party where I collapsed." I was surprised to hear a note of irritation in my voice. "I was in

235

the hospital nearly a week, Arne. Why didn't you come to see me?"

"I don't like hospitals."

"I've been at home for weeks. Why didn't you come see me there?"

He shrugged.

"You didn't even call."

He stared into the distance. "You got pregnant, Mazie."

"That's the reason I collapsed."

"I know. I heard all about it."

"So why didn't you come see me?"

"Getting pregnant outside of marriage is a sin. I couldn't act like what you did was okay."

"You avoided me because I got pregnant? You can't be serious."

"A young life ended because you had to have your moment of pleasure."

"I didn't have control of that. It just happened."

"You sinned and a baby died."

"That was no baby."

"In the eyes of the church it was a sacred life."

"I can't believe I'm hearing this. You sound like the Pope!"

"God will forgive you."

"I don't need anyone's forgiveness, especially yours. You think you're so smart. You live in your protected little world, so self-righteous, believing you can pass judgment on everyone else. You don't know everything, Arne. The real world is a messy place."

I turned away, hurrying down the street and to my car without another word. In minutes I was retracing my route out of town once again. Streets that had seemed open and comfortable only a short time before felt staid and oppressive, the houses lining them dull and lifeless. The church with the white crosses appeared and then vanished from view. I felt my past falling away like the white lines along the highway as I pulled onto the road, heading west.

Thirty-two

I wished for Betty Belle, Mister or even Doctor as I hurried into the soaring hospital atrium, but they were all long-passed. Gothic windows along a broad hallway stretched before me, reaching toward a vaulted ceiling far overhead. Outside, the white walls of a spare cactus garden reflected the midday sun. Nuns in traditional black and white habits huddled together in groups of two or three, talking in hushed tones. I felt like I was back in church.

I soon stood near the door to Roddy's room trying to gather my thoughts. He was out of the coma and I knew from speaking to the doctor that surgery was not an option. Roddy's next step involved a regimen of chemotherapy stretched over several months, a process that would leave him violently ill, with little chance for success. I wanted to sound encouraging when I first broke the news but all I could think of was how hard it would be for him and, if I dared admit it, for me as well. I took a breath and stepped through the doorway.

Inside the room the curtains were drawn and the room nearly dark in spite of the hour. What I assumed to be a bed formed a dark rectangle against the far wall, glowing monitors and blinking lights on either side only adding to the confusion. I felt my way into the room as footsteps from the hallway echoed nearer. Just as I flipped on the lights Quit appeared in the doorway like an apparition. Roddy stirred and sat upright.

"I was laying here wondering when you would show up, Mazie."

"Roddy, have you taken up as a vampire now?" I nodded Quit into the room. "It's noon outside but dark as a cave in here."

"I do feel like a vampire in this place."

"I'm not surprised, the way you have it all closed up." I pulled the curtains aside.

"Why should I care? I'm not planning on staying."

"Well, you're here now so I suppose I'll ask how you feel."

"Like I'm ready to go home." He frowned and slapped his knee. "I was hoping I'd never set foot in a hospital again."

I pulled a chair next to the bed and sat. "Roddy, we need to talk about that."

"Who did you bring along?"

"Quit has come to see you."

Quit stepped into the room. "Hello dad, how are you feeling?"

Roddy tilted his head and I could see by the flutter in his eyes his mind was working fast. He fingered the edge of the sheet like a rosary. I leaned forward, about to say something more when he held up a hand as if blessing me.

"So you finally decided to come see me." He chopped the air with his hand. "Why now, Quit?"

"What do you mean?"

"It's a simple question. Why are you here?"

"You're in the hospital."

"You wait until I'm flat on my back and you have the advantage, then you come."

Quit took a step back. "I'm here. Do you want me to leave?"

"I don't want your pity."

"You're sick. I can't be concerned about you?"

"I won't let you or anyone else use this cancer to define who I am. If you stay, treat me like you would if I didn't have it. Otherwise, leave now."

"You always have to be in control." Quit sneered.

"You'll treat me with respect." Roddy growled. "I'm your father."

"Oh, and you did a fine job didn't you?"

"Stop it, both of you!" I stood. "There are things, important things that we need to talk about."

Roddy again raised his hand in blessing. "I won't go through chemotherapy again, Mazie so save your breath."

I sat back, surprised. "How did you know that's what I was going to say?"

"An old chess player learns to anticipate every move."

"The doctor says it's your only option, Roddy."

"Not exactly. I can go home instead."

Quit stepped toward the bed. "You can't just give up."

"I can do whatever I want to."

"You're a damn fool. Without the therapy you'll die." Quit grabbed the rail. "Instead, you're just going to give up on your life."

"I call it taking control of my life, not giving up."

"You can't mean it." Quit turned to me. "He can't mean it, Mazie. Maybe he's psychotic or something because of the tumor."

"Don't talk about me like I'm not here!" Roddy grabbed the rail and shook it. "I can choose how I want to live and how I want to die."

Quit slammed his hand on the bed. "You don't know what you're saying, you crazy old coot."

"Don't call me an old coot. I know exactly what I'm saying. This is not my first time in the ring, you know."

"That's a damn selfish attitude, Mazie. I'm not one to stand around listening to a crazy man go on."

With that Quit turned and walked out the door. As I watched his shadow disappear down the hall I wondered how two grown men could act like such children. I walked to the bedside and leaned against the rail. Roddy still faced the door, a stunned look on his face.

I bent towards him. "That was real mature of you, brother."

"Quit has always brought out the anger in me. He's nothing like Angie was." he grumbled.

"Well, she's not here and he is." I touched his shoulder. "Do you want to spend your time together like that?"

Roddy turned to me, his voice soft. "I know it's hard for him to accept, Mazie but I've had plenty of time to think it through."

"I know you have, Roddy but you're not finished. You still need to find a way to help Quit understand. You can see how he is…"

I stopped when I heard approaching footsteps, thinking Quit had decided to return. Instead, Des appeared in the doorway. I wanted to walk over and hug him as lonesome for support as I felt but I just stood there. He tilted his head to the side and gestured across the room with his arm.

"I declare, Roddy you sure know how to live the good life. I drive all the way down here expecting the worst and instead find you in this swank hotel talking to the best looking woman in the place - and there are a lot of good looking women around here, trust me. Can we order room service? I'm starved."

Roddy sat up. "What are you doing here, Des?"

"Like I said, I was looking for a good looking woman and I found one."

"Knock it off, Des and tell me what you want." I sat down, as if waiting for an answer.

"Mazie, you could use a lesson or two in taking a compliment gracefully." He stepped over to the bed. "I just wanted to see if I could help in some way."

Roddy leaned toward him. "Why sure you can, Des. I'll pay you to give me a ride home."

Des glanced at me but continued facing Roddy. "Are you telling me they're going to let you out just like that?"

"Sure, let's go."

"I can't do that, Roddy. I asked at the front desk and the doctor said you'll need to start the first round of chemotherapy as soon as possible."

"I call it torture and I'm going to pass."

"But why, Roddy? The doctor said you need those treatments right away."

Roddy turned to me, a pitiful look on his face. "Take me home Mazie, please."

"Are you sure that's what you want, Roddy?"

"Take me home, Mazie. Don't make me beg."

Des looked from me to Roddy and back, pointing to each of us in turn. "You're not really going to take him, are you?"

I held up my hand. "Des please don't make this personal because it's not. You're sweet to come here and offer to help but I'm asking you to wait for us outside. Roddy and I need to be alone for a minute."

"I hope you know what you're doing, Mazie." Des nodded and gestured toward the door. "I'll be in the hall."

I grabbed the bedrail, pulling myself up. "Will you talk to Quit and help him understand what you've decided?"

Roddy rubbed his face with both hands. "It won't be easy. I'm sure he wouldn't admit it but he's all twisted up inside about something, maybe seeing me again, maybe something else."

"That's all the more reason to do what you can. You're his father after all."

He nodded. "I'll talk to him but I doubt it'll do any good."

"I'll be right back."

I walked out the door and found Des pacing the floor halfway down the hall. Without a word he took me by the shoulders, drawing me near. I had forgotten how good it felt to be held. After what seemed a long time he pulled away, holding me at arm's length and peering into my face. His blue eyes sparkled above his nose, still bent but somehow appealing. I shook off the urge to cry.

"I have some news for you, Mazie." Des held up his hands. "Linc called this morning and asked me to tell you about a call he got from the Nutt brothers. Grita's land is now free and clear of any legal problems so she can do whatever she likes with it. A developer even approached the brothers with a handsome offer to buy the place just to

241

access the aquifer. You were right about the value of that groundwater. Linc thought she should hear the news from you but he hopes she'll hold onto the land as part of her heritage."

"I'd go tell her but I have other things on my mind just now." I sighed.

"I know you do."

"Will you help me, Des? Doing what Roddy asks won't be easy but it's what's right."

"I trust you, Mazie."

"You don't need to go see Hannie Hereford or some other woman friend?"

"Now why would you bring up Hannie just now? I'm here, so tell me how I can help."

"Just stay nearby, that's all."

"All you have to do is ask, Mazie Goforth."

"I don't know why you put up with me, Des."

He cocked his head and winked. "Well Mazie, I can't deny that I've wondered that same thing myself."

Thirty-three

Palm trees are surprisingly resilient, able to survive intense desert heat as well as frequent onslaughts by typhoons and hurricanes. Successful throughout tropical and subtropical regions, there are over three thousand species, some growing to over a hundred feet in height. While living in the palm-draped garage apartment behind Betty Belle and Mister, I never imagined that years later I would again be surrounded by palms. Somehow, I felt comforted by their presence.

Cam lifted the last Sabal palm into the bed of the truck, securing the tailgate and then turning toward the house as if someone had just called his name. I followed his gaze up the hill. Since Roddy's return home Cam had spent his spare time hovering around my brother like a lost child. I wondered if he somehow felt responsible for Roddy's decision to ignore the doctor's advice and come home. I might have asked except I needed to focus on work and I needed him to do the same. With all the unexpected running around here and there, we had gotten more than a little behind in tending the nursery and filling orders. As Nacho liked to remind us, palm trees are like people and don't fare well when neglected. I couldn't help but glance past Cam and toward the house again as I held out an invoice, shaking it in front of him.

"Try to get there before they close up for the day but don't speed. I don't want you to lose your license, or worse."

He took the invoice and studied it before looking up at the house again. I could see the worry in his face, as well as the resistance. Cam was too young to accept that little could be done for Roddy, much less that he had returned home against the doctor's advice. I searched my mind for something to say but found nothing. I had yet to face that future myself. Roddy and I had spent so much of our lives at odds I never thought we'd learn to get along but his return had changed everything, leaving my thoughts as clouded as my emotions.

Cam folded the paper and stuffed it in his shirt pocket. "I'll just go see if Roddy needs anything from the store."

I sighed. "Alright but make it fast or you'll be too late."

As I watched Cam walk up the hill, I wondered if he hoped to find Grita as well. She had been avoiding him. Earlier in the day she and I had again talked about what she intended to do about her pregnancy. Not only had she yet to tell Cam, she also was plagued with guilt over any decision her mother might have opposed. As Grita saw it, keeping the baby was the only option if she was to honor her mother's memory.

"I think mom would want me to keep the baby, Mazie."

I realized I could no longer put off telling her Sephie was her adopted mother.

"Grita, there's something you need to know. I should've told you before now but the time was never right."

"Mazie, you sound so serious."

As I repeated what Linc had told me, Grita's face gradually shifted away from worry, as if she already knew what I was about to say. She sighed and turned from me, gazing across the hills and beyond to the broken horizon. I touched her shoulder.

"I know it must be a shock. Are you alright, Grita?"

She smiled at me. "Don't you see, Mazie? It doesn't matter. As far as I'm concerned she'll always be my mother."

"She was the only mother you knew."

"That's right. Have you told Quit?"

I nodded. "Why do you ask?"

"This may sound strange but I thought he might be my father." She shook her head. "Now I know I was wrong."

"Lucky for you."

She chuckled. "Oh Mazie, he's not so bad."

Cam disappeared through the door as I stood facing the house and thinking back to that moment when Quit's voice echoed from inside the barn. I turned and walked the short distance to the open double doors where Nacho stood just inside, leaning against the wall. In the middle of the room Quit paced, motioning toward the loft with both arms. Once Nacho saw me he nodded toward the dark end of the barn.

"Take a look at this."

I squinted into the dim interior. Once my eyes adjusted, I spotted Winston standing at the edge of the loft, balancing a bag of mulch on its side and slowly shaking his head. Quit stopped and stood below with his arms open.

"Come on Winston, we can do this."

"Sir, the bag is heavy."

"Just tilt it over the edge and I'll do the rest."

"Sir, the bag will fall."

"That's the idea, Winston. I'm trying some of your British efficiency. We can't waste time climbing up and down that ladder."

"Sir, the bag will fail."

"You're repeating yourself, Winston. I get the idea. Go ahead and..."

"He said fail not fall." I interrupted.

Quit glanced over his shoulder at me. "Mazie, if Winston and I need your help we'll ask for it."

Winston looked to where I stood with Nacho. "But sirs."

"Winston, must I remind you that I'm not a sir?" I shook my finger at him. "In any event, Quit is the boss so you'd better do what he says."

Nacho nodded in agreement while trying to stifle a smile. I did the same. Winston shrugged once before giving the bag a gentle push and in an instant the sack toppled off the loft, landing squarely in Quit's arms and exploding in a cloud of dust. He stumbled back, hacking the air with one hand and holding the empty bag with the other while trying to keep from choking. Except for his eyes, the fine dirt covered his face like a mask. Mumbling incoherently he threw down the bag and hurried toward the door, looking like a coalmine refugee. Once he reached the doorway he turned to us, holding up a single blackened finger.

"Not a word from either of you, not now, not ever."

I nodded to Nacho and we followed Quit out the door.

"Yes sir, not a word." I called up the hill. "We'll be sure to never mention it, right Nacho? No talk of British efficiency or falling or failing, no sir, nothing at all."

Quit was halfway up the hill when Cam stepped of my house. As soon as he spotted Quit his face broke into a broad grin that soon turned into a high-pitched, hyena-like laughter that had him doubled over. He slapped the porch railing, shaking his head.

"You look like a giant raccoon, Quit. What the heck happened?"

"Ask Mazie." He grumbled and kept walking.

"Come on and get moving." I waved to Cam. "You'll be late."

He trotted down the hill and I held the door open as he climbed into the truck. I glanced at the door to my house once more and leaned into the cab.

"How is he, Cam?"

"You mean Roddy? He asked me to get some chocolate for him." He beamed. "I think he's going to be alright, Mazie. He looks good."

"You know what the doctors said, Cam."

"Doctors don't know everything." He turned the engine. "We're going to have a game or two after I get back."

"That's good. Now get moving."

As I watched Cam pull onto the road, Nacho appeared beside me looking as if he had something on his mind. He rubbed his hand across his face, smoothing his thick mustache. I guessed that he was worried about Cam. I was right.

246

"I heard what Cam said about your brother. When you're young you can make yourself believe anything. I saw guys in 'Nam fool themselves about their chances over and over." He shrugged. "It was a way to survive."

"You think Cam is fooling himself about Roddy?"

"You heard what he said about doctors."

"Now that I think about it, Roddy did look a little better this morning. Maybe Cam sees something we can't."

"I don't know about that but I do know he looks up to Roddy. Cam is awful young to be on his own with no family. He'll take it hard if Roddy passes on."

"I know he will." I studied his face. "You were about Cam's age when you went into the service, weren't you?"

"Yeah, but you grow up quick when you're getting shot at. I had a father back at home too."

"Do you think I should talk to Roddy about him?"

"Cam will listen to whatever Roddy has to say."

"Maybe Roddy can find something to say that will help, although I have no idea what it might be."

"Maybe he can." He nodded. "Cam's a different kid than when he first came here and Roddy has a lot to do with it."

I walked up the stairs and onto the porch just as Roddy pushed open the door. I searched for any sign of health in the sharp angles of his pale cheeks but found little in his face other than an odd urgency that seemed to animate his entire body. He held up a bony hand that trembled like a goodbye wave.

"Mazie, I was on my way to see you."

"Well, I'm here to see you too so we're even." I peered into his face. "Is anything wrong? Are you feeling okay/"

"Sit down, Mazie."

He motioned towards the end of the porch and we made our way to two chairs opposite the swing. I tried to think of what I wanted to say and how to say it but my mind kept turning away from any thought of the future despite my efforts. I studied Roddy's face again, convincing myself I could see some slight improvement in his color. His eyes darted here and there as his mind worked out his next move. He chopped the air with his hand as he spoke.

"Now what's on your mind, Mazie?"

"I'm worried about Cam. It's just that, uh…he'll have, uh…he's changed so much." I stammered. "How will he, uh…what will become of him, Roddy?"

"Calm yourself, Mazie. Cam will be alright."

"Quit worries me too. Just because he's older doesn't mean he can handle things any better." I leaned towards him. "Have you talked to him?"

"Mazie, it's you I'm worried about."

"Me?" I asked, surprised. "Why on earth would you worry about me, Roddy?"

"What will you do with yourself when I'm gone?"

I took a breath, trying to take in those words but my mind zigzagged here and there like a pinball to avoid facing them squarely. I grabbed the arms of the chair to steady myself.

"What will I do? Why, I'll do whatever needs doing." I sat back, frustrated. "I came up here to talk about Cam, not me."

"Mazie, find someone, someone you care for, someone who'll care for you." He blessed the space in front of me. "Don't do like I have. Life is too hard to go through alone."

"But Roddy, I'm fine being on my own."

"You're an exceptional woman, Mazie but you've been alone too long. You keep people at a distance. Let someone know you, who you truly are, the real person underneath all that independence before it's too late."

"I don't keep a distance or whatever you said. I'm just strong-minded. I like doing things my own way."

"You keep people away, Mazie. You don't let them in."

"I care about people. I don't keep them away."

"You do care about people, Mazie but that's just the problem. It keeps the focus off you so you don't have to let on who you really are."

"What's gotten into you, Roddy? In all your life you've never talked to me like this."

"I have to say what I need to now or I never will. There's something more, Mazie." He reached out, finding my hand. "I can never make up for my leaving Quit and Angie like I did. I was wrong to be so selfish. I was wrong to saddle you with taking care of them."

"You don't have to explain, Roddy."

"There is no excuse for what I did but I have to say this and you're the only one I can say it to." He squeezed my hand tight, as if I might get up and leave.

"Alright."

"Back then, the thought of living out the rest of my life here as a widower was more than I could stand. I felt like I was suffocating. I married too young and once I became single again the chance to really taste life before I died haunted me day and night. I couldn't eat. I couldn't sleep. One day I finally gave in to it and left."

"That was a long time ago, Roddy."

"It doesn't seem so to me. You understand me, don't you?"

"I understand."

With that he sank into his chair, seeming to vanish into his rumpled clothes, so I let him sit in silence. After a moment he dropped my hand, stood and started toward the door.

"I have to go lay down now." He chopped the air.

"But Roddy, what about Cam?"

"Find someone, Mazie." He called through the doorway.

I ambled back to the barn, frustrated and confused with all I'd heard. I decided work would be just the distraction I needed to clear my mind. An hour later as I stepped out of the greenhouse no better off than when I started, I noticed the truck parked next to my house. I guessed that Cam had been eager to get back in time for a quick game of chess before dinner, parking it there instead of the usual spot next to the barn. I checked on the greenhouse and was just beginning to sort through the remaining invoices when I heard footsteps behind me. I turned to find Cam standing in the doorway.

"Did Roddy manage to take your queen again?" I thumbed through the papers as I spoke.

"He's gone, Mazie."

"I know you were looking forward to a game. Maybe Grita took him into town for something."

"No Mazie, he's gone."

I looked up from the counter. Cam held to the doorframe, his knuckles white against the stained wood. I braced myself on the counter.

"Cam, what are you saying?"

"He's gone, Mazie." his voice broke. "I found him sitting at the kitchen table with his board set up, ready for a game."

"How can that be? I was with him only an hour ago and he seemed fine." I paced a tight circle.

"I thought he would be alright."

"Where is Grita?"

"She's with him now. She came in right after I found him." He shook his head. "That's why I didn't get down here sooner. She couldn't stop crying."

"Roddy is gone?" I mumbled to myself.

"I'm sorry, Mazie."

I closed my eyes and tried to collect my thoughts but Roddy's words kept crowding in. I could almost feel him standing next to me. Nothing seemed real. I wanted Cam to just walk away so the day would return to what it had been. Then Quit's voice calling my name echoed through the open door, at once snapping me out of my confusion. I shuddered to think how he would take the news. I wiped my eyes with the back of my hand as I stepped past Cam and through the door into the last light of day.

Thirty-four

Like a break that defies mending, a strange feeling of separateness came over me as I stepped away from Roddy's grave and turned to face the horizon. The world I had known until that moment had changed. My new world held an unfamiliar sense of freedom tinged with sadness followed by guilt. Of the two of us, I was the one left.

In a black clerical suit, Gus stood at the center of a small crowd that still hovered around the gravesite as I made my way down the hill to the familiar stand of sycamore trees, their smooth limbs glowing like bones in the harsh light of midday. The few remaining leaves overhead shook before a light breeze, filling the air with the sound of rushing water. I watched the sun play across the thread of river and tried to clear my mind of everything but the present moment. A crow called from far below.

I stood there for some time lost in the light-filled scene until a hand slid across my shoulder and lingered on the back of my neck. I turned to find Len squinting at me through the dappled sunlight, a slight smile on his lips. Without a word he took me in his arms and held me, his body tight against mine while the ground melted beneath my feet. I fell into him, tears filling my eyes. An instant later an image of him standing at the bar in Dizzy's, his arm around some woman, crowded itself into my thoughts and I pushed away, wiping my eyes with the back of my hand. They were the first tears I'd shed for my brother.

"As soon as I heard about Roddy I wanted to see you," he lightly touched my arm. "I know how hard it is when you lose family."

"There's only Quit and me left now," I mumbled. "And he'll probably be leaving any day."

"I know how alone you must feel right now, Mazie. Let me do something for you. I owe you that much."

"You don't owe me anything, Len. I've decided to let go of the past. It's time for me to live life as it is while I can."

"Then let me cook you dinner."

I knew better than to accept but was tempted in spite of myself so I let the question stand as I studied Len's handsome face. He still looked delicious as ever and seemed sincere enough. I was wondering if time with an old friend was just what I needed when a distant voice called my name. I turned to see Grita waving me up the hill. Len glanced at his watch.

"I'm running late. I probably shouldn't have come at all but I wanted to see you." He took my hand. "Let me be your friend, Mazie. Come for dinner."

He started out across the dry grass toward a sleek coupe parked away from the other cars. The thought that his car cost more than my house crossed my mind and I pondered how it is that importing is so lucrative while teaching is most certainly not. Grita's voice pulled me from my thought and I looked up to see her, Des and Zoe walking toward me. Des stopped and cast a quick glance my way before watching Len pull from the curb and vanish through the gate. I wondered what was going through his mind. He probably wondered the same about me as he walked up and took my hand.

"Mazie, my dear, is there anything I can do for you on such a melancholy day?"

I squinted at him. "Des, you're sounding a bit like Rhett Butler."

He cocked his head, smiling past his bent nose. "Frankly Mazie, a man could do worse."

"Who was that, Mazie?" Grita nodded toward the gate as she drew nearer.

"Just an old friend."

Zoe stepped next to Grita. "He looked familiar, but everyone starts to look familiar if you wait tables long enough."

"Zoe and I have talked Quit into going to an equine therapy session." Grita grinned as if she'd won the lottery.

"Good, he needs all the therapy he can get."

"Afterwards we're going to have a wake for Roddy at Dizzy's Bar."

"Who thought up that?"

Zoe put her arm around Grita. "She had the idea and I think it's a good one. I know I'd rather have people celebrate over me than cry over me."

"You're too young to drink." I frowned at Grita, thinking of her pregnancy.

"Zoe says she can make me drinks without the alcohol."

I turned to Des. "Are you going to be there?"

"Why, uh…well, uh…not exactly. I have to, uh… I just can't." Des stammered.

I had never seen Des so flustered. He seemed to be all motion, turning from me to the gravesite and back again, his arms gesturing wildly. He turned once again and I followed his gaze up the hill to where Hannie Hereford stood in the shadow of a distant live oak. I felt my cheeks flush as it dawned on me that I had scarcely noticed the crowd or who Des had come with, and as I turned to face him a choking sadness crept into my throat.

"Oh, I see. You already have plans." I mumbled.

"Well yes, I do need to get going." He patted my arm. "Mazie, I'm truly sorry about Roddy. Let me know if I can do anything for you."

I watched Des walk away, realizing for the first time the many ways I had neglected his friendship. Close to my age but a bit older, he understood the disappointments and loses that often visit us as time passes, the end of our youth, the loss of a brother. I needed a friend like Des and yet I had pushed him away.

"Why don't you come see my horses do their therapy, Mazie? It'll do you good." Zoe took my hand. "Then we'll drink a toast to Roddy."

"Will you come with us, please?" Grita pleaded.

Grita and Zoe were worried about me. I could see it in their eyes. Their words still hung in the chill air as the world seemed to collapse around me and for a moment I could scarcely breathe for the closeness. I needed time, time below an open sky, time with a cold wind on my face.

"I know you both want to help but I need to be alone just now."

"Alright, Mazie. We'll be at Dizzy's in a couple of hours if you can make it." Zoe turned to leave, pulling Grita with her.

I stood for a time watching sunlight flicker through the massive cottonwoods scattered along the riverbank below, then I walked to my car. As I pulled through the cemetery gate and onto the highway, I had no thought of where I would go. Without thinking, I turned north toward the lake. A crisp fall wind whipped through the window as I followed the highway centerline, thinking of nothing.

I crossed the long bridge spanning the river a half mile downstream from the dam, the dull metal supports shedding light in brief flashes, and turned west into the dense brush country. Trees vibrating in the chill breeze cast furtive shadows that danced across the blacktop in the low winter sun. Glimpses of the lake, its surface restless before the wind, appeared through the windshield and vanished between dense cedar breaks and stands of Live oak. The yellow centerline seemed to reel me in.

I had lapsed into a thoughtless trance when two whitetail bucks, one chasing the other, came out of nowhere, leaping off a low cliff and directly into my path. Without thinking I swerved onto the shoulder and the car slid to one side and then back onto the road, careening left at a sharp angle. In an instant I found myself crashing through the low brush bordering the opposite shoulder, narrowly missing a thick post oak before coming to a rough stop. Dust surrounded the car in a dense cloud. With difficulty I released one hand and then the other from the steering wheel while trying to keep from shaking. I struggled to release the seatbelt, finally jerking it free. My ragged breathing and the low hiss of the engine seemed the only sounds.

As soon as I stepped out of the car into the tall grass, a sharp pain shot up my ankle. I had to grab the door to keep from falling. After a moment I tested the ankle again and it held, the pain lessening with each step. In spite of the overgrown location, I could see that the car tilted at an odd angle so I walked around to the passenger side and parted the grass. The front tire was completely flat and although the rest of the car seemed intact, I knew right away the rocky ground would not allow the changing of a tire. I wanted to cry.

I had no idea where I was. I surveyed the road and then hobbled toward a sharp bend a quarter of a mile beyond to get a better view. As I approached the far end on the curve, I began to feel like I had been there before. The roadway was far from familiar and yet my mind began piecing together the next view before I could actually see it. I rounded a thick stand of juniper and knew before looking that Len's house lay just ahead. I peeked around a nearby clump of bushes and sure enough, there it was.

The human mind is a mysterious contraption and I had somehow brought myself to Len without actually deciding to do so. Maybe that was the only way I could avoid talking myself out of it. As it was, I had little choice but to see if he was in. My ankle felt a good deal better but I didn't want to test my luck trying to make the next house. I retraced my steps from the last visit, walking up the stairs and banging on the heavy wooden door. In what seemed like no time, Len stood in front of me looking better than ever. Maybe it was the near wreck or maybe I'd reached my emotional limit but at that moment all I wanted was for Len to take me up the stairs to that four-poster bed. He stared at me with that sly smile on his lips without saying a word. I wondered if he could read my mind. A hint of worry flashed across his face as he surveyed the road in both directions before closing the door.

"Mazie, I didn't expect you so soon but I'm glad you're here." He took my hand and led me inside. "You look like you could use a drink."

"Now Len, I don't need a drink anymore than you do." I lied.

"Then you'll join me. As it happens, I just opened a bottle of very expensive Scotch." He stepped to the bar but again glanced toward the front of the house before pouring two large tumblers of the brown whiskey. "Where'd you park? I don't see your car."

I decided to avoid mention of the accident just then even though I knew I'd eventually have to ask Len for a ride. The last thing I wanted was his sympathy. Something had taken hold of me and all I wanted right then was to experience life without a care for tomorrow. Nearly wrecking my car had sobered me but only briefly. I could feel a careless freedom lying just out of my reach and I meant to grab hold of it if I could.

While Len finished at the bar, I headed straight for the big leather couch I had avoided before. A shimmering vista, both lake and sky, filled the arching windows with a luminous blue. Crystalline sunlight angled across the airy room as Len sat next to me and we toasted the day. I felt a brief stab of guilt for enjoying myself so soon after Roddy's passing but then the thought of death only made me want to appreciate whatever came along all the more.

"Mazie, you're looking a bit wild and very sexy." Len leaned back to get a better view.

"You're not looking so bad yourself, Len."

"You seem changed, even from when we spoke earlier. I can't put my finger on what's different about you but I like it."

"Everything looks better in this beautiful place."

"The beauty I see is sitting right here."

I gulped Scotch and settled back into the cool leather, its odor wild and pungent. Len cast another furtive glance toward the road and then focused on me. As he set his drink aside and shifted closer, I realized I was still wearing my coat which now felt like a sauna. I gulped the rest of my Scotch and stood.

"I'm burning up all of a sudden. It must be your expensive Scotch." I dropped my coat on the table.

"I was hoping it was me."

He grabbed my arm, pulling me to him and an instant later we were on the couch making out like teenagers, fumbling with buttons and breathing hard. I felt transported back to that warm sea we had once floated while my mind raced with images I tried to ignore. Len leaned me back onto the couch, a half-smile on his lips and started to unbutton his shirt. I reached for his drink and finished it in one gulp.

Just as he found the last button, a flash of light dashed across the ceiling followed by screeching tires and slamming car doors. Len jumped up, stumbling backwards and crashing into the table. He righted himself and grabbed my coat and then me by the arm, rushing me across the room and down the hallway as quick as we could move. Pushing through the back door and down the landing, we raced toward a detached garage where he thrust me into the wall-like brush just beyond the lawn's edge.

"Run!" He hissed before turning back toward the house.

I parted the nearest branches and stepped into a dense thicket, soon vanishing into a pool of half-light and shadow. Moving away from Len's house with as little noise as I could manage, I crept through a cedar break scattered with persimmon and the sharp spines of agarita. Gusts of cold air rattled the juniper branches around me like bones. I paralleled the road, heading for my car as shouts floated overhead, the actual words lost in the wind. I had no idea who was shouting or what I'd do when I reached my car but I was determined to keep moving. My mind raced, almost keeping pace with my heart.

As I crept along a narrow deer trail cast deep in shadow, I began to make out the crackling of a police radio. I peered through the trees, trying to gauge the direction of my car and I angled away from the sound in a looping arc. Now and then the howl of a car engine floated past, ghostlike on the unseen road ahead. Bare branches pulled at my clothes like tiny hands.

The deep shade lightened and then vanished altogether as I parted the branches edging the thicket and stepped onto the road. I looked one way and then the other. I had overshot my car and could just make out the rear bumper behind a distant cedar a hundred yards beyond. I paused to check my cell phone for service but found it useless. As I neared the car a sheriff's deputy rounded the curve, slowing and pulling to the edge of the road. My heart jumped into my throat as he stopped and leaned out the window.

"Having trouble with your car?"

"I missed the deer but blew a tire." I tried to sound relaxed.

"I'd offer to help but we're working a crime scene up the road." He nodded up the road as he stuffed his lower lip with snuff.

"Should I be worried?"

"Not hardly. The feds busted some feller from up north on money laundering and fraud. Evidently, he got himself mixed up with the Mexican drug cartels." He spit out the window and wiped his mouth with the back of his hand. "They say he's lucky we got to him first."

"I suppose it was lucky for me those deer came along before I got that far." I could feel the sweat trickle down the back of my neck in spite of the chill air.

"I have to get moving but I can call a wrecker for you."

"Can you call a friend instead?" I gave him Nacho's number.

"I'll do that. You take care now." He spit again and pulled back onto the highway.

As I watched the deputy disappear around a distant bend in the road I leaned against the hood of my car, trying to calm my rapid breath. Turning in the direction of the house I had just left, unseen behind a great mass of trees, I imagined Len sitting in the backseat of a police cruiser with his hands bound and his shirt still half-buttoned, watching the life he knew dissolve before his eyes. Just then a black sedan rounded the curve, a single red light flashing beneath the windshield. As it passed I could just make out Len's head pressed against the rear passenger window, his eyes turning as they locked onto me, his face marked with what seemed a tinge of regret. Then he was gone.

Thirty-five

Less than two weeks after Roddy's funeral, Nacho and I were in the barn preparing a delivery of cycads, one of the more ancient palm-like plants, when Quit and Zoe walked in. They had been spending time together at Zoe's equine therapy clinics and Quit had mellowed a bit, although his anger could still bubble up without warning, thrashing him about until he was spent. Zoe even had managed to get him on horseback again.

"Zoe roped me into scaring little kids with horses again, Mazie. Can ya'll handle the rest of this delivery?"

"It's only a load of rare cycads that'll cost us a fortune if Nacho and I don't get them delivered on time, but go ahead and have your fun."

"You call riding herd on a bunch of screaming munchkins fun?" He frowned as if he meant it. "There's no telling how many diseases those runts carry around at any one time. I told Zoe I might have to run the whole lot through a vat of flea dip if I get coughed at or sneezed on again."

Zoe looked at me and rolled her eyes. "As soon as Quit shows up, they forget all about me and Rosie. They can't get enough of him, especially one little girl with cerebral palsy. For the longest time she wouldn't do a thing for me but Quit has her riding like a pro."

"I admit Callie has taken to me."

"Well Quit, there's no accounting for taste." I quipped. "I'm surprised you even remember how to get on a horse."

"Quit looks as comfortable on a horse as anyone I've seen." Zoe beamed. "He's a big help."

"It's just like riding a bicycle. Before you know it you're right where you left off."

"Would that be flat on your back?"

260

He ignored me. "Nacho, can you ride herd on things around here while I'm away?"

I nudged Nacho. "Quit, with all this talk of horses you're starting to sound like a bad John Wayne movie."

He frowned at me. "There are no bad John Wayne movies."

"Speaking of horses, we'd better go or we'll be late." Zoe took Quit by the arm.

I watched them walk away, laughing and smiling together, and wondered where it might lead. They had just eased Zoe's truck onto the highway when Winston rushed in, flushed and out of breath. He tried his best to speak between gasps. Nacho held up a finger, placing his free hand on Winston's shoulder. Winston seemed to relax a bit.

"Take a few breaths before trying to talk, Winston."

Winston gulped a mouthful of air and turned to me, his red face covered in sweat. "Sir, a fight, sir."

After Nacho's seizure, I had learned to trust Winston's judgment and I knew he had something important to say. I walked around the table to where he stood as Nacho bent down, facing him at eye level.

"Winston, tell us who is fighting."

Winston took another ragged breath. "A knife, he has a knife."

I dropped the invoice on the table. "That doesn't sound good."

Nacho's voice was calm. "Where, Winston, where are they?"

He pointed. "Greenhouse."

An instant later, the piercing sound of Grita's voice yelling my name echoed from down the hill. We rushed through the back door and toward the small greenhouse not thirty yards beyond, leaving Winston where he stood. Blurred figures danced through the hazy hothouse glass. I rounded the far side a few feet behind Nacho and came upon Cam and a young man I had never seen before thrashing about on the ground, Grita to one side, poised as if ready to run, the red image of a hand still visible on her cheek. A low growl came out of nowhere as Cam jammed his blood-soaked forearm against the man's throat and grabbed for the free outstretched arm, the hand beyond clutching a black-handled knife. The scene took my breath away.

I stood, not knowing what to do. Just then Cam freed his forearm, rearing back and striking the man across the jaw in a blur of motion. The man reeled to one side but then recovered, kicking Cam away and swiping at him in a flash of gleaming metal. The blade passed just under Cam's chin. They scrambled to their feet and squared off before realizing we stood nearby. Nacho picked up a dowel rod leaning against the wall and stepped forward, positioning himself between Cam and the man. He held the dowel loosely with one hand, tilting it up and down like a seesaw.

"Que tal, mano?" Nacho's voice held no threat.

"I don't speak no Spanish, dude." The man waved his knife in a figure eight. "Get out of my way."

Cam took a step forward. "This is between me and him, Nacho."

"Not this time, Cam." He continued facing the man. "Mazie, I want you to take Grita and Cam to the barn."

I went to where Cam stood, pulling him back several yards and turning him to face me without a word. Once I looked him in the eye, I knew he would leave without an argument. I motioned Grita to join us as we began walking toward the barn. Behind us, Nacho continued talking to the man. Once we reached the end of the building, I motioned them through the barn and told them to wait inside my house. I turned back to where Nacho faced the man.

"Grita, you're not leaving." The man yelled past his already swollen jaw. "You hear me, bitch?"

Nacho ignored the comment and took a step closer. "Como se llama, chico?"

"Like I said, I don't speak no Spanish."

"No? You should learn. It might come in handy."

"What the hell for, ordering tacos?"

"It saved my life in 'Nam."

"Why do I need Spanish when I got this?" He waved the knife again.

"What's your name, junior?"

"It sure as hell isn't junior, old man. Who the hell are you?"

"My name's Nacho."

He chuckled. "What kind of stupid name is that?"

"It's my name. What's yours?"

"It's Manny and you're in my way."

"Your way is that way, Manny." Nacho nodded toward the road.

"No man, I'm not leaving here without Grita." He tossed the knife from hand to hand. "You don't want to get hurt, do you old man?"

"Take it easy, Manny." Nacho held up a hand. "She doesn't want to talk to you. Just lay down the blade and walk away. That's all you have to do."

He shook his head. "She's going with me."

He pointed the knife at Nacho and began moving toward the barn. I scarcely noticed the dowel as it snapped down hard on Manny's wrist, sending the knife skittering along the ground. Nacho swung the rod back in a blur, raking across Manny's ribs with a dull crack. He doubled over, stumbling back and onto the ground in a cloud of dust. Nacho walked over to him.

"Don't hit me again, man!" Manny held up his hand.

"I didn't want to hit you in the first place, Manny. All you have to do is leave."

"Okay, okay, I'll go." He climbed to his feet.

"You'll leave Grita alone too."

"Sure, sure, no problem."

He hurried off down the road where a beat up motorcycle leaned against a tree, kicked it to a start and sped away in a haze of exhaust. Nacho sat hard on a nearby

263

bench, his elbows on his knees. I walked across the small space and sat next to him.

"Where'd you learn to do that?"

"My physical therapist is a martial arts expert. She thought it would be helpful in my therapy." He took a deep breath. "I pretty much figured it had been a waste of time until now."

"Well, that seizure was good for something then."

He nodded. "I guess so."

I leaned forward to face him. "Do you want to call the sheriff about that boy?"

"I was in all kinds of trouble when I was a kid and I got through it alright, so I hate to hurt his chances." He shook his head. "Even so, I don't like the look of him, Mazie. He could still be a problem."

"That's what worries me. I believe I'll give them a call."

"He's a minor so they'll probably make it a low priority."

"First, I'll tell Grita to stay watchful for a while. I think I'll tell Caspar too." I patted him on the shoulder. "I'll bet you didn't know you signed up for guard duty when you took this job."

"Cam is like a son to me, Mazie. I won't stand by and watch him get hurt. I couldn't live with myself if I did."

"That's why I like you, Nacho."

"You like me because I'll deliver those cycads while you're off socializing."

As I walked through the barn and up the hill to my house, I spotted Cam watching me from the front porch steps, his arm wrapped in a blood-stained bandage. I looked for Grita and soon realized her car was no longer parked where it had been. A chill ran up my neck as I hurried toward the house.

"Where's Grita?" I called up the hill.

"She left." Cam called back.

"I thought you would both wait in the house." I said between breaths.

"She bandaged up my arm and took off. I tried to talk her out of leaving, Mazie but she wouldn't listen. I've never seen her so worked up."

I sat next to him. "She had reason to be, seeing you nearly get your throat cut."

"I had no choice but to step in. He slapped her, Mazie. He slapped her hard. I can't tolerate that." He rubbed his raw knuckles. "I got in a couple of good shots on him before you and Nacho showed up."

"You should be glad we got there when we did. Nacho took care of the situation and the young man left without anyone else getting hurt."

"If he does anything to harm Grita, I'll kill him."

"Cam, don't say such a thing. You won't do anything foolish, will you?"

He shook his head. "No, Mazie."

"I know you're a man of your word, Cam so I'm glad to hear it." I stood and started walking toward my car. "Will you come with me to find her?"

Thirty-six

Water, the most abundant compound on the planet, covers three quarters of the world's surface. It's the basis of life and the only natural substance to exist in all three states: liquid, gas and solid. A typical puffy cloud floating by on a summer day weighs as much as eighty elephants. A person can drown in only a puddle of water. Ice has ten phases.

For reasons I couldn't explain, thoughts of water filled my mind as Cam and I drove the road to Caspar's house. Below the broken horizon, a silver ribbon of river flashed briefly through the mass of trees. Twisting yellow leaves dotted the bare-boned branches that stretched over the road like clutching hands. The blacktop dipped and then rose again, bending sharply to the left before reaching Caspar's house.

There was no one about as I pulled into the drive. I turned toward the porch, expecting to see Caspar limping down the steps when I noticed the partially open front door. To the right of the porch, a black shape lay partially hidden by the grass. Grita's car was nowhere in sight.

"What's that?" Cam pointed to the dark form.

"Something's wrong, Cam. Grita's car is gone and the front door is open." I set the brake and got out, pointing to the dark shape. "Go see what that is while I look for Grita."

Before I had reached the front steps, Cam called to me.

"Mazie, you'd better get over here."

I retraced my steps, hurrying to where he stood over Caspar's dog, Priddy. She lay on her side, a small hole just behind her right shoulder. I bent forward to get a better look.

"Good lord Cam, she's been shot."

"Why would someone shoot an old worn out dog, Mazie?"

I turned without answering and headed for the front porch, my mind reeling with worry. As I neared the house, I could see a shoe blocking the door and for a brief moment wondered why Caspar would want the door propped open. Then I realized there was more than one shoe. I ran up the steps, flinging the screen door aside and pushing past. Caspar lay just inside. I feared he was dead too but he stirred, groaning as he pushed up on one elbow. I bent down to help him.

"Caspar, what's happened?"

He looked at me for a moment as if he'd never seen me before. Cam pushed through the door, kneeling beside us and taking Caspar's hand in both of his. After a moment Cam helped him stand, moving him to a nearby chair.

"Mazie, where is Grita?" Caspar whispered.

"Her car is gone."

"I checked and she's not in her apartment." Cam paced the room.

"What happened here, Caspar?" I knelt beside him.

"I don't remember how I got on that dang floor."

"What do you remember?"

"I was in the kitchen and I heard yelling out back, so I go to see who it was. Grita and her old boyfriend were there and I could see she was angry and upset, wit them dang tears in her eyes, telling him to leave. I can't have that, Mazie."

"Are you sure it was him?"

He nodded. "I had to chase him off before so I know what to do. I went and got that dang pistol out of the closet and went to the front door, so I could surprise him. I opened the door to go out and then I don't remember not'ing. Now I got this big headache."

Cam stopped pacing. "Where's the pistol, Caspar."

He rubbed the back of his head. "I had it right there in my hand when I opened that door. That dang gun got to be here somewhere."

Cam searched the room in short order and then the porch. After a moment, he stepped back through the door, shaking his head. I turned to Caspar.

"Caspar, we found Priddy out front. She was shot dead. I believe that boy has the gun."

"We got to go find Grita." He tried to stand but fell back into the chair with a groan. "That boy must have her."

"Caspar, we need to take you to the hospital."

"No Mazie, I just got a little knock on my hard old head." He looked from me to Cam. "Go find her. Go find Grita."

"Where do we look, Caspar?"

"That boy's family has a ranch out west, somewhere south of Junction. I don't know the name but a place called Horse Camp Waterhole is close by. A damn coward will go hide, Mazie. That's where he will take her."

"Okay, Caspar." I put my hand on his shoulder. "You stay put. Can you use the phone?"

"My head hurts but I can still see wit my glasses here." He pulled a pair of reading glasses from a nearby side table.

"Call the sheriff and tell him what's happened."

I tried to clear my mind as we hurried to the car. Although I believed Caspar was right, I knew we'd never find the ranch on our own. We needed detailed maps of the area and I knew who had them. Cam had the same thought.

"You can't find that ranch without a good map, Mazie."

"You're right and I know where we can find one."

As I pulled the door closed, I glanced at the black shape of Priddy and shuddered at what might become of Grita. I backed out and turned the car toward town when Quit's truck rounded the curve at a fierce rate, slinging a spray of gravel far into the weeds. He slid to a rough stop next to me and leaned toward the open window. Cam opened the passenger door.

"Nacho told me what happened. How's Grita?"

"Give us a minute, Quit."

I set the brake and got out.

"Cam, take the car to Des Clymer's office. He can show you the location of the place Caspar mentioned. At least, I hope he can."

"Are you going after her?"

I nodded.

"I want to go, Mazie."

"Cam, I need you to listen to me." I took him by the arm. "I'm not about to let you anywhere near that boy if I can help it, and right now I need your help. Grita needs your help. This is the best way you can do that."

"What do you need Des for?" Quit set the brake and got out.

I ignored him. "Will you help me, Cam?"

He nodded and moved behind the steering wheel. "I'll call you once I get there."

"You'll be our navigator."

"You're right, Mazie. It's the quickest way to find her."

"Let's hope it works." I slammed the door.

Cam sped off and I climbed into the cab next to Quit, pulling the door closed before calling Nacho to tell him what had happened and asking him to check on Caspar right away. I repeated the story to Quit as we sped toward the Junction highway. We had soon passed the town of Mountain Home, climbing the edge of the Edwards Plateau as the land around us seemed to fall away in all directions. The top of Graveyard Mountain capped the distant horizon as we turned west, following a steep ridge, the headwaters of the Frio River on one side, the Llano on the other. Horse Camp Waterhole was somewhere in the canyons below. Although I had always loved the look of the land west of Junction, I could see little of its beauty as my mind swirled with worry. Almost mirroring my thoughts, a bank of low clouds moved overhead, turning the knotted landscape gray.

Quit had just started down the steep side of an unnamed canyon when my phone rang. I was relieved to know we still had service. Cam's voice echoed in my ear as Des called out directions in the background. I imagined the wild gestures that no doubt accompanied his words and realized with a start how much I had grown to rely on him. I pushed the thought from my mind as we rounded a bend and the sign for Horse Camp Waterhole loomed ahead.

"There it is." I called into the phone as I pointed out the sign. "We must be near the place, Cam. What's our next move?"

"The map shows several properties surrounding the lake but we can't tell anymore than that." He sighed. "You're on your own from here on."

"Alright, you're breaking up anyway."

"Mazie?"

"What is it, Cam?"

"Des says he wants you back in one piece so don't do anything foolish. That's me saying it too."

"We'll be careful, Cam."

"But find her, Mazie."

"Tell Des I'll see him soon."

Half an hour later Quit was again angling down a narrow gravel road as we peered through barbed wire and thick stands of scrub oak for anything that might lead us to Grita. The road soon became more of a path and a cloud of dust towered behind us like a white flag. We had already tried two other roads with no luck, the few ranch houses we were able to see yielding no sign of Grita or her car, and as we neared the end of the path, I worried we might never find her.

"That ranch is close by, Mazie. I believe I can feel it." Quit sounded less than certain.

"What if we figured wrong and they went somewhere else? What if he took her to Mexico? We'd never see her again."

We rounded a curve to find a short, coffee-colored man stooped over a torn fence, the sinew of his thin arms straining against the pull of the wire. A scraggly beard showed white against his dark face. Quit slowed the truck, pulling off the road near where the man bent as if frozen in place. Other than his shaking arms, he stood still, statue-like. Sweat dripped from the tip of his nose. After a moment he released the wire and stood, swaying a bit as he turned toward us. He motioned us to him with a swipe of his bony arm.

"He looks like he needs a hand." Quit opened the door.

"We don't have time for socializing, Quit." I called after him.

He stuck his head back into the car. "He may know something that'll help us find Grita.

I frowned at him. "Sounds like a long shot, not to mention wasting time we don't have."

"I can work and talk at the same time."

I followed him to the front of the truck.

"Looks like that fence is being ornery." Quit called to the man.

"This fence is even older than me but he fights like el toro. We old men can get stubborn. I don't mind as long as he keeps my goats from getting out."

Quit stepped over to the fence. "The two of us can probably pull that wire back into place."

"Si, I was hoping you would give me a help."

I watched as Quit leaned all his weight into the goat wire while the man strained to hammer it back into place. As they worked, I peered toward the end of the road and thought I could make out the shine of a metal roof through the trees. A quarter mile from where we stood, the road ended in a rocky drive that disappeared beyond a cracked and faded wooden gate. When Quit and the man stood up to admire their work, I stepped in front of them and pointed toward the end of the road.

"Do you know who lives there?"

"Excuse me for being so rude." He took my hand, making a slight bow. "My name is Solomon Ordonez."

"I'm Mazie Goforth and this is my nephew, Quit."

271

He shook Quit's hand. "Nobody lives at that ranch but a boy comes out here sometimes. I don't know his name but he is trouble, I think."

"Is he there now?"

He nodded. "A car went by here not five minutes ago. I think it was him but he has only a motorcycle so I'm not sure. He had a girl with him this time."

"A girl with dark hair?"

"A very pretty girl." He smiled. "I am old but my eyes, they still work."

"Quit, we're right behind them." I pulled out my phone. "I'm calling the sheriff."

Solomon held up his hand. "Your phone will not work here. You have to go ten miles to get a signal. Why do you want the sheriff?"

Quit gestured toward the road. "That girl you saw is a friend of ours. We think that boy kidnapped her. We mean to get her back."

I held up the phone. "I can drive to where there's a signal."

Quit shook his head. "Mazie, I'm not waiting for the sheriff. It could take you an hour to make the call and then a deputy will take another two, if he shows at all."

"I would go to the sheriff for you but I let my cousin borrow my truck." Solomon pointed across the fence. "All I have is my horse."

"You have a horse?"

He pointed into the brush. "Si, she is saddled and waiting by a tree where the grass grows good. Her name is Nunca."

Quit rubbed his jaw. "Can I borrow her?"

Solomon scratched his beard and studied Quit. "Nunca is a good horse. In Spanish, her name means 'nothing'. I named her that because she never gives me any trouble. What do you want with her?"

"She could help us get our friend back. I'll pay for the use of her."

"No, I am glad to help. You tell me what else I can do and I do it."

Quit held up his hand. "No Solomon, thank you. I appreciate the use of your horse but we best handle this ourselves."

"My cousin, he will come back soon and I will go find the sheriff."

"We appreciate your help."

"I will get Nunca for you now." He climbed through the fence and disappeared into the brush.

Quit drove to the end of the road, blocking the wooden gate with the truck while I watched Solomon lead Nunca over a cattle guard of slatted metal pipe that crossed his driveway. Her sorrel coat glistened under the dim cloud-strewn sky. Solomon patted her neck handed while he the reins to Quit, his rough hand raising a small cloud of dust.

"Nunca, you listen to these good people and do what they tell you." He turned toward the fence. "I got to go tend my goats now we got this fence fixed up."

Thirty-seven

Quit opened the broken down wooden gate, leading Nunca through and down the drive a few yards before returning to latch the gate. Nunca snorted warily while she waited but her brown eyes remained large and calm. Only her nervous ears betrayed her reticence. Quit spoke to her in a near-whisper and I was surprised to see he had a natural ease with her, a horse he had never before seen. She still looked at me askance. Quit checked the saddle and then slipped his foot into a stirrup, swinging onto Nunca's back with little effort. He turned to me, taking his foot from the stirrup while holding out his hand.

He nodded toward the horse's side. "Okay Mazie, just put your foot in and I'll pull you up."

"Are you sure you know what you're doing, Quit? What if she bolts?"

"Do you want to find Grita or just stand there complaining?"

He was right. I had wasted too much time already so I did what he said and before I knew what had happened I was on the back of a horse for the first time in my life. Although a bit wobbly, I felt my confidence grow as Nunca turned and trotted into the high grass edging a thick cedar break.

Quit cut through the trees, keeping a dense wall of brush between us and the house. Now and then we could make out its dim outline against the gray horizon. Somewhere past the house was Horse Camp Waterhole, a small spring-fed lake caught between rugged limestone hills flanking either side of a steep valley. Nunca crept along noiselessly, as if she knew why we were there. Quit pulled the reins to one side and she drove through a thick wall of cedars without pause, emerging into a clearing under half a dozen sprawling live oaks, their branches touching the ground. I felt as if we had entered a green cave. Quit swung his leg over the front of the saddle and slid to the ground. I did the same and soon stood next to him.

"The house is over there." He pointed through one side of the green wall surrounding us. "Let's take a look but try to be quiet, Mazie."

He frowned as a twig snapped beneath my foot. Once he had tied the reins to a nearby branch, we crept through the inside edge of the thicket, parting the branches just enough to view the small home. The low-slung house had a deep porch covering three sides and a wide stone chimney rising above the fourth. It sat not thirty yards beyond, a single light burning in what looked to be the kitchen window. Grita's car stood nearby, the doors hanging wide open but there was no one about. As I peered at each window, hoping for a sign of her, the emptiness of the scene fluttered inside my chest like a trapped bird.

"Quit, I don't see any sign of Grita. Where could she be?"

"She's here, Mazie. I'm trying to see a way into that house."

"Don't forget he probably has Grita's big pistol."

"Well, at least Nacho took the switchblade away from him." He edged back and sat, his legs splayed.

I turned to face him. "What do we do now?"

"We wait. I want to get a look at him before we do anything. I also have an idea why those car doors are hanging open. If I'm right it'll make this a lot easier. I'll give him five minutes."

As we crouched beneath the trees watching for any movement in or near the house, I wondered at the strange turns a life can take. When Angie was still alive, I never thought I'd see Quit again. Yet here we sat, trying to help a girl he once believed might be his daughter but instead proved otherwise. The difference mattered little at that moment. I wanted to believe he was no longer the angry, belligerent young man I had grown accustomed to but I

275

knew people don't magically change all at once. If change happens, and it often doesn't, it's a gradual, almost invisible process. Then again, I knew there were always exceptions. I studied him as he peered through the trees and wondered again at his past. He turned to me at just that moment.

"Mazie, what's on your mind?"

"What do you mean?"

"You look like you have something to say and it's just busting to get out, so out with it."

"What did you do before you came back here?"

"I got paid to photograph places, events, whatever the magazines wanted."

He turned from my gaze, staring into space in the way I'd seen so many times before, but he kept talking.

"I was in Afghanistan."

"Why did you leave?"

"I got the letter about Angie. You know that."

"What's the real reason?"

"What do you mean?"

"Why don't you have any cameras? Why don't you ever talk about photography or where you traveled or the people you met?"

He looked at me for what seemed forever but was really only seconds. The look on his face sent chills down my spine and I started to wish I'd kept my thoughts to myself.

"I was getting shots of the devastation in a small town I thought was safe until it came under fire. I found out later I had misread the map and mistakenly entered a live fire zone. One second I was standing on a peaceful, deserted street in a pretty little town like you might see in any travel ad and the next I was falling to the ground in a cloud of explosions and small arms fire.

"Bullets were whizzing all around so I took cover in a brick entryway. That's when I spotted a little girl squatting behind a trash can directly across the road from me. She looked to be ten or eleven, with thick black hair and dark eyes. She stared at me, terrified, as if she expected me to help her. I motioned her toward me and she started to stand but then froze with fear, unable to move. I could see I would have to go to her but I couldn't make myself move. I could hardly breathe. I finally got the courage to try and had just started out the doorway when a sniper round went whining just above my head. I jumped back to cover.

"A moment later a mortar exploded nearby, filling the street with dust. I could barely see the end of the entryway much less the other side of the street. Once the dust cleared, I could see the girl again but she was sitting away from the trash barrel with her back against the wall. I waved for her to move back to cover and she just stared at me like there was nothing in the world wrong. That's when I noticed the blood pooling next to her. I started out the doorway again and a mortar exploded nearby, knocking me to the ground, then another and then nothing.

"The next thing I remember, I was someplace unfamiliar and a medic was waving smelling salts in my face, saying something without making a sound. I was totally deaf and had stitches up one leg. My hearing gradually came back and as soon as I could walk again I got a ride back to my apartment, burned all my photos and smashed all my cameras. I booked the next flight to Europe and then disappeared into a country where I couldn't speak the language. That's where I was when I got the letter about Angie."

"That sounds like a nightmare."

"It is a nightmare and it comes to visit whenever it wants."

"I'm so sorry, Quit. Forgive me for prying."

"I should have helped her, Mazie."

"What could you have done except gotten yourself killed?"

"I should've done something."

A door slammed behind us and Quit jumped up, pulling a branch aside and peering through the wall of brush. I moved next to him, squinting through the trees as Grita carried a cardboard box to the car. Manny followed with a duffle bag, the big pistol jammed under his belt. They went back inside and returned with two more boxes, placing them in the back seat. Then he pushed Grita into the passenger seat. As Manny turned back toward the house Quit grabbed my arm, pulling me toward Nunca.

"Quick Mazie, climb up." He grabbed the stirrup.

"What are we going to do?"

"We'll hide out near the gate and wait for them. When he stops we'll have a chance to grab Grita."

"It sounds risky, Quit."

"These bully types are cowards." He waved off my worry. "Once he sees we mean business, he'll run. As long as we have Grita, I don't care what he does."

Quit spurred the horse into a quick but quiet trot, her hooves cushioned by a damp layer of fallen leaves. In less than a minute, we stood between a stand of thick junipers, their fir-like branches crowding Nunca's face. The gate was just beyond. Quit held my arm as I pulled my leg past the saddle and slid to the ground.

"When he gets out of the car, I'll go right at him. A big horse on the run ought to distract him enough for you to get Grita out of the way and back to where we were just now."

The car rumbled up behind us, slowing as it approached the gate. Nunca shifted restlessly and snorted into the junipers. Quit leaned forward and ran his hand along her neck, trying to calm her. The car stopped abruptly and sat idling as Manny opened the door and peered at the truck beyond the gate as if it was a mirage. He turned to his left and right, and for a moment I feared he would see us but he moved around the car door and took a step toward the gate before stopping.

"Get ready, Mazie." Quit whispered.

I crouched low, trying to get a look at Grita through the reflected light of the back windshield. When I finally spotted her, she was turning in her seat as if expecting someone. She knew we were close. As I stood, Nunca's muscles tensed as if ready to jump. Then I felt Quit's hand on my shoulder. I leaned to one side and looked around him as Manny climbed back behind the wheel. The car roared forward, turning a tight half-circle and spraying gravel in all directions before racing back down the drive. Quit grabbed my arm and pulled me up onto Nunca's back as if I weighed nothing.

"There must be another way out." He turned the horse on her heels. "We have to get there first."

I hung to Quit with all my strength as he spurred Nunca to a full gallop. In seconds we were flying above the tall grass, taking an angled course behind a long line of trees and toward the lakeshore beyond. The car flashed through narrow breaks in the brush, speeding along the drive and trailing a ragged plume of dust. Ahead, a broad pasture opened up as the wall of trees fell away.

Without losing a step, Quit turned Nunca sharply left and around the trees. I thought we still had a long stretch of pasture left before reaching the drive but in a flash we were in the road, the car surprisingly close and bearing down fast. By instinct Nunca turned toward the sound, barely able to keep her footing in the loose gravel. Quit strained against the reins, struggling to move her away in time. I believe we might have made it too, but a blast from Grita's big pistol cracked the cold air, turning Nunca in a half-circle as the bullet slammed into her side. A searing pain shot through my leg.

In that fraction of a second I spotted Grita grabbing for the gun just before a second blast shattered the windshield, blocking my view. The next instant Nunca's back legs gave way, throwing us onto the lakeside rocks as Manny veered sharply left and onto a short bluff above the water. I felt time pause. The car seemed to hesitate as if suspended above the lake like an injured diver. A second later I watched as it smashed into the agitated water. I tried to stand but fell back as Quit scrambled to his feet, running toward the lake like a madman while the car slipped beneath the dark surface. He dove in and disappeared, following the slowing trail of bubbles, surfaced and dove again, and then again. I lay there watching as the surface calmed to quicksilver beneath the leaden sky. A suffocating stillness enveloped me. I struggled to my feet but the world swirled before my eyes in streaks of gray, then brilliant white, before disappearing altogether. I slipped into a deep well.

Thirty-eight

Wind threaded through bare trees like rushing water, filling the air with sad but beautiful music as I limped toward the empty corral. The sky beyond held not a single cloud. For the first time in a month I was walking without crutches but I felt like an old woman. I reached for the fence, grabbing it with both hands and glancing around to see if anyone had noticed. Even something as simple as walking was a chore. Still, I was glad to have back my freedom. I heard footsteps behind me and turned to see Zoe walking through the nearby open-air barn. She had her boots on.

"Look at you, up and about already." She called as she walked to where I stood.

"That all depends on how you define up and about."

She stopped and looked me over. "Standing and talking will do for someone that almost bled to death."

"I wish it had turned out differently." I shook my head. "I somehow feel responsible."

"Mazie, that boy nearly killed you. He would have shot you all if he hadn't drowned." She took my hand in hers. "You and Grita are lucky to be alive."

"She told me she doesn't know whether to feel sad that she miscarried or relieved that Manny won't hurt her again."

"After what he did, I don't believe she would've kept that baby even if she hadn't miscarried."

"How does she seem to you, Zoe? Will she be alright?"

"It won't be easy but she'll be alright."

"Will we?" I took a breath. "Why did it have to happen, Zoe?"

"I don't know but it did and we have to face that fact."

Her voice was matter of fact though her eyes brimmed with tears. She brushed them away like she would a fly. For a moment, I wondered if I'd somehow offended her but then realized Zoe was trying to help me. I needed to face what I'd been through and see it clearly, if I could. I vowed to try.

I wanted to say more to Zoe but could see in her sad yet beautiful eyes this was not the time. A hard look at reality lay somewhere in our future and it was all we could do to acknowledge its dim presence. She seemed to sense it too and took my hand.

"You're a strong woman, Mazie. You'll get through this."

"I'm not feeling so strong these days."

"Nearly dying can do that to a person."

A door closed behind us and I turned to see Des saunter into the barn, his new boots stirring a cloud of dust. He stopped and held up one arm, looking like a Roman orator about to hold forth.

"Why, I see a vision. Two beauties bathed in sunlight, waiting for a real cowboy to walk in."

Zoe rolled her eyes. "And we're still waiting."

"Des, you remind me of my old uncle Doctor." I was grateful for the distraction. "He loved to make an entrance. I believe he should've been an actor."

Des walked to where we stood. "I've long thought I have a talent for acting. I can see myself..."

"Acting up is more like it." Zoe interrupted. "I thought you were bringing over the horses. The kids will be here soon."

"I was told to wait in here."

"Wait for what?" Zoe looked around the corral.

A horse whinnied nearby and I turned to see Grita round the corner leading a sorrel mare with a small, helmeted rider perched on top. Other volunteers with horses and riders followed close behind, the children grinning broadly as they swayed back and forth in their saddles. Grita led her horse to one side while Zoe moved to join her. I turned to Des, searching his ruddy face. He looked past his crooked nose into my eyes and offered a reassuring smile.

"Try not to look so sad, Mazie."

"Am I that obvious?"

"Grita told me she got into a college in Austin."

I nodded. "Linc helped her. It's a program for students that are the first in their family to attend college. She'll be leaving soon and Cam is going with her."

"That's good news, isn't it?"

"I only wish Quit was here to see it. I can't believe he's gone, Des. Why did he have to go back for that boy?" I put my hand to my mouth. "Why couldn't he save Grita and leave it at that?"

"You would've done the same, Mazie. Quit couldn't just leave him to drown. Bad or not, he was still a kid."

"I sometimes find myself thinking Quit will come walking around the corner at any moment and, as usual, find something to complain about."

"I know how hard it must be for you, Mazie, losing Roddy and then Quit like you did." He took my hand and turned me toward the corral. "But look at that young woman. Grita wouldn't be standing there if Quit hadn't saved her. And she wouldn't be on her way to college if it wasn't for you."

"I hope I've been an influence, even if only a small one."

"More than you know. I can see it even if you can't."

"But soon she'll be gone too, and so will Cam. What will I do then, Des?"

He chuckled. "Austin isn't far, Mazie."

I knew he was right. "I suppose I'll just have to adjust."

"Things change Mazie, sometimes for worse but mostly for better."

"I'd like to believe that's true."

He studied me for a moment. "Whatever should happen, you don't have to face it alone."

I felt my face pale as I looked into his lively blue eyes and without warning tears spilled down my cheeks in a torrent. I swept them aside with a trembling hand, terrified

I might lose control. The air surrounding us seemed to vibrate. I tried to speak but all that I had never said to Des caught in my throat and instead went swirling through my mind like a wild river. After a moment I took a ragged breath, managing a meager smile.

"Don't you decide to move away too." I croaked.

He took my hand. "I'm not going anywhere."

"Come on Mazie, give it a try." Grita called. I turned to see her wink at the little girl in the saddle.

Des gave my hand a squeeze and let go as he stepped away. Looking across the corral at Grita, her satin hair spilling down her shoulders like rain, I felt the future pulling at me.

"What do you have up your sleeve, Grita?" I called to her. "You have an evil look about you."

"Mazie, she's ready to help you if you'll allow it. Isn't that right, Callie?"

The girl giggled and nodded while one of her arms flailed about as if it belonged to someone else. As far as I could tell, she neither noticed nor cared.

"Who says I need any help?"

Grita gave Callie a frown. "Mazie doesn't think she needs any help but we know better, huh Callie? All you have to do is take hold of Callie's hand and walk alongside. You'll be feeling better before you know it."

Once Callie turned her round, expectant face to me, I had no choice but to limp across to where Grita stood holding the reins. She took firm grasp of my hand while I reached to the saddle and steadied myself with the other. The next instant Callie's small fingers wrapped around my thumb. I tried to let go of Grita but she held tight as we walked a broad circle together. Sunlight filtered through the bare trees, throwing a dense filigree of shadow at our feet. A raven called from somewhere near and I turned to see Des leaning against the tall fence, his head cocked to one side, his eyes shining blue as the winter sky.